*continued . . .*

SCIENCE FICTION

FANTASY

MAR 1 0 2011

*Ace Books by Walter Greatshell*

XOMBIES: APOCALYPSE BLUES
XOMBIES: APOCALYPTICON
XOMBIES: APOCALYPSO

MAD SKILLS

# XOMBIES:
## APOCALYPSO

**Walter Greatshell**

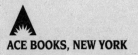

ACE BOOKS, NEW YORK

**THE BERKLEY PUBLISHING GROUP**
**Published by the Penguin Group**
**Penguin Group (USA) Inc.**
**375 Hudson Street, New York, New York 10014, USA**

Penguin Group (Canada), 90 Eglinton Avenue East, Suite 700, Toronto, Ontario M4P 2Y3, Canada
(a division of Pearson Penguin Canada Inc.)
Penguin Books Ltd., 80 Strand, London WC2R 0RL, England
Penguin Group Ireland, 25 St. Stephen's Green, Dublin 2, Ireland (a division of Penguin Books Ltd.)
Penguin Group (Australia), 250 Camberwell Road, Camberwell, Victoria 3124, Australia
(a division of Pearson Australia Group Pty. Ltd.)
Penguin Books India Pvt. Ltd., 11 Community Centre, Panchsheel Park, New Delhi—110 017, India
Penguin Group (NZ), 67 Apollo Drive, Rosedale, North Shore 0632, New Zealand
(a division of Pearson New Zealand Ltd.)
Penguin Books (South Africa) (Pty.) Ltd., 24 Sturdee Avenue, Rosebank, Johannesburg 2196,
South Africa

Penguin Books Ltd., Registered Offices: 80 Strand, London WC2R 0RL, England

This is a work of fiction. Names, characters, places, and incidents either are the product of the author's imagination or are used fictitiously, and any resemblance to actual persons, living or dead, business establishments, events, or locales is entirely coincidental. The publisher does not have any control over and does not assume any responsibility for author or third-party websites or their content.

XOMBIES: APOCALYPSO

An Ace Book / published by arrangement with the author

PRINTING HISTORY
Ace mass-market edition / March 2011

Copyright © 2011 by Walter Greatshell.
Cover art by Cliff Nielsen.
Cover design by Lesley Worrell.
Interior text design by Tiffany Estreicher.

ISBN: 978-0-441-02013-3

ACE
Ace Books are published by The Berkley Publishing Group,
a division of Penguin Group (USA) Inc.,
375 Hudson Street, New York, New York 10014.
ACE and the "A" design are trademarks of Penguin Group (USA) Inc.

PRINTED IN THE UNITED STATES OF AMERICA

10  9  8  7  6  5  4  3  2  1

*To my wife, Cindy; my son, Max;*
*and also to the gang of talented apes I hang out*
*with on Saturday nights: Dave, Steve, Adam, and Dan.*
*I'm proud to be one of you.*

# ACKNOWLEDGMENTS

Some books come easy; others come hard. This one was hard. I don't know why, except that maybe because it was the third book of a trilogy, the fifth book I'd ever had published, and the summation of everything I'd written to this point, there was a lot I wanted to pour into it—much too much, as it turned out. If it's true, as the French say, that "one must suffer in order to be beautiful," then any beauty achieved here is thanks to my long-suffering editor, Danielle Stockley, and the rest of the talented staff at Ace Books. I'd also like to thank my agent, Laurie McLean, and, most of all, you, my readers, for joining me on this adventure.

How is it possible for you to have accompanied me all this time without coming to perceive that all the things that have to do with knights-errant appear to be mad, foolish, and chimerical, everything being done by contraries? Not that they are so in reality; it is simply that there are always a lot of enchanters going about among us, changing things and giving them a deceitful appearance, directing them as suits their fancy, depending upon whether they wish to favor or destroy us.

—Cervantes, *Don Quixote*

Comedy is not pretty.

—Steve Martin

**PART I**

Loveville

# CHAPTER **ONE**

## DREADNAUTS

There was no boat. There was no crew. There was only a shared dream, fragile as a bubble in an endless sea. And there was no sea, just ripples of time and space—the bottomless, shoreless reach of eternity.

And Beatles music.

Suspended in the depths like a black thought, the USS *No-Name* echoed with the murky strains of "Eleanor Rigby." Within its vast hull, we all listened, everyone equally intent, equally inert, whether whole or in pieces, all motionless as corpses in the smothering dark, embedded like fossils amid the roots of a tree—which was what the boat had become: a single organism of cold flesh and metal, blue limbs intermingled with blue steel, organs with plumbing, sinew with cable, bone with bracing. The flesh persisted, the flesh was permanent—the metal somewhat less so. Water trickled in, pooling blackly in the bilge.

In the airless environment, a creeping patina of blue rust became more evident by the day . . . at least in the areas where lights still functioned. Nobody cared. There was a short somewhere, many shorts, all neglected, life-support systems ignored and faltering . . . for there was no life left to support.

It didn't matter as long as the reactor still burned, the screw still turned, and the music still played. That music was our residual humanity made manifest; it was the sound of hope: hope of finding the living and relieving their mortal woes, the damned seeking the doomed and spreading the seed of Maenad salvation . . . before it was too late. Such was our mission.

Such were we missionaries.

All at once, the music stopped. From miles away, far across the void, down from the world of light and air, came a new sound, a deep electronic vibration low enough to be detectable even through water. A sound meant specifically for submarines to hear: an Ultra Low Frequency radio signal.

In the belly of the boat, a rusty, cracked voice: "Can you hear that?"

"Yes."

"Sounds like an invitation."

"Let's RSVP."

The glittering blue surface of the sea spread in all directions to the thin circumference of the horizon, swells rolling in long regiments under the sun. In the middle of this enormity, a giraffe-speckled pole rose from the water—the boat's radio antenna. It scanned the heavens for the least electronic whisper and immediately fixed upon the loudest signal. This was routed to the AV console in the radio shack, where Reggie Jinnah played it for a small audience that included Captain Harvey Coombs, Dr. Alice Langhorne, and me. All of us Xombies. Reggie's mates, three other Anglo-Pakistani musicians who formerly comprised the Beatles tribute band known as the Blackpudlians, waited in the background, having been using the room as a makeshift music studio.

On the video screen, we could see an image of a man. He was a very familiar man, a man we had not seen since the height of the Agent X pandemic and never expected to see again. A man I had seen shoot himself on national television.

The superimposed caption read, PRESIDENT OF THE UNITED STATES.

"Turn up the sound," I said.

"Sorry." Reggie hit a switch. Now we could hear the man's familiar voice:

"—time to correct the mistakes of the past. We are re-building humanity one soul at a time, just as we are rebuild-ing civilization one brick at a time, and we can choose the kind of society we want it to be. Do we want another soci-ety doomed to failure? A society based on fear and lies? Or do we want one based on reason and truth? Not a society of exploitation, corruption, and waste, but a federation of free peoples in which the Golden Rule prevails; a society in tune with nature, run on green principles of clean energy and self-sustaining agriculture, and serving the highest goals of mankind, for which everyone shares the burden and the benefits. If you can hear this, you are invited to join our grand endeavor. We are located in the heart of Washington, DC, a place we now call Xanadu. In Xanadu, we have learned to live in harmony with Xombies as we have with each other, not as adversaries or exploiters but as fellow cit-izens of the Earth, celebrating the diversity of all beings, for all beings play a precious role in building the future. If you still live in fear, hatred, or despair, join our growing family and learn the meaning of freedom."

This was followed by a long series of diverse and attrac-tive faces—men, women, and children, of many races, styles, and physical types—all saying the same thing: "I am Xanadu." At the end, the president came back, closing with, "We are Xanadu. And we welcome you."

"Sounds bloody good to me," said Reggie. "Where do I sign up?"

# CHAPTER **TWO**

## TWO DEAD BOYS

Two boys missed the boat.

Unlike all their shipmates, Todd and Ray were neither dead nor undead. They were very much alive, thank you, though a casual observer might not have deduced this fact from their ghoulish appearance—in fact, such an observer would have had to be forgiven an involuntary shudder at the sight of two such unspeakable monstrosities as Todd Holmes and Raymond Despineau.

But there were no observers, casual or otherwise, to shudder or deduce anything. Other than the two teenagers, the entire riverfront was deserted. Neither man nor Ex-man walked its urban shores, the place having been recently cleansed of its inhabitants. Whether alive or dead, red-blooded or blue-, all had been caught up in the Reapers' recent Waterloo and swept downriver to the sea.

All except Todd and Ray, who had missed the boat.

Let me tell you how they looked: Imagine a pair of seven-foot-tall rag dolls; pumpkin-headed monstrosities with black-ened knotholes for eyes and gaping, raggedy mouths. Scarlike seams crisscrossed their bodies, stitched shut with shiny metal staples. Their naked, veinous flesh was weirdly active, a crazy quilt of mismatched skin samples, some with hair, some without; some with nipples or moles or freckles or ears or faces, some without; but every part alive with tics and twitches and grand-mal spasms, several square yards of jerky meat, all aflutter with the animating energy of Maenad Cytosis—the original Agent X.

Like beauty, this ugliness was only skin-deep. It was a shell of undead tissue that clung to each boy's mesh-armored body like a thick excrescence of living coral, a literal power suit that amplified his strength to Maenad proportions. But that was the secondary purpose of Reaper outerwear. The prime purpose was that it allowed the boys to walk among Xombies unmolested. It was camouflage.

Each suit had been carved from live-caught Xombies, tailored to spec, and worn by a foot soldier of the Moguls during their scavenging raids. Todd and Ray had stolen the awful, offal garments in order to make their escape, only to be trapped inside the grisly vehicles of their flight. Now the Reapers were all dead, their barge sunk, and the submarine, which had been the boys' last hope, was a floating flytrap, a five-hundred-foot-long Pandora's box. Witnessing the annihilation of the Reapers, the boys had been hesitant to go anywhere near the thing . . . until they realized the only other choice was to be abandoned in this no-man's-land of Providence, Rhode Island.

Great.

"This is so not cool, man," groaned Ray, watching the U-boat vanish in the distance. Hell-ship or not, there was clearly some sort of intelligent control at the helm, whether human or otherwise. "What are we gonna do now?"

"Try to chill. I'm thinking."

"Awesome."

"It'll take all day for the sub to get out of the bay. Maybe we can find a boat and catch up with it."

"How? Those Reaper dudes scooped up every boat in the harbor when they abandoned their barge. They all got trashed. Face it, we missed our chance."

"Then we can take a car and beat the submarine down to Newport. There must be tons of boats there."

"And then what? You saw what happened to those guys who attacked the sub."

"Yeah." Todd wished he could forget it. He and Ray had witnessed the horrible spectacle from shore: those bulging masses of flesh that rose from the boat's missile bays and exploded into a thousand frenzied tentacles, yanking El Dopa's assault force down to oblivion. "What the hell *was* that?"

"I don't know, but something's seriously wrong in there. Whatever it is, I don't want a closer look."

"Well, where would you like to go?"

"I just want to get out of this suit. I'm thirsty, man."

"Me, too. Let's just start by finding a drink."

"How the hell are we gonna be able to drink anything wearing these helmets?"

"It's called a *straw*, doofus."

They left the waterfront area of India Point and headed inland on Gano Street. There were several small businesses along the way, including a donut shop and a convenience store. It was the same street that had been swarming with Xombies a few days earlier, when the boys had first come ashore seeking supplies. Bad idea. They didn't have the Reaper suits then and were completely defenseless against the blue onslaught that wiped out over thirty boys in under thirty minutes. It was the meat-armored Reapers who saved their lives.

This time there were neither Reapers nor Xombies, and no reason to fear them even if there were. The boys were covered.

Todd and Ray checked the donut shop first. They were unsurprised to find the four-month-old pastries inedible, but were disappointed to find the drink coolers cleaned out and the sink taps dry.

"Look out—zombie donuts!" Todd yelled, pitching Munchkins at Ray's flesh helmet. The stale balls exploded into crumbs.

"Hey, cut it out, man," Ray said lethargically.

Todd threw a few more, but Ray could not be incited to a donut war, so Todd gave up. They went next door to the convenience store, heartened by the big Pepsi sign out front. Nothing—it was even worse than the donut shop.

"What the hell, man."

There were not even any remains of food—rats, mice, and maggots had erased all organic matter. Anything canned or bottled had been efficiently looted; the shelves were empty. And the pillaging had happened recently, a few days ago at most; the mud tracks were fresh. This wasn't the act of random looters in the heat of panic. It was Reapers.

"Shit, man, that's right," Todd said. "We're not gonna find anything around here—the Reapers reaped it all. They stripped this whole area, remember?"

"Awesome."

"But they couldn't have gone through every house. Come on, we just have to go door-to-door."

"You mean break into people's homes, Holmes?"

"Yeah, why not? It's not like they're coming back."

"I don't know . . . it's like desecrating the dead or something."

"Not really. It's just putting stuff to good use that would otherwise go to waste."

"Hey, Todd?"

"Yeah?"

"I have to go to the bathroom."

"I know; I've been holding my piss for the last hour."

"It's not just piss."

"Well, just try to hold it."

"Too late."

They were prisoners of the flesh, golems of raw meat, doomed to wander the wasteland until they drowned in their own filth. Ray expected to die a little sooner, having been shot through the side, but this was only speculation since there was no way of examining or treating the wound. At least it didn't hurt, and the bleeding had stopped, so there was that.

Out of forty boys who had come ashore, just these two survived. Did they survive out of superior skill or intelligence? Was it their unusual grit that enabled them to outlast their fellows? Were the others just weak?

No—much as they might have wished it were so, both Todd and Ray knew they were nothing special. This was what haunted them: the thought that stronger, smarter, and more deserving boys had died in their stead. Brave dudes like Sal DeLuca and Kyle Hancock had sacrificed themselves so that lazy nubs like Todd and Ray could escape. It wasn't fair. But as Todd shuffled along the barren streets of his hometown, staring out through misshapen eyeholes at the living nightmare that was his only companion, and knew that he, too, was a horror, both of them damned to this ridiculous, incomprehensible fate, he realized there was perhaps some justice to it after all.

Maybe the dead were the lucky ones.

As they turned a corner, they encountered a blue Elvis. Elvis was dressed in a blue-and-white polyester suit covered with sequins, a gold-lined cape, and boots of blue suede.

Blue Elvis asked, "You boys lookin' for someone?"

"Who the hell are you?" Ray asked.

Todd said, "Don't talk to that Xombie, man, are you crazy?"

"He asked me a question."

"Ignore it and keep walking."

Elvis stayed with them like a persistent panhandler. "You fellas look lost," he said. "Maybe I can help you find what you're looking for."

Todd spun on him. "What the hell kind of Xombie are you? Get the fuck away from us, man."

"Now what kind of way is that to talk to a fellow traveler

on the road of life?" The blue man suddenly became very animated, running ahead and calling their attention to a seething mass of ants around a crack in the asphalt. "Take a look here, right here. You know what this is? This is a war we've got going here, with two races killin' each other: the Black and the Red. I been watching 'em all day." He shook his slick-coiffed head. "Look at 'em go, man!"

"I hate bugs," said Ray.

"*Hate?* They're just doing what comes natural. Hate is in their DNA, just like it's in ours. Only way to stop 'em from fighting is to change their fundamental genetic structure. They won't do it voluntarily, I can tell you! But *hate*, gee whiz. How can you hate anything in this beautiful world?" He took off his sunglasses, wiping an imaginary tear. "Especially knowing it's all gonna be gone soon."

"Oh shit," Ray hissed. "It's him. Todd, I think it's *him*."

"Who?"

"*Miska!*"

"No way." Todd turned to the blue man. "You're Uri Miska?"

"I'm partial to folks callin' me the King."

"See, it's not him."

"Just kidding!" The man shook his head affably. In a British accent, he declaimed, "The king is dead! Long live the king!"

Todd said, "Come on, let's get out of here."

The man blocked their way, bowing stiffly. "Uraeus Miska, at your service!"

"What? Seriously?"

"Surprised? Yes, it's me. To paraphrase another great emancipator: I *had* a dream." He raised his arms to the sky. "A dream to which all men expired!"

Todd hissed, "This is bullshit. Dude is crazy."

"Congratulations!" Miska cried.

"What for?"

"Finding me. They say a good man is hard to find. Considering how many people keep finding me, I must not be very good . . . or perhaps it's that I make myself too conspicuous. What do you think?" He struck a heroic pose.

Ray couldn't hold back anymore. "Oh my God," he said. "Can you help us? We need to get out of these suits."

"Why? Clothes make the man."

"Seriously, sir, we're in trouble. If you help us, we'll do whatever we can to help you."

"What makes you think I can help you . . . or you me?"

"You're a scientist! You're famous! You invented Agent X!"

"I had nothing to do with those 'suits'—that's somebody else's workmanship. Check the deli. I hope you got a money-back guarantee."

"They're not ours! We only stole them so we could get away!"

"Hoist by your own petard, eh?"

"You have to help us, *please*."

"Well, let me think about it. Sit down, and I'll tell you a story. Did you know we're standing on the site of a battle? Before the ants, I mean. This was the War between the Black and the Blue."

"Come *on*, man!" In desperation, Todd said, "Help us or we'll kill you."

"That would be a neat trick," Miska said. "Come now—sit, sit."

The boys suddenly jerked into motion like meat puppets, their bodies wrenched against their will as the flesh armor moved them. Insanely strong and none too gentle, it forced them to plop down cross-legged across from Miska.

"What the fuck, man!" Todd cried, in pain. He felt like he had been wrung out like a wet sponge.

Weeping, Ray groaned, "Awesome."

"Sorry," Miska said, sitting down himself. "I'm still getting the hang of it."

"What is this, man? What the hell are you doing to us?"

"That flesh you're wearing answers to me. Isn't that something? I originally developed the technology to control prosthetic implants. Every Maenad morphocyte is an independent nanotransceiver, tuned to an electrode array in my cerebral cortex. It triggers a cellular rather than a neuromuscular response, which allows a rather extraordinary degree of control. It's just a matter of mastering the complexity— learning to ride a bike. Or a million bikes. The cells themselves amplify and relay the signal, promulgating in iron-rich hemoglobin and even the Earth itself to form a vast, wireless data array—a true cellular network. What I call my Billion-Fingered Fist."

Mind reeling, Todd asked, "Are you saying you can control the Xombies?"

"Yes."

"You fuck! You made them kill our friends and families, you motherfucker! You killed *everybody*!"

"I know, it sounds pretty bad when you put it that way. I suppose that explains why folks are so mad at me."

"Fuck you! You might as well kill us, too, you asshole!"

"Who said anything about killing anyone? I never killed anyone. How do these things get started? No one has been killed. Do you understand? Literally, no one who has been inoculated with Agent X has died."

"No, they've just become Xombies, which is worse!"

"Worse than death? I think you would have to consult them about that. They are quite content, believe me."

"But they're not even human! They're monsters!"

"Monsters? Human beings are monsters. Did you ever watch MTV? Unlike Will Rogers, I never met a man I liked very much, which is why it is so ironic that I should be the one to save the human race from annihilation when the end comes."

"What the hell are you talking about?"

"Oh yes—haven't you heard? The end is coming. From

up there. The end of life on Earth: every bird and bee and monarch butterfly blown to smithereens, not with a whimper but with a bang. The only survivors will be deep-sea tube worms and some hardy bacteria . . . and perhaps my Xombies."

Ray said, "You mean that Big Enchilada thing the Reapers talked about?"

The blue man looked at him, then burst into laughter. "Big Enchilada? Really? That's what they're calling it? No 'Hammer of God' or 'Shiva the Destroyer.' Big Enchilada, wow." Sobering up, he said, "The word is 'Enceladus.' Let's call it a Trojan horse, which will unleash an enemy of unknown proportions or intentions. All I know is that they *aimed* for us. They are coming, and we must be prepared to stop them."

"Them who? Aliens or something?"

"Or something."

"Stop them how?"

"With my fist. Quiet now, boys, and let me tell you the story of the Sadie Hawkins Day Massacre."

Uri Miska closed his eyes as if summoning unseen forces, then began to speak:

"Imagine a line of Humvees with roof-mounted fifty-caliber machine guns, armored personnel carriers with swiveling weapons turrets, actual tanks, all driving down the streets of Providence. Some of the vehicles were flying American flags or were painted with crosses and Bible quotes. The weather was so warm and sunny it was like summer in January, a regular Fourth of July parade. And like any parade, there were cheering spectators . . . only in this case the spectators were naked and blue.

"Not too many at first. It was hardly worth the soldiers' ammunition to shoot them, for they splattered like rotten melons and were squashed to pulp beneath the treads. But from every corner of the city more Xombies were flying in,

Xombies by the thousands, their bare feet hardly touching the ground and their blue hands outstretched as if magnetically drawn to all that clanking steel.

"Many of the creatures had been migrating out of the city along the interstate and were now drawn back by this sudden bonanza of red-blooded fighting men, this traveling carnival of destruction. And as the unstoppable naked horde descended upon the immovable mechanized force, the female Xombies—Furies, Harpies, Maenads—winnowed themselves from the main group, holding back in the shadows as the less-circumspect males charged forward.

"These males closed in from all directions, rounding corners and converging ever tighter, the narrow canyons of downtown funneling the crowd into an undifferentiated flowing mass, a tsunami of blue bodies that filled the urban grid like a caustic fluid, scouring everything in its path. Then they were there, pouring onto Westminster from all sides, surrounding the mobile column and falling upon it.

"The turkey shoot commenced. Harrowing spikes of ammunition blazed straight into the densest centers of the mob, rendering them instantly into bursting globes of jelly, with limbs and heads and other large fragments raining down like chaff. Ground-floor windows disintegrated all along the street, stores and restaurants gutted by blizzards of steel. In a matter of minutes, and ten million rounds of ammo, the entire mass of creatures was cut down. The vehicles continued on, having barely paused to engage the enemy. Random burps of gunfire continued as more Xombies were sighted, but the battle was over."

Miska held up his finger, then slowly wagged it. "Or maybe not. As the column's wheels drove over its semi-liquefied adversary, movement could be seen in the remains: All those sundered body parts were still very much in the fight.

"Mangled sinew stuck to heavy treads; tendons wound

around drive shafts like taffy, gummed up brakes and springs and mounted guns; animated gristle wiggled up under chassis, fouling engine rods and clogging exhaust pipes; bony hands scuttled spiderlike over fuse boxes, pulling wires willy-nilly; veiny cauls of flesh covered windshields and viewports.

"The war machine seized up. Not every vehicle was equally vulnerable, but those that were blocked the rest, so that very soon the whole enterprise ground to a halt.

"Masked men with long-necked acetylene torches got out and played their superhot jets over the carpet of crawling meat, fanning it off vehicles and creating a clean zone for the mechanics to work. The stench of burnt flesh filled the air. At first, the technique seemed to be working: The disarticulated foe pushed back to form a seething dam around the cleared area, but every time the firemen let up for only a second, the line broke down, invaded by slithering masses of viscera. As the gruesome dam grew higher, it became more impossible to police all the sneaking incursions . . . and the psychological effect of that wall of talking heads and slurping entrails must have been terrible.

"Very soon, the defenses started to break down. Men were beset by slippery fragments worming under their pants and into their orifices. The vehicles were also infested, so that their crews had to turn their attention from the threat outside to more immediate pestilence in the cockpits. It became a farce, every man battling an invisible enemy, ripping at his own clothes like an alcoholic with delirium tremens.

"At last the order was given to retreat. Crazed men piled back into overcrowded truck cabs with their crazed fellows, pursued by waves of squirming chum. Guns blasted indiscriminately at the enveloping mass as the column surged forward and crashed together, panicked gunners shooting each other, and the heavier vehicles pushing lighter ones out of the way or just driving over them. Acetylene tanks exploded, setting off boxes of shells, which ignited leaking fuel—a chain of fiery explosions ripped through the column. Two tracked vehicles—an Abrams tank and a Bradley Fighting Vehicle—broke through and hurtled up the street, wreathed in mantles of flame and frying meat.

"Several blocks up, Westminster ended at a T-intersection on Empire Street, where there was an Irish pub and a National Guard recruiting office. The Abrams was there first, but did not stop, did not turn, did not even slow down, but just blindly rammed the brick face of the federal building, smashing through the support columns, and the Bradley followed it right in, causing the whole structure to avalanche down on them both. The last sound was the popping of ammo in the fires . . . with perhaps a few conclusive pistol shots mixed in.

"That was a turning point in human history—the first battle of meat versus machines, where the point went to the meat.

"The next battle was very different. The men had learned their lesson. It began two weeks later, and was initiated by a single unarmed truck: an ice-cream truck. Like any ice-cream truck, it had a loudspeaker on top, blasting the familiar tinkly version of 'When the Saints Go Marching In.' Unlike an ordinary Mister Softee wagon, this one was pulling a flatbed trailer with a large chain-link cage on it, a portable dog kennel. The cage did not contain dogs, however, but human beings—specifically, women. Innocent women incarcerated for the threat posed by their sex. They appeared to be praying.

"The reason for their prayers soon became apparent. Following close behind the truck was an enormous mass of running Xombies. It looked like a naked, blue Boston Marathon.

"Approaching the site of the previous battle, the truck turned off the music and slowed down, allowing a man in back to release the trailer hitch. The cage came free, rolling to a stop as the truck peeled away.

"Now the trapped women could only wait as the following horde caught up with them: Xombies tall and short, fat and thin, young and old. Xombies of all kinds except for one specific group: the initial women carriers of Agent X, the Maenads, who had gone rogue spontaneously, then spread the disease to everyone they could catch . . . and kiss. Once again, these less-impulsive multitudes were holding back, watching from the shadows.

"Unlike them, I could not stand to watch as the cage was surrounded. The worst weren't even the running dead but the crawling ones—the blasted remnants left over from the earlier fight, whose bodies had half frozen and healed together in strange, awful configurations and now came scuttling out of burnt storefronts like a freak invasion.

"In seconds, the kennel was an ovum buried under a thousand competing sperm. The victims could be heard screaming as the cage crumpled . . . and then all vanished in a blinding flash.

"It was fire. White-hot fire as bright as the sun. Brilliant sparks rained down like a shower of stars, burning through anything they touched, incinerating skin and hair and turning Xombies into roamin' candles, great balls of fire, their bodies consumed even from within by tumors of malignant flame. Inhuman torches fled the bonfire, shedding layers of flesh like dead leaves until there was nothing left to combust, and they toppled into paper-doll silhouettes of molten slag.

"Down at the river, there were more fireworks. Floating braziers which had once been piled with firewood for the pleasure of strolling tourists were now loaded with living, praying females, attracting an audience of avid blue spectators down the riverbanks and into the knee-deep scum, where there was no escape from the incendiary barrage that was loosed upon them, a glowing hailstorm that obliterated anything and everything in that blazing, boiling trench.

"On the opposite end of town, hung above the street, a pair of giant masks forged out of steel grating—playhouse faces of comedy and tragedy—were likewise packed with live girls and allowed to gather a tremendous cult before a tanker truck on the rooftop was detonated, showering jellied fire on the whole congregation.

"Such fire traps had been set in cities all over America, all over the world, and in one day they immolated millions of Xombies, perhaps tens of millions . . . plus thousands of uninfected women.

"Providence burned, or parts of it. It's an old city, built in the days of brick and stone, and its walls are resistant to fire. Many newer buildings disappeared, in some areas whole blocks, but after a few days of heavy sleet and snow, the inferno sputtered out. And then it was over. Whatever tarlike deposits remained soon froze solid and were covered with a thick crust of ice. Providence was purified.

"That was when the men emerged, the instigators of the holocaust. They were a peculiar confederacy of men, whose chief point in common was that they had all survived the plague because of their isolation from women and who now believed that this was nothing less than divine providence: Agent X was God's punishment for original sin. Women were the enemy, instruments of Satan, and it was only right and proper to burn them in order to save their immortal souls. This was a very timely gospel, and many desperate people joined the church, including not a few women."

Todd asked, "Why are you telling us all this?"

"Because these people are still around, even after all these months. I drove them out of Providence, sent them fleeing into the wilderness, but they are coming back. In fact, they are experiencing a bit of a renaissance these days, spreading their gospel far and wide like some kind of traveling revival show. Revival in the literal sense—they are restoring Xombies to mortal life."

"Restoring Xombies! You mean *curing* them?"

"Yes, but not just any Xombies. They are mainly baptizing Xombie Moguls—elderly tycoons who had the foresight to embalm themselves in Agent X prior to the plague. Restored to life, these men still have tremendous resources at their command, and they no longer need guns, they don't need fences, and they don't need to wrap themselves in dead meat to stay alive. But they do need women—immune women—in order to retain their humanity . . . and to procreate. Do you understand what that means?"

"They're shit out of luck?"

"It means they are a threat to the survival of our species. They survived the plague, but they can't survive Enceladus. They may be immune to Agent X, but they are perfectly vulnerable to ordinary injury and death, and every day the number of new Immunes increases. Xombies will not touch them, nor can I."

Todd said, "Maybe you should try explaining all this to them."

"Oh, I have. But after how I terrorized them and chased them out of town, they are not conducive to helpful hints. In fact, they think I'm the Devil and have come back to slay me. No, I cannot help them. But maybe someone else can."

Suddenly Todd and Ray felt their suits stiffen, seams popping, and abruptly the flesh capsules of their helmets burst open like giant milkweed pods, revealing their startled, sweaty faces, then split downward and peeled off their bodies as though sheared away by invisible blades. The liberated meat jerked violently loose from under their seated butts and scuttled away in a blur of peculiar, flapping locomotion.

Freed from the restraining flesh, the two boys cried out in relief and immediately tore the wire cages off their heads so they could rub their filth-encrusted faces. Ray checked his gunshot wound and found that it was almost healed, a healthy pink dimple in his side. Then he froze.

Both boys froze, hearts stopped in unison. *Listen.* There

was a sound in the distance—the mournful, impossible, un-mistakable sound of a train whistle. A train was coming! Just on the other side of the hill. And if there was a train, there were people; where there were people, there was life. Ray's shocked eyes met Todd's, and they came to an instant, un-spoken agreement: *Run.*

They ran.

# CHAPTER **THREE**

## XMAS

**W**e are creatures of habit. Immortality is not something you learn overnight. There are stages, similar to the five stages of dying: Denial, anger, bargaining, depression, acceptance—not necessarily in that order. And there is an extra one: fear. It's scary to wake up dead. For that was how we all thought of it, despite Dr. Langhorne's explanations. You were alive or you were dead, and since we no longer fit the definition of life, we had to be ghouls, zombies, revenants, none other than the ever-loving Living Dead.

I say that all these things had to play themselves out, and there were many little melodramas before the strange new dialectic was resolved. Boys being boys. We were on the boat a long time working it through.

Being human was a craving most found hard to ignore: the comforting, pointless routines of eating, drinking, dressing, breathing. Hoping, praying, hurting, doubting. Loving and hating. In my case, reading and writing. We liked our mortal identities, frailties and all, and were deeply afraid of losing ourselves.

Eating, yes. What do you think, we didn't eat? Zombies aren't magic—there's no such thing as a perpetual-motion machine; everything that moves requires a push. Most unreformed Exes get around this by moving as little as possible, existing in a fugue state that allows them to subsist for a long time on the stored energy of their residual human tissue as well as elements in the air, every pore soaking up gases and microparticles like a sponge, taking in nitrogen and carbon dioxide and even ambient light, and off-gassing a bit of ionized oxygen—the undead are regular air purifiers. Environmentally semiconscious!

We on the boat, however, had daily duties to perform. The cost in energy was such that we had to supplement "light soup" with more substantial food. I say "had to"— the truth is we ate less for physical nourishment than to sate the hunger in our souls. Eating was an act of nostalgia. We could as easily have gotten our calories by glugging diesel oil or chewing rubber boots—our bodies were capable of rendering almost any organic-based substance into motive force. For that matter, we could have taken bites out of each other . . . and some did. Since pain was no longer an issue, and even the grossest injury did not lead to death, cannibalism was a sin comparable to stealing from the cookie jar. Except cookies don't grow back.

Little by little, everybody began to relax. To surrender. And in surrendering to realize we were free. Free of pain, free of disease, free of old age, free of death. Free even of the Xombie curse—with no human crew left, Dr. Langhorne decided there was no need for me to continue donating my blood serum. I was doubtful about this, having developed a maternal bond with my blood recipients. It was hard to just cut the cord.

Despite my qualms, they remained entirely placid, choosing to stay on the boat rather than to join the wild ones ashore—which was yet another freedom: the freedom of choice. Many other freedoms we could not yet comprehend, but for now, this alone was enough, an existence not only rid of pain but with the prospect of joy. The joy of saving others.

On my command, the boat emptied like an uncorked

cask. Men and boys erupted from the hatches and spilled over the side like hairless lemmings, plummeting to the bottom and clambering forward through swaying eelgrass as through a meadow, leaving clouds of roiled silt. They emerged from the water draped in seaweed and nipping crabs, their splashes making prisms in the sun. Mounting the bank, they lined up on dry land and waited.

It was the moment we had dreamed of in life . . . and beyond death. The crucial first step toward restoring our lost humanity and returning home. *Home.* What was home anymore? We only knew what it was not: Home was not the cold bowels of a submarine or the colder void of eternity. Home was not anyplace we had left behind. Because without our loved ones, our houses were only haunted shells.

After the battle with the Reapers, we had briefly considered putting ashore in Providence to look for surviving family members and friends, whom we could indoctrinate into our tribe. The simple truth of the matter was, the population of rational undead could only grow as long as there were mortal human beings to inoculate. Otherwise, those "undecideds" would likely die and be lost forever. Thus it was crucial to find such people and save them . . . even from themselves.

Easier said than done. Our loved ones had scattered along with the rest of humankind. And as the survivors dwindled, the feral Xombies moved on as well, leaving the coasts and migrating inland, heading west and south as if driven by some powerful compulsion. We denizens of the boat felt this, too, this need to move on. Some simply left and never returned.

Home was elsewhere, a sanctuary beyond our reckoning. There were no words for it. The nearest thing was love, an emotion we had all but forgotten and knew only through its absence—a vague residual ache in hearts that had long since ceased to beat.

Flashes of remembrance struck me like electric shocks, that familiar sad face looming out of the mist. *Come on in, Sillybean, the water's fine.* The past reaching out its long-fingered hand to stroke my cheek.

*Just a dream,* I reminded myself, as I suddenly found myself sitting at a table overlooking a ballroom floor. The band was playing "Hey Jude," and the moment was rich with the luster of its own impermanence. Moments were priceless when you knew they were finite. That hand, that face.

It was my mother. It was our last Christmas Eve, and Mummy had heard of a fancy dress ball at the Biltmore Hotel. *Come on, sourpuss! Better than moping at home!* So we assembled our best outfits and traipsed to the high-priced citadel that was the Biltmore . . . only to be stopped cold by the admission charge: forty-five dollars a person.

I was furious—it was so typical of my mother, so typical I didn't bother whining about it because I knew perfectly well that that ninety dollars would wipe us out for the rest of the month. There was just no way.

We retreated in shame under the sneering noses of door-men and parking attendants and waiting hoi polloi. *Well! What do you want to do now?* Mummy asked. Her jaunty game face was painful to behold. *I don't care,* I said. Re-splendently tacky in our party dresses, we walked to a coffee shop. It was a grubby, forlorn place, and as I sat there with my mother amid the homeless and other beat-down human refuse of the season, I thought, *Our natural habitat.* I raised the cracked vinyl menu like a shield. *Six ounces of USDA Choice Sirloin, grilled to perfection and served with your choice of—*

*Hey.*

Mummy hadn't touched her menu. She was looking at me with that light in her eyes.

*What?*

*Let's go.*

*Where?*
*Back. Up there.*
*We can't afford it.*
*Oh pooh. We'll figure that out later. Let's just go.*
*Really?*
*Come on!*

We fled the dive, running back to the hotel, trailing laughter and flouncing satin.

Winded, we entered the ballroom. It was the most beautiful thing I had ever seen, all dim-lit opulence, with candles and tuxedoes and tall windows overlooking the city. We were shown a table, and treated as if we belonged in such society. My mother was clearly at ease, having assumed a poise I had never seen before, navigating the etiquette traps with perfect confidence. We ate dinner, prime rib, then sat for a long time, just breathing it all in, watching people dance. The band was good, and when the piano player struck up a cabaret rendition of "Hey Jude," my mother stood up and reached out her hand and said, *Let's dance.* I had never danced before, but I was caught up in it, trusting that the need to believe was enough.

And it was.


*This is it.*

I waited until all the others were ashore before I left the bridge. It was the first time I had ever been alone on the submarine, and I listened to the foam-padded silence with something like worry.

Could it be possible to live again? I was afraid to find out. To abandon the boat was to put hope to the test—and if hope failed, what then? All that was left was to give up. Give up all trace of the girl I once was; shed Lulu Pangloss like a dead skin. Go native. That was what gnawed at me and ate me up inside: How easy it would be to let go. Surrender to the Xombie.

*Don't give up the ship,* I thought. More like, *Don't let the door hit your ass on the way out.*

Whatever happened, I would likely never see this ship again. The orphaned steel behemoth would sit here and rust, hatches open to the elements, wallowing with the tides until hard weather heeled her over, and water filled the hull. Then she would settle to the shallow bottom, every intake plugged with mud and the great gold propellers crusted thick with oysters and lurid orange sea squirts. Eventually, the boat would silt over entirely and join the shore, sprouting grasses and wooded slash so that her fairwater would become a brushy hillock, red with sumac and rusty edges, reeking of rotten iron. And in her belly the fallow reactor would crack and seep radiation into the environment, its brittle control rods breaking under the pressure of invading sediments. But the clay would also contain the poison, forming a solid cast within the chamber and hardening around the decaying metalworks, effectively fossilizing them. A million years hence, only the extruded patterns would remain, pressed in rocky strata miles from the sea.

Finishing my final walk-through, I stumbled across my mother. It was as though she were waiting for me.

Entering the reactor room, I almost jumped at the sight of a wild-haired blue Fury hanging from the ceiling. The last time I had met her was in the slime pit of the Reaper barge, and we hadn't been able to communicate verbally. The time before that, I was still a human girl, and she was the monstrous Xombie chasing me. We hadn't talked much then either—she was barely capable of speech. But since then, she had recovered most of her wits . . . if not her looks.

"Mummy," I said. "We're going ashore now."

She didn't react, just staring at me.

I said, "We're probably not coming back."

She tipped her head sideways and closed her eyes. I started to leave, and she said, "Lulu."

"What?"

"Fred Cowper's not your father."

A strange chill blew through me, the ghost of a human feeling. "What do you mean?"

"Fred Cowper and I never had any children together. He wasn't capable. You never met your real father, the father of my children. His name was Al Despineau. Alaric Despineau."

*"Alaric?"* That was my hated middle name. "What do you mean, 'children'? How many children do you have?"

"None, anymore."

"What does that mean? I'm here."

"You are dead, my darling, and so is the past. There is no changing it now; it's fixed and dilated. I'm so sorry."

Mummy fled into the dark.

# CHAPTER **FOUR**

## PEPPERLAND

Fred Cowper was incommunicado when I found him, dead to the world and unavailable for comment. Frustrating, but Xombies were notoriously unreliable that way, able to tune out indefinitely just when you needed to talk to them. Stuffing Fred's head in a ditty bag along with a few other necessities, I left the ship. Albemarle and the crew had rigged lines across the water, and I easily crossed this rope bridge to shore. Everyone was waiting for me there, as if only I could provide the answers they sought. I knew they would stand that way for hours, days, unless I told them what to do next. Time meant nothing to any of them, not even me. Time was totally arbitrary unless you forced it to mean something—unless you divided it into portions and measured it out like medicine. That was the human thing to do.

I assembled us all on the beach. Even in my own altered state, I thought we looked weird in the daylight, like creatures dredged out of the deep sea. Not liking the word "Xombies," we had chosen to call ourselves Dreadnauts, but this forbidding moniker had more recently been amended by the four Brits to Dreadnuts. There were three categories of us: Dark Blue, Bright Blue, and Clear.

The Dark Blues were those who had been violently infected with the original strain of Agent X. Their bodies "died" in the process, starved of oxygen while Maenad microbes hacked their cell nuclei and rewrote their DNA. With their drowned blue flesh and unblinking black eyes, they were the most Xombie-like in appearance, though with regular infusions of my blood serum, their higher faculties had gradually returned. They just had to relearn everything.

Along with Big Ed Albemarle and the boys who died with me at Thule, there were some thousand or so other Dark Blues on board, all new arrivals. Most of them were in bad shape—either missing major pieces or barely pieced together. They were leftovers from the recent Reaper madness. My mother was among them.

The Bright Blues were those like yours truly, who had either been passively infiltrated from within by Agent X spores (and this would apply to all the billions of first-generation female Maenads), or been deliberately inoculated with Uri Miska's "Tonic" before brain damage could occur. I met both criteria, and knew that intelligence alone was no buffer against X-mania, since in the seconds before the Tonic kicked in, I had strangled the first man I saw. Horrible. I didn't like to think of that even though I realized there was a higher purpose to it all.

Uri Miska had developed Agent X as humanity's only defense against the coming cataclysm—the Big Enchilada—which would kill all life on Earth. Since we weren't alive, we might survive. Xombies, that is. Black gold. Texas tea. This vague knowledge had been communicated to all of us through increasingly intense, dreamlike visions, and most on board believed it even if they did not fully comprehend it.

There were only two Bright Blues on board: I and Fred Cowper—or rather, Fred Cowper's decapitated head. In our perfect blueness, Fred and I were not grotesque so much as beautifully strange—living Hindu deities. Or so I chose to think about it.

But the Clears . . . the Clears were something different, something nobody understood yet—not even themselves.

They had the same regenerative capacity as the rest of us, the same apparent immortality, but without any of the negative side effects. They weren't blue. They never needed daily doses of my blood to function. They looked and felt completely human . . . until they suddenly turned their bodies inside out, changed colors like chameleons, or split in two and joined seamlessly back together.

As they learned to control it, their flesh answered their will to a degree that we Blues could only marvel at. Since Clears had only just begun to grasp their potential, it was an alarming process of discovery—a few mirrors were broken out of sheer fright.

Socially, there was a peculiar division between Blues and Clears. Unable to convert each other, we were in a race for the last dregs of humankind. Having taken an early lead, Blues were far ahead, but Clears were clearly faster, having taken over our original Navy crew and all the civilian refugees in a matter of hours.

Dr. Alice Langhorne (a Clear herself) had traced their mutant strain back to a single carrier, a young refugee boy named Bobby Rubio, who had been picked up in Providence.

Bobby seemed to have no idea why he was different and still refused to talk about where or how he might have been "infected." Langhorne didn't think it was possible he could have been born that way, but a lot of people liked the idea that little Bobby was the next stage of human evolution, that the world might save itself.


As we commandeered a fleet of abandoned vehicles and headed inland along the road, I began to have a strange sensation. This was the first time I had been ashore in months, and the sight of all these quaint houses and shops caused weird flutters of emotion that I recognized as goose bumps. Goose bumps!

I wasn't alone: My fellow travelers were experiencing

similar jitters of anticipation. If anything at all remained
of the America we once knew, this might be where we'd
find it.

The buildings and cars ahead showed minor traces of
damage: wires down, tilted utility poles, scattered debris.
Unlike some other cities we had seen, there were few signs
of panicked fight or flight—it all happened too fast. No
backed-up traffic or buildings burned to the ground. Except
for drifts of sand blown in from the dunes, it all looked
pretty normal.

The wind kicked up, raising a cloud of dust that momen-
tarily blotted out the sun. In that orange gloom, the signs
disappeared, the cars disappeared, the *road* disappeared.
This wasn't sand; it was ash. Ash from afar, carried on the
wind from the heartland, residue of a thousand burnt cities
all over America.

We came to the outskirts of a town called Exmore, along
the main highway that ran the length of the peninsula to
Cape Charles. There were no barricades, no security of any
kind. No life.

Through the settling haze, we began to make out a line of
human figures along the highway, still and silent as statues,
ankle deep in ash. Not humans—Xombies. They were inert
as lampposts, completely dormant, staring at nothing.

"Pepperland," said one of the Blackpudlians.

"Trucks a-comin'!" shouted Robles.

Then we could all sense it: a convoy of heavy vehicles
roaring toward us down US 13. They were bright with headlights and the life auras of their passengers—several dozen
human beings.

We automatically went into action, Blues and Clears
racing for the chance to add new members to our respective
teams. Hurriedly blocking the road, we took positions on
either side and hunkered flat in the ditches. As the trucks
neared, I could see that they were completely unprotected,
no armaments of any kind. It was too good to be true. When

the first one shifted down, we were all over that thing like
ants on a half-melted Popsicle.

Or we would have been, had the people in that truck not
suddenly glowed with a strange poison that robbed us of
our strength. The closer we got to them, the weaker we
became, so that the fastest and strongest of us fell the hard-
est, tumbling off the truck like frost-killed spiders.

Adding to our trouble, the dormant Xombies suddenly
sprang to life and attacked us. One came at me, and when
Lemuel smashed it with a sledgehammer, I realized it was
only part Xombie. The other part was machinery, a mass of
wires and gadgets stuffed into a gutted Xombie body. A
remote-controlled meat puppet! The flesh had been crudely
stapled back together, leaving small apertures for cameras,
radio antennae . . . and weapons.

Those weapons opened fire, taking out targets with pre-
cise bursts of metal pellets, electrically propelled at a zillion
rounds per second. Each blast sounded like a single shot but
was actually a patterned stream of ammo that cut through
flesh and bone like a superfast jigsaw. Anything it hit came
apart as though run through a sieve. When the ammo ran
out, they had false limbs that ejected bladed weapons that
slashed us to the bone. Worst of all, they tagged us with la-
sers, opening us to fire from the sky—an orbiting attack
drone. All around me, my Xomboys started exploding like
popcorn.

Too late, I realized what it was: Immunes. We had heard
rumors of Immunes from the Reapers, and I had refused
to believe they really existed, thinking immunity was just
more mortal wishfulness. But there could be no doubt about
it: There were Immunes in those trucks . . . or people tainted
with immune blood. Either way, we couldn't touch them;
our own bodies wouldn't allow it.

The poor miserable humans had come up with a perfect
defense. They had made it impossible for us to save them,
as if suffering and death were the most beautiful prizes they

could imagine. They had won. It was so tragic, I almost wished I could die with them.

But I couldn't.

As shrapnel riddled my torso, I remembered what Alice Langhorne had told me about Xombies when we first met: ". . . a bag of obsolete parts governed by a solid-state master." My body was not the fragile human form it had once been, but a completely arbitrary assemblage of cells. This was a disturbing thought as it threatened my very identity: Who was Lulu Pangloss if not this girl, this body, this face? How could she exist if she was a stranger to herself, some random, amorphous blob? It was too troubling to contemplate. So I had refused to face it, clinging to my mortal conception of myself, using my Maenad abilities as if they were party tricks, busying myself with plans and hopes and dreams.

Well, perhaps it was time to wake up.

That was it—I ordered a general retreat, and we ran for the vehicles. What was left of us.

# CHAPTER **FIVE**

## LOVEVILLE

Half the tires were flat, but we kept driving on them until the dragging treads started to catch fire. Then we had to get off and stand around while the buses burned. Looking at the map, I noticed there was a place called Hollywood not too far away—Hollywood, Maryland. My mother used to take me to Hollywood. The real one. The memory was enough to start me moving again, and my evident purpose compelled the others to follow.

Hiking cross-country, we found a gasoline terminal and commandeered a fuel barge. Maneuvering the barge was tricky in places; the river was full of carbonized ruin that had washed down from Baltimore, its banks and shoals festooned with trash. But as we navigated downstream, the river widened, and the junk dispersed.

After a few miles, we put ashore in a cove and started walking toward Hollywood. It was a semirural area, checkered with farms that were now meadows, encroached upon by suburban developments that would croach no more.

Breasting the tall grass, surrounded by the hiss of locusts, we came to a town called Loveville, and that was it. We had all had enough. It wasn't that we were tired—just tired of seeking something we knew didn't exist. Tired of being disappointed. Screw Hollywood. This was a pleasant little town, with schools and churches and grocery stores.

The sign said, WELCOME TO LOVEVILLE—what more could one want?

"What are we doing, Lulu?" asked Bobby. "What are we looking for?"

I had no good answer. Listening to the birds and the bees, I said, "I think this may be it."

"What?"

"We're home."

For the first few weeks, very little happened. We existed in a dream state, some of us wandering around like sleepwalkers, others barely moving, all mesmerized by patterns of energy underlying the material world. With a little concentration, it was possible to make out the quantum-mechanical webwork that connected everything to everything else—the literal fabric of time and space. Actually, it was more like a vast harp, warping and rippling and swirling as the planet moved, vibrating a deep B minor chord from the depths of the galaxy. It called to us, promising gorgeous oblivion, but most were not ready to go . . . yet. We were torn between two worlds, unwilling or unable to commit to either and thus trapped in between. In limbo.

But perhaps we were underestimating ourselves. What if we didn't have to wait for the answers we craved but could invent whatever life we wanted and simply start living it? What if we could *create* the best of all possible worlds? Customize a reality that suited our peculiar needs?

Alice Langhorne called a meeting:

"Lulu has brought something to my attention," she announced. "Something that must be addressed if we are to continue as a group. We believe the present situation is becoming untenable. It's too difficult trying to graft our previous lives onto this new set of circumstances. We failed at it on the sub, we failed at it in Providence, and we're failing at it here. We aren't the people we used to be, and it's no use pretending we are. The incongruities are too . . . awkward. We need a less-fraught model to follow; otherwise, we'll all crack up."

There was silence—the truth of it was plain to all.

Langhorne continued, "Obviously, this is uncharted territory. We're not only reinventing ourselves, we're inventing an entirely new mode of existence—one that goes far beyond anything our human psyches can comprehend. It's not a damn makeover. The only frame of reference we have is mythical: zombies, vampires, angels—that kind of Hollywood baloney. We all know the reality is not quite so . . . glamorous. We think something profound is going to happen, some kind of Armageddon, and we were altered to survive it. So we're just hanging around, waiting for the other shoe to drop. Cosmic loitering. And if we're not careful, we'll all disappear right up our own black holes."

Julian Noteiro stepped forward. "So what did Lulu suggest?"

"That we need a new script to follow—something that touches upon all the basic aspects of human society without all the oppressive limitations of that society. A stylebook that we can live by, day to day, to keep our humanity intact. So we don't lose it."

"You mean like the Bible?"

"Not exactly." Langhorne picked up a stack of magazines out of a carton and slapped them down on the table. They were old comic books with titles like *LOVE* and *PEP* and *PALS 'N' GALS*. "Lulu was thinking of something a little easier—something more along these lines."

The crowd came forward, inspecting the comics as though they were peculiar alien artifacts. Inside the box were many more comics, as well as vintage paperback books and

DVDs of old television shows. On top were discs of *The Andy Griffith Show* and *I Love Lucy*.

Langhorne said, "Let's get started, shall we?"

I sat alone in the dark, reminiscing as I watched dawn creep over the horizon.

Xombies didn't sleep. Nor could it be said that we were ever truly awake—not in the human sense. Xombies did not live in the present. Our minds wandered freely in time and space; they drifted in and out. I knew the human conception of reality was a façade erected by mortal minds to block contact with the inconceivable vastness of genuine reality. Living creatures needed this mechanism in order to forget they were doomed. Xombies did not. So in that sense it could be said that Xombies were deeply awake and that human consciousness was a mode of dreaming. A delusion.

My mother came back to me again and again. This time we were driving to McDonald's in a borrowed Cadillac. I remembered: My mother got a job working as a housekeeper for a family in Lake Tahoe. It was a large house on a remote mountain road, and I shared a cozy room over the garage with the children of the family who owned the place. The three girls welcomed me like a sister, and their unexpected generosity filled my parched heart. Even the local elementary school was incredible, a woodsy, progressive place where the kids were friendly and the teachers funny and sane. One day, while the family was away, I made the mistake of trying to climb a steep gravel bluff, lost my footing, and slid to the bottom, badly skinning both knees. My mother found me bleeding on the doorstep and rushed me to the bathtub, where she washed the wounds and dabbed them with Mercurochrome. Once I was patched up, stiff with pain, my mother said, *You know what this means, don't you?*

*What?* I sniffled.

*You get a wish. A freebie.*

I was propped on the couch in front of the TV, watching pornographic close-ups of golden fries. *I want a Filet-O-Fish,* I said.

*Honey, the nearest McDonald's is fifty miles away.*

*What about the Caddy?* I meant the family Cadillac, a pristine black limo that never left the garage except on the most special occasions—the Baxters used their two other cars for getting around. The Caddy was strictly for show.

*Lulu, you know I'm not allowed to use that car. Mr. Baxter specifically said so.*

My tone turned tragic; waifish tears welled up. *Why not? It's just a quick ride into town and back. They'll never even know.*

*You must be kidding. You know what'll happen if they find out?*

*How could they find out? They're in Sacramento.* Sensing my mother waver, I crooned, *Mummy, you promised—pleeeeze?*

It was a thrillingly short drive: Halfway down the mountain, the Caddy ran out of gas.

We were forced to abandon the car, flagging down a passing motorist for a ride to town and paying a service station to deliver fuel. By the time we got back to the car, it had been towed. The police thought it was a stolen vehicle because the Baxters had left word they would be out of town, and the car had been vandalized. Then there was the hefty impound fee. My mother tried first to charm, then to bluster her way out, and I cranked up the waterworks, but it was no use. We had no money; we were stuck. The only way to get the car back was to call the Baxters and explain the whole situation. It was not fun. The look on Mummy's face as she hung up the phone made it utterly clear that our life in Lake Tahoe was soon to be over. So much for the joyride. But already I was adjusting to the new reality, walling off the humiliating dismissal—*fuckit,* I thought.

My attention shifted to the golden arches across the street—Mummy still had a few bucks left.

My blue lips parted, mouthing the words of that long-ago child: *Mummy? I'm still hungry.*

I heard a noise. Somewhere down the block, an unmuffled two-stroke engine sputtered to life. Then another, and another, all working their way up the street. It was an unpleasant and deeply familiar sound—one I had not heard since I was alive.

Lawn mowers.

Opening the kitchen window, I leaned out to see all the crew from the boat pushing lawn mowers across their new lawns. It was still quite dark out, and the landscape was shaded deep blue under a paler sky pricked with stars. I could smell exhaust and cut grass. The stars were the only lights—there was no electricity yet.

As the mowers completed their work, and the sun cleared the rooftops, I heard a different sound, like gunshots in the distance—it was the backfiring of an old car. A moment later, the vehicle chugged into view, turning up my street.

It was an antique car, a red jalopy with the top down, squeaking and rattling as if its engine were shaking it to pieces. The spoked wheels were visibly out of alignment, and the exhaust pipe spewed a contrail of noxious fumes.

The car stopped in front of my house. I could see Jake Bartholomew in the driver's seat; he set the brake and gave the horn a toot. Jake's passengers jumped out and came up the walk—they were Sal DeLuca and Lemuel Sanchez.

Sal was wearing a peculiar hat, its felt brim turned up and cut to resemble a king's crown, with colorful buttons pinned around it like jewels. Lemuel's hair had been cropped short and bleached blond, and he was dressed in a football jersey that said QUARTERBACK. They knocked on the door.

This was unusual. The door was unlocked; nobody announced themselves anymore. Human courtesies such as respect for privacy were meaningless, especially after the forced intimacies of living together on the sub. I turned to see Alice Langhorne gliding down the stairs like a ghost. The usually austere woman was wearing a pleated pink dress and a frilly apron, but the most alarming change was her head of curlers.

"I'll get it," Langhorne said. Opening the front door, she said, "Good morning, boys."

"Good morning, Mrs. Langhorne. Is Lulu around?"

"That's *Ms.* Langhorne. And she certainly is. Lulu!"

"What?"

"Lemuel and Sal are here to pick you up."

"Pick me up? For what?"

"Boys?"

As if reciting from a script, Sal said, "Miz Langhorne asked us to ask you if you would do us the honor of letting you drive us—I mean, letting *us* drive *you*, heh heh—to school."

"*School?* Are you demented? What do you—" Langhorne jabbed me in the back. *Hard.* "Oh. Right. School, really?"

Alice Langhorne nodded grimly.

"All right," I said. "Hang on." I stepped into my shoes. "I'm ready; let's go."

"No you are not, young lady."

"What now?"

"You can't go to school like that. You march right upstairs and put on a clean dress and brush your hair. The boys will wait. Won't you?"

"Yes, Miz Langhorne."

Knowing it was pointless to argue, I climbed the stairs while Alice invited the boys in and offered them milk and cookies. Little Bobby Rubio was at the top of the stairs, staring down.

"Are you going to play school?" he asked me, as I brushed past.

"I guess so."

"Can I play, too?"

"Go ask Alice."

I went into my designated room and examined the clothes in the closet. They had belonged to a girl exactly my size though much younger. Taking off my filthy velvet dress, I put on a clean cotton one—a sunny yellow number with black polka dots. Then I brushed my hair into some semblance of order and tied it with a bow. Flying back downstairs, I was intercepted by Langhorne, who spit-shined my face and handed me a sack lunch before letting me out the door.

"Have a nice day at school!" she called after us.

Getting into the car, I was struck anew by the boys' weirdly preppy appearance. Jake's copper-colored hair was parted into two lobes in front and buzzed short at the sides, the stubble shaved in a peculiar grid pattern. He wore a V-neck sweater over a dress shirt, baggy golf pants, and brown-and-white gaiters.

"Hi, Jake," I said.

"Hi, Lulu. What do you think of Bess?"

"Bess?" My first thought was Basic Enlisted Submarine School.

"Bessie, my new car—well, maybe not *new* . . ."

"Oh. Nice."

"Nice? You wouldn't believe what we went through to find this thing and get it running. It's a Model T Roadster—is that awesome or what? We looked up antique car dealers in three different counties before we found it."

"Why?"

"Why? Why do you think?" He waved a comic book in my face. "Mood! Atmosphere! The power of suggestion! It's an experiment in Xombie psychology, and we're the subjects. Haven't the officers drilled you about this?"

"No. Just Langhorne."

"Oh." Abashed, Jake said, "Well, we all got the full spiel during the night—you're lucky you missed it."

Lucky. Right. Well, I supposed I had no one but myself to

blame. They drove me through deserted neighborhoods to the local high school. Arriving, I was surprised to see hundreds of students milling around the entrance. I was not used to seeing Xombies wearing clothes, much less carrying books and backpacks. From a distance, they did not resemble Xombies at all. Only about fifty of them were from the boat, the rest were freshly groomed strangers.

Crowd noise was muted; there was little talking and less laughter. Harvey Coombs, Dan Robles, Ed Albemarle, and several other officers from the boat were patrolling the crowd like ominous shepherds, preventing anyone from straying too far.

"Hi, Ed," I said, as Albemarle passed me.

Lemuel hissed, "We're supposed to call him *Principal* Albemarle."

"Oh, really?" As Fred Cowper's proxy on the sub, I was accustomed to giving the orders, not taking them. "What happens if I don't?"

"Then you get sent to Detention."

"Ah . . ."

Clearly, most of these "students" were random Xombies rustled up during the night and given a crash course in campus life. With no humans around, they were quite docile—in fact, hard to distinguish from the treated Blues. It really brought home the fact that in a totally human-free world, my blood was no longer needed to keep the peace. I was obsolete. I wasn't sure how I felt about that or what it would mean for me.

The bell rang, and everyone started filing inside. Waiting my turn at the back of the line, I noticed a car racing toward the school. It was a silver Jaguar with the top down. As it screeched into a handicapped parking slot, the driver vaulted out of his seat and landed lightly on the sidewalk. Despite his aviator sunglasses and disco outfit, I recognized Kyle Hancock.

Kyle strutted up the path like an urban cowboy, and

when he reached me, he threw his arm around my shoulder, and said, "Hello, baaaaby. Can I have a burger with that shake?"

Shrugging his arm off, I said, "Smooth. Who are you supposed to be? Superfly?"

"I'm MC Ricky Ricardo, honey. The Afro-Cuban Revolution. *Babaloooo!* Question is, who are *you* supposed to be?"

"That's actually a good question . . ."

"Well, in that case, why don't you and I blow this chicken shack and take a ride in my X-K-E?" He put his arm back around my shoulder and tried to steer me away.

I resisted slightly, but it was more trouble than it was worth. Actually, I was glad for the excuse to get out of school. Just then, a large hand settled on the back of Kyle's neck. Before the boy could react, the hand squeezed tight and hoisted him off his feet.

It was Lemuel. Shaking Kyle like a rat, the larger boy said, "Nobody messes with my girl." Then he punched Kyle square in the face. Kyle's sunglasses fractured, mirrored shards embedding in flesh and bone as his nose squashed flat and his face actually inverted. He bounced off Lemuel's fist and sailed backward across the grass. The crowd watched all this impassively, then turned away.

"Gee," I said. "You really didn't have to do that."

"I kind of did," said Lemuel sheepishly. "It's in the book."

Picking glass out of his face, Kyle yelled, "But you didn't have to mean it!"

The first day of school was always a little strange. New classes, new faces, new locker combinations—it was a lot to learn. Unless you just didn't care. That was the challenge of Xombie High: teaching those who had no reason to work. The time factor alone was nearly impossible since Maenad consciousness was not easily synched to a clock.

Five minutes here, an hour there—it was like posting stop signs for the wind.

To a Xombie, the rate at which time passed was completely optional. We were not trapped in the here and now, chained to the present like students watching a clock. Exes were never bored or impatient because if we didn't like what was going on, we simply skipped ahead in time, leaving our inert bodies for however long was necessary—hours, days, weeks . . . perhaps years or centuries—until body and mind could reunite under more pleasant circumstances. To us, this leap was instantaneous; there was no mental gap.

Therefore, in order for school to function, we had to deliberately imprison our minds in the present and obey a schedule, like circus lions jumping through hoops. For us creatures from the boat, this was not so difficult—we were accustomed to a degree of effort and self-control. The challenge was that we were expected to impart this work ethic to the wild-caught Exes, the free-range and the rogue, who had no such inhibitions.

Fortunately, the newbies learned fast. All of us did. At least at first, Langhorne's experiment was far more successful than I ever imagined possible. With no actual humans around to distract us or remind us what monsters we were, we eagerly convinced ourselves we were people again. Nostalgia spread among us like a new disease, so that even the zombiest of Xombies was soon putting on hair gel and yammering "Gosh!" and "Gee whiz!"

Classes were fairly interesting, and there were only two subjects being taught: Xombiology 101 and Ex Ed. The first was a kind of Xombies for Dummies tutorial on everything that was known about the Maenad condition, given by the resident authority, Alice Langhorne, PhD. The second was a primer on how to create a utopian society by modeling idealized human behavior, such as that found in "wholesome" 1950s Americana. Not just comic books, but television shows, movies, and children's literature. The idea was to use these materials as How-to-Be-Human handbooks—make it so simple even a Xombie could understand. It helped that wild Xombies had a moony fascination with Clears and were inclined to do what they said.

All day long, Langhorne addressed variations of the same question: What was the purpose of all this?

To which she would reply, "The purpose is to have a purpose."

"That's it?" Julian Noteiro asked on Day One. "So what we're doing is just totally arbitrary?"

"Not at all, Julian. We are preserving certain familiar archetypes—just as our bodies are preserving human physical characteristics, which are equally obsolete. We are doing this because each of us is an archive of human traits—a walking, talking time capsule—and someday our survival as a species may depend on how much we remember of being human."

"But what if we don't want to be human?"

"Then we may forfeit that choice forever. That's the challenge we must confront: whether to jettison the mortal definition of humanity—its 'soul,' if you will—or try to preserve it. Life as a Xombie is very inviting—we all feel the pull. No need to think, no need to worry or wonder or doubt. No need to do anything but float in eternal bliss—that euphoria which some of you have taken to calling the 'Gulf of Toyland.' The problem is, our minds are not equipped for infinity, and I believe there's a danger of getting lost in it, losing our way back. The only landmark in all of time is our residual humanity—that's our sole point of reference, our one small island in an eternal sea. Lose touch with that, and we drift out into the unknown, our finite consciousness expanding outward until it disperses like smoke, leaving our bodies empty vessels, ripe for plucking by whatever alien will is constantly insinuating itself upon us. In other words, we will become true zombies—that's zombies with a 'z'—mindless slaves to that controlling intelligence."

"How do you know that intelligence isn't God?"

"Yeah," others agreed, "maybe it's God. Maybe we're supposed to submit to His will."

"Maybe," Langhorne said. "Or maybe it's the Devil, did you think of that? Although in a contest between the Devil and Uri Miska, I'd put my money on Miska."

At lunchtime, I went into the cafeteria. There was no food being served, but many students had brought their own lunches, according to instructions. Since Xombies only needed a tiny fraction of all this food we were eating, most of it passed right through us undigested. The bathrooms became popular student hangouts.

In the cafeteria, I noticed something odd. Blues and Clears were not sitting together.

All my original Dreadnauts had assembled at one table, and I automatically went over there.

"What's going on?" I asked Julian Noteiro.

He was tentatively peeling a hard-boiled egg. I wondered where he had found it. "What do you mean?" he asked.

"I mean why is the room divided up like this?"

"Oh, that. Yeah. I didn't really notice."

I went to a table of Clears and sat down. These were all boys from the boat, not strangers, and I knew most of their names. Speaking to a guy named Virgil Kinkaide, I asked, "Why aren't you guys sitting with any Blues?"

They ignored me.

"Excuse me," I said. "I believe I asked you a question."

Instead of answering, they all got up and stationed themselves at another table. Intrigued, I followed and sat down with them again. When they tried to get up once more, I grabbed Virgil by the ear and slammed his head down on the table, pinning his neck with my elbow.

"What do you think you're *doing*?" he squealed.

"What is this? Why can't I sit with you?"

"You're Blue."

"What?"

"Blues and Clears don't sit together. Go sit at a Blue table."

"Are you serious?"

"Blues sit with Blues, Clears sit with Clears—everybody knows that."

"Why?"

He seemed reluctant to answer.

"Who came up with this?"

"All of us. Yesterday, on the bus."

"I wasn't on the bus."

"Well, now you know. So deal with it."

*Interesting,* I thought.

After lunch we had Gym, which initially consisted of tryouts for various sports teams: football, baseball, track and field, gymnastics. I recoiled from any of these, having only negative associations with school athletics programs. But there was also to be a marching band. When I saw that the band consisted entirely of Clear guys, I immediately signed up.

"You can't do that," said the Clear band captain, a bearded Ex named Henry Bartholomew, whose nephew Jake was one of my best Blues.

"I just did."

"Well, go and unsign. We're full up."

"I'm staying. So deal with it."

"There's no way. What are you, ten years old?"

"I'm eighteen." But he refused to admit me until I said, "I have an idea. Why don't you go complain to Principal Albemarle?"

Instead of facing big blue Ed, he disbanded the band. After that, the Clears withdrew from most official school activities, forming clubs of their own.

I could sympathize to a degree. In this world, Blue was normal; Blue was the mainstream. Clears could, of course, choose to look Blue, camouflage themselves to resemble everyone else, but that required constant effort on their part, a burden none of the rest of us was subjected to. So it was either accept the strain of conforming, or give up and be . . . different. They chose to be different.

I chose to join the cheerleading squad. I was intrigued by the idea of being a cheerleader, as it was something I never would have considered in my mortal life, when my physical awkwardness, small size, and bad attitude relegated me to the society of misfits, making anything to do with sports or "school spirit" loathsome. Also, my mother called cheerleading "Red State porn."

After school, Lemuel came up to me, and haltingly asked, "D'uh, hey, Lulu, would you like to go to the malt shop with me?"

"Jesus, Lemuel, cut the moron act."

"Sorry—it's just that Dr. Langhorne wants us to stay in character. We're supposed to be examples to the others."

"Are you sure that's all it is?"

"Well . . ."

"Because I'm not really your girlfriend, you know. I mean, if there even is such a thing anymore as boyfriends and girlfriends. I don't have those feelings; I'm sorry."

"You don't have those feelings, or you just don't have those feelings for me?"

"I don't know. What the hell difference does it make?"

"It makes a difference to me."

"Fine! I have no feelings."

Lemuel seemed slightly placated. "So how about the malt shop? A bunch of us are going."

"Yeah, sure, why not? Malt shop—unbelievable!"

When we arrived at the malt shop, the joint was humming—literally. There was a large generator out front spewing exhaust. But the power was on, the neon sign was lit, and the jukebox was playing "Sugar Sugar." It looked cozy and hospitable, but once inside I could see that Blues were only sitting with Blues, and Clears with Clears. Sal DeLuca sat slumped at the lunch counter, arguing with Emilio Monte, who was dressed like a short-order cook.

"I ain't makin' no fifteen hamburgers," Emilio said.

"But you have to," Sal insisted, pointing his finger at the pages of a comic book. "It's right here. It's my *character*."

"I don't care if it's your character, the point is I got no *meat*, kid. No meat, no buns, no cheese, no lettuce, no onions, no tomato. Also no gas to cook it on, you understand? All I got is whatever's left in tin cans. The refrigerators work, but there ain't nothing in 'em. You bring me a cow and a charcoal grill, and I'll make as many hamburgers as you can eat."

"Well, what do you have?"

"Ah," Monte said, raising a finger. He leaned down behind the counter and emerged with a box of crackers and a big glass jar. "How do you feel about pickle chips on stale Saltines?"

Before Sal could reply, the door burst open. From out of the darkness, a large, skinned carcass slid across the checker-tiled floor, leaving a red swash. It was a deer—a big buck.

"There're your hamburgers, Emil," said former commander Harvey Coombs. He was wearing a coonskin cap and holding a propane gas cylinder on one shoulder. Following behind were Dan Robles and Phil Tran, both dragging sacks of foraged wild goods: potatoes, onions, carrots, various greens. There was a whole truckload of the stuff outside.

The dead animal shocked us—death of any kind was disturbing to those who could not die. I suspected this was one of Langhorne's tests.

As the restaurant went silent, Emilio Monte stormed out from behind the counter, yelling, "I just waxed this floor!" Ranting about the mess, he slipped on blood and went airborne, crackers flying, and landed flat on his back. The pickle jar shattered, launching sliced gherkins in all directions.

Sal said, "That's no way to make a buck!"

Everyone laughed and laughed. The new Xombies were slower on the uptake, but quickly caught on, screeching like hyenas. Then the laughter abruptly petered out. The scene was over, no point running it into the ground.

# CHAPTER **SIX**

## REBELS WITHOUT A CAUSE

So the days progressed, emulsifying one into the next, until the habits of the world we were creating became ingrained. Not *real* . . . but at least routine. Many things needed to be scavenged, so the females were always begging the males to take them "shopping," which was the pretext by which stores were pillaged for fifties geek-chic costumes and props, Xomboys cooling their heels while Ex-girls posed in outfit after outfit, store after store, with the boys teetering behind them under mountains of boxes and shopping bags. This was multiplied many times over, as there were many boys playing the same roles: nine Archies, for instance, and twice that many Jugheads (the girls were fewer, more closely matching the number of female characters, though Betty and Veronica were disproportionately represented). There were also Fonzies, Beavers, Opies, Charlie Browns, Lucys, Blondies, Flintstones, Jetsons, Bradys, Munsters, Mary Worths, Gidgets, Gilligans, Daisy Maes, Li'l Abners, Richie Riches, Little Audreys, Little Orphan Annies, and Little Lulus. Why the hell, I asked myself, wasn't I a Little Lulu instead of a fucking Midge?

At the end of every week, the excess goods were distributed throughout the community in the form of gifts. Every Sunday was Christmas in Loveville. In short order, the town was cleaned up, spruced up, and lit up—Officer Arlo Fisk led a delegation of undead nuclear engineers to the nearby Calvert Cliffs Nuclear Power Station, getting the plant going at a small fraction of its capacity . . . but more than enough for the needs of the town.

On Saturdays, the entire population went to the beach, taking over a cove of the Potomac with our coolers and beach blankets and sun umbrellas. Archies danced around as if the sand was hot, and Reggies rubbed lotion on the girls' backs. I suffered Ex-Lemuel's oafish attentions, knowing I was expected to be his fictional "steady," which was annoying because he took it all a bit too seriously, just as he did the Monday night football games—few of the players he tackled left the field in one piece.

Lemuel had not been the same since drowning in icy slush up at Thule; of all the Dreadnauts, he was always the least pacified by my blood. I would have much preferred spending more time with the aloof Julian Noteiro, but in the persona of brainiac Dilton Doily, he was always busy tending to the technical demands of Loveville. He actually avoided me—he *shunned* me . . . so I shunned him right back. But my annoyance grew as this silent treatment continued, until one day I couldn't hold it in anymore.

"What is your problem?" I demanded.

Refusing to look at me, he said, "My problem?"

"Please! Ever since we arrived here, you've been very aloof with me."

"Aloof?" He mulled over the word. "Aloof . . . hm."

"It means removed or distant or—"

"I know what it means. Here's the thing, Lulu: *I'm not human.* You're not human. We are a mockery of everything that's human, our existence is pointless, and we are condemned to live this way forever. And you ask me why I'm *aloof*?"

"No, I get all that. And I also know you were an aloof kind of guy even before the world fell apart—fine. What I don't understand is why you have to treat me differently from everybody else. You work fine with others, you talk with others, you *make an effort* with others. Why do you have to be such a total Xomboid with me?"

"Lulu, I don't know what you want from me. This whole thing is your idea—I'm just playing my part."

"*My* idea? What whole thing?"

"You can cut out the innocent waif act—nobody buys it anymore."

"No, seriously, what whole thing? You lost me."

"Are you kidding? Lulu, you're in command. You brought us here. You gave Langhorne free rein to use us as rats in her mind-control experiment."

"Me? No! I'm nothing more than a liaison for Fred Cowper. He's the captain."

"That head can't be captain. Fred Cowper did not lead us here. You did."

"That's ridiculous. When did this funny farm become my responsibility? I'm not in charge. I'm not qualified to be in charge."

"Absolutely. That's why Langhorne's picked up the slack; she's the only one willing to step up. That's why we're hemorrhaging people right and left."

"What are you talking about?"

"The new Blues are heading for the hills, we lose a few every day. We're marooned—no one's in charge."

"Well, I don't hear any suggestions coming from you."

"Nobody listens to my suggestions. You want advice? Why don't you go ask your boyfriend?"

"D'uh, somebody talkin' about me?"

A large hand spun Julian around, and a right haymaker knocked him clean out of his shoes.

"Goddammit!" I yelled. "Stop that, Lemuel! What the hell's the matter with you?"

"I can't help it," Lemuel said, looking stricken. "I have these *feelings* . . ."

"Well, you have to control them! This is getting way out of hand!"

"I know. It's just that . . . I think I love you, Lulu."

"Oh God."

"I know! It's impossible. But I can't help myself. I feel like I'm starving all the time, then if I see you with somebody else, it just makes me lose it, I'm sorry."

"We've all talked about this. It's only because I'm the last girl you knew before you died."

"But it isn't just that! It really isn't. I really, really love you—I've loved you since I first saw you, but the more I got to know you, the more I loved you. And ever since I died, it's only gotten worse—you're the only thing I think about, the only thing in the world that can still hurt me. I mean actual, physical pain. You make me feel human. It's like every cell of my body craves you, and it takes everything I've got to restrain myself from grabbing you and holding you and kissing you—"

"I get it, I get it, stop."

"No! You don't get it! If you knew what I was going through, you couldn't treat me the way you do. You would love me back! Please love me, Lulu—you have to love me." He lunged forward and caught me in his arms. My Maenad flesh recoiled, but Lemuel did not let go.

"Lemuel—*oof!*—lay off! I told you I can't love you like that!"

"Yes, you can! You just have to try! I'll show you!"

Clutching me in his right arm, he used the other to unzip his varsity jacket, revealing a heart-shaped door in his chest. It was silver, elaborately engraved, and in fact was the lid of a fancy music box. Lemuel's blue flesh puckered around it.

As I watched in dismay, he opened the lid and reached inside.

To the plinking of Bach, Lemuel said, "I give you my heart, Lulu."

Before I knew what was happening, I felt a cold, slippery object being pressed into my hand. It squirmed like a living creature.

"Now I just need you to give me yours . . ."

I was about to leap right out of my skin, when suddenly a large circular saw came out of nowhere and chopped Lemuel's head off.

It was Julian. He proceeded to cut Lemuel's still-standing body in half lengthwise, then to remove his limbs from his bisected trunk. It was fast work. Shutting down the saw and flipping up his splattered visor, Julian said, "That oughta hold him for a while."

"That's why I don't bother with girls," said Sal DeLuca, who was walking by with an enormous submarine sandwich. "They really make a guy go to pieces." Bystanders laughed.

"Shut up, Sal," I said, dropping the heart and looking for someplace to wipe my hand. "Why don't you go do something useful?" As Jughead, Sal did nothing but sleep and eat, seemingly grateful to dispense with all effort.

"Gee whiz," he said, "have a heart."

I almost caught him.


On Sundays, everybody went to church, where we learned all about the Father, the Son, and Casper the Friendly Ghost. In the evenings, we held sing-alongs around a bonfire, the officers handing out ukuleles and leading the crowd in Don Ho numbers. Every now and then a rogue Xombie would join the party, but this happened less and less as the weeks went by. The Xombies were pulling out—a mass exodus to the west. The only way to make them stay would have been to inoculate them with my blood serum. Most of these Xombies were male; the female ones were much more elusive, if not gone altogether.

Or so we thought.

One evening in late September, just as the first cool snap came through, I was lying naked on the highest point for miles around: the water tower. I had staked out this spot as the best place to commune with the heavens, and even to a non-Xombie, it would have been a beautiful view—in fact, teens from the surrounding towns had been climbing it for years, as evinced by the graffiti they left behind.

A hundred feet above the ground, I lay spread-eagled on the cold steel surface, my body just as cold and passive as the metal, the flesh of my back wedded to it, using the tower to amplify the stellar chorus—in effect, making myself an antenna, channeling the strange vibrations through hair and toes and fingertips straight to my dead blue heart.

*Lulu,* a silent voice said. It caused my heart to jump.

*Who? What?* I asked.

*Come away with us. You don't belong here.*

The voice was not coming from above but from below. Peeling myself off the metal, I crawled to the edge of the tower and looked down. Even in the darkness, I could clearly make out figures skittering up the ladder. They were Maenads—female Xombies. More Maenads than I had ever seen.

"What do you want?" I called down.

"To free you," the leader replied.

"I'm already free."

"No, you have another purpose."

"Which is what?"

"To help complete the Hex."

"The what now?"

"It's all right, Lulu," the lead Maenad said, cresting the tower. She was a black silhouette in the moonlight, her skin like metal and her wild hair gleaming like a crown. "We'll show you."

Others rose over the edge, fanning out to encircle me, pressing me toward the center. As they closed in, I felt a vestigial tingle that I recognized as fear. The mortal fear of

Xombies. For an instant, I even considered jumping off the tower, but then thought, *Why?* I was as much a monster as any of them; what possible reason did I have to be afraid?

They pressed in on me, getting too close, and I raised my hands to keep our distance. The two Maenads on either side of me took my hands, gripping tightly. My flesh shriveled at their touch, and I twisted wildly to break free. Two more of them seized my kicking feet, and all of a sudden I felt an electric force shooting through me. It surged up my arms and legs like water through a fire hose, jerking my limbs taut, flooding my heart, and filling my head to bursting.

I fell backward, and they fell with me, all of us connected like paper dolls, a web of six-sided figures draped like lace across the steel dome of the tower. Facing the sky, I said, "Oh."

We were one, linked not just with each other but with other hexagons all over the world. Streaming live and jacked into the Agent X network—the proliferating mass of cyanotic rust that had already infected the human race and was now spreading like wildfire in the iron-rich veins of our very planet. This blue rust was merely the visible manifestation of the indestructible Maenad morphocyte. It was everywhere now, fusing the billions of Maenads into an information complex greater than the entire Internet, drawing power from Earth's magnetic field. Soon it would be able to focus that power, channel it, exploit it.

But to what end?

As if in answer to my unspoken question, I could suddenly see masses of strange black objects floating in the sky. They looked like enormous embryos—pulsating, alive, and intricately organic. Hundreds, thousands of them were rising off the land like so many spores, rising in streams from multiple sources all over the world.

I didn't see them with my eyes but with the eyes of a billion others, vast Hexes of Maenads, and as I watched, I could see the first of them actually leaving the bonds of the

Earth, pushed by collective thought alone, rising beyond
the highest reaches of the atmosphere and accelerating into
space. Heedless of gravity, heedless of time.

For that brief moment, I knew everything.


A little later, I was sitting on a second-story ledge over
the drugstore, just watching the show. That was what I
thought of this experiment of Langhorne's: It was a play,
some kind of performance art, so we might as well enjoy it.
*All the world's a stage,* I mused, as Julian Noteiro passed
beneath me.

In a hurry as usual, Julian sensed my eyes on him and
looked up. "Hi, Midge."

I froze, then dropped from the ledge to the sidewalk.
"Whoa," I said, getting up and brushing myself off, "whoa,
whoa, whoa, whoa, whoa—*what*?"

"I'm sorry?" Julian said, reluctantly pausing.

"Did you just call me Midge?"

"Uh . . . yes?"

"Let's get this straight, once and for all," I said, jabbing
a finger in his chest. "Nobody calls me Midge. All *right*?
Midge is not a name, it's an insect. I may be short, but I
refuse to be called Midge for the rest of eternity. I am not
Midge. My name is Lulu, get it?"

"Okay, sure, Lulu."

"Also, I am not 'going steady' with Lemuel, in case you
were under that impression."

"You mean Big Moose?"

"No! I mean Lemuel! I'm Lulu, you're Julian, and he's
Lemuel. My *friend* Lemuel—not my boyfriend. I didn't ask
for a boyfriend, I don't need a boyfriend, and I don't want
a boyfriend. Period! Case closed! End of story!"

Without warning, I kissed him.

Apropos of nothing, I leaned forward and *kissed* him,
and it was like two car batteries joined at the wrong termi-

nals: Electricity arced from our lips, our hair crackled, our flesh ran liquid, and boiling acid seethed in our veins. We *burned*. Flesh sizzled against flesh as every Maenad cell in our bodies recoiled against the forbidden contact.

Julian screamed in pain, fighting to break free. But just when I thought we had to die, to explode, *something* . . . the wall burst, the defenses cracked wide, and instead of being forced apart, we fused harder, melting one into the other until I didn't know where I ended and Julian began . . . and I didn't care. At once I understood that there was something beyond the X barrier—something awful and wonderful and utterly strange. Something no one knew about.

Suddenly, a wedge came between us. In a frazzle of molten strands, we were split in two, roots sundered and our gorgeous circuit cleaved apart by Lemuel's brute sword— actually a NO PARKING sign planted in a can of concrete. While we were still stunned, Lemuel slashed again, chopping Julian's upraised arm off at the shoulder, then reversed the weapon and clubbed the slighter boy to the sidewalk.

Blind and barely sensible, I tried to intervene, leaping on Lemuel's back and locking arms around his freshly scarred neck, but what would have crushed a human throat had no effect on my fellow Dreadnaut.

Ignoring me, Lemuel seized Julian by his head and swung him in a circle, leaning against the centrifugal force like an Olympic hammer thrower before hurling him through the drugstore's plate-glass window.

"Lemuel, Lemuel, stop!" I cried. "It's just a game!"

The big boy wasn't listening, still intent on Julian. With manic ferocity, he vaulted over the sill and was hit in midleap by an old-fashioned, enameled-steel candy machine. It cracked his skull like a Goober-filled shillelagh, and as he went down, it struck him again for good measure, thick glass and thicker skull fracturing together in a burst of brain matter and candy-coated peanuts.

"What the hell do you people think you're doing?" asked

Alice Langhorne, setting down the vending machine and helping Julian to his feet. "Oh shit, did you just lose your arm? Unbelievable—that's gonna take a week to mend. Can't I even go to the drugstore in peace? Let me tell you, I'm getting a little tired of all the horseplay, people. This is not in the story—there's no dismemberment in *Archie*, I can tell you. If this continues, we're going to have to start taking away privileges. You want to be benched all season? Yes, I'm talking to you, Moose."

Things were getting out of control.

Lemuel's jealousy was just the tip of the iceberg: the weekly football games were Coliseums of rampant carnage, two dozen Mooses going berserk on each other, and the lost body parts raked into a pile until their owners could claim them.

Then there was the conspicuous consumption of the Reggies, Veronicas, and Richie Riches, who were engaged in a race to see who could acquire the most stuff, all of them amassing huge stockpiles of worthless "valuables": jewelry, designer clothes, original art, antique furniture, cars, boats, planes, and enormous estates in which to hoard it all. If one mansion got too cluttered, they took over another.

Likewise, the wasteful appetites of the Jugheads and Dagwoods were depleting the food supply for miles around, and they contributed nothing to the common good except perhaps a comforting example of human repose . . . and the occasional clever quip.

On the other hand, the blond Bettys were the workhorses of the community, volunteering for the most onerous tasks (such as helping the Veronicas get more stuff) and doing it all with a smile. In fact, the Bettys would have been perfect if not for their unhealthy obsession with the Archies . . . an increasingly violent obsession, which caused them to do almost anything for an Archie's attention, such as jump in front of a speeding car or set themselves on fire—especially if an Archie told them to do it.

The Diltons, on the other hand, had no real faults, being the junior problem solvers and tech wizards of the neighborhood—Julian Noteiro was top Dilton. All they lacked was a sense of fellowship; their clinical solutions sometimes lacked consideration for social niceties; they were cold, clinical nerds.

Then there were the Archies.

Archies were the stars of the town, the planets around which all the other stories orbited. An Archie might be hated or he might be loved, but everyone knew that he among us all was the name on the masthead. Archie was the Hero, the Holy Fool, the Boy Next Door, and Jake played him to the hilt. Jake Bartholomew had been born to play Archie— he even looked like Archie.

But there were other Archies out there, and some of these gingers took great license with the brand. Archie is a bumbler, yes, so at first their accidental catastrophes were taken lightly—it was accepted that no vase, sculpture, or windowpane was safe with an Archie nearby, and ladders were acknowledged instruments of havoc. But the harmless blunders soon escalated to unnecessary heights of mayhem: The school science lab exploded, destroying Dr. Langhorne's research, along with a wing of the building; then a fireworks display went haywire, causing a wildfire that burned down half the village. Both times it was an Archie that caused it.

That was just the beginning: Soon neighboring towns burned, bridges sagged, dams broke, and power lines went down—all in the wake of well-meaning involvement by Archies.

The Weatherbees, Flutesnoots, Grundys, and various other authority figures attempted to rein in these extreme manifestations of "character," to channel them in more positive directions, but this only led to more opportunities for destruction. By the same token, increasing restrictions and curfews on one Archie just made the others act up. There was talk of eliminating the role of Archie altogether, replacing him with a less-destructive persona. But it was too late; the play had developed its own momentum and could not be controlled. It was like a runaway train, careening faster and faster to some unknown end.

The end came on a Monday night, right after the football game.

After a bad call, the game degenerated into a brawl, with players fighting and hooligans running onto the field with weapons. A tanker truck was driven onto the field, scattering the combatants and smashing through the goalposts before ramming the stands and exploding.

Flaming spectators swarmed down and made it a riot, then the whole population joined in and made it a war. The battle migrated from the stadium to the center of town, everyone savaging everyone else and being savaged in turn. All traces of Archie and the gang were erased. All the nice outfits were ripped to shreds (if not burned away entirely), all the neat houses were trashed, and all the tidy townsfolk were reduced to antic horrors, frenzied skeletons jigging to the music of The Monkees.

Perhaps because of the jukebox, they left the malt shop for last . . . but finally its time came. As if by some prearranged signal, the mob poured in, breaking down the door and crashing through the windows. The cash register became a weapon; plates and silverware became missiles. The level of crazed destruction was far beyond that of ordinary Xombies—this was violence for the sake of violence, man-sized ants attacking each other and spiraling into even more extreme havoc, so that to a human witness, the scene would have been a blur, a chaos-making whirlwind.

"Stop," I said.

The mob came at me, rearing up with everything it had to slice, dice, and make julienne fries.

"I SAID STOP." My voice had a power over them; they bumped into it like hitting an invisible wall.

Then the power went out.

Just like that, the lights winked off, the music died. Anything running on electricity clunked to a halt. All at once, Loveville was silent but for the crackling of flames. Somewhere in that silence, a telephone rang—it was the malt shop's pay phone.

Grumbling, Emilio Monte answered it, saying, "Hello? Yeah. Uh-huh. Uh-huh . . . uh-huh . . . uh-huh—no shit. Okay . . . I'll tell 'em."

He hung up and just stood there, ruminating over whatever he had just heard, while everyone else in the room waited expectantly in the dark, frozen in midfight. It was the first time the phone had ever rung. At last, Emilio picked his way through the wreckage of his shop, footsteps clinking on dishes and broken glass.

"Attention," he said. "I got an announcement to make. That was Arlo Fisk on the phone, calling from the nuclear plant. He says he's under attack."

"Under attack! By who?" I asked.

"Another boomer. It's a French boat—*Triomphante*-class. Arlo says they entered the reactor facility and routed his team. Says they stole the fuel rods, cleaned the place out."

"Were they Xombies?" asked the charred corpse of Harvey Coombs.

"No. Just ordinary humans."

This caused a stir.

Coombs said, "We should go after them!"

Alice Langhorne scoffed, "How? Swim?"

"No! Return to our boat! Get her reasonably shipshape, and start a search pattern."

"That other sub will be halfway to Africa by the time we do all that."

"Well, we have to do *something*. Look at us!"

"Coombs is right," said Phil Tran. "If we ever want to catch them, we need to act like we give a damn."

Dan Robles said, "Isn't acting what we've just been doing? And look where it got us."

I said, "That's because we've been ignoring the elephant in the room. *It's not about us.* Our story ended with our human lives. We no longer require care and feeding, and pretending otherwise is frustrating us to madness. Stop acting. Stop *trying* so hard. We are already free. Let's focus on freeing *them*."

Heads nodded, a change swept the room. *Yes, free them, free them.*

The tension ebbed like pressure dropping in an airplane, giving way to intense relief. Ravaged ghouls smiled. In letting go our humanity, we briefly felt the joy of being alive.

In minutes, a caravan of vehicles was pulling out of Loveville. For the first time, the town looked truly post-apocalyptic, streets littered with debris, buildings and cars engulfed in flames, fire hydrants spewing. By morning, there would be nothing left.

**PART II**
# Divine Providence

# CHAPTER **SEVEN**

## PROPHETS

Ditching Uri Miska and not daring to look back, Todd Holmes and Ray Despineau bolted for the train station as fast as their wobbly legs could carry them.

"Wait, man, wait—look!" Ray was pointing at two of the bicycles recently abandoned by their friends.

"Yes! Grab 'em!"

It was somewhat disturbing to be riding bikes again; the boys were still traumatized, waiting to be jumped any second by Xombies. Riding up the hill was a nerve-wracking slog, but on the downside, they flew.

Spread out before them was the center of Providence: on the left, the clustered towers of downtown; on the right, the marble-domed State House; between them the canal leading to Waterplace Park and the Providence Place Mall—and the train station.

Blazing down Waterman Street, the two boys hurtled between abandoned cars and shot across the junction of two creeks, cutting through empty parking lots up to the train station's main entrance. The train itself was in the tunnel underneath the building, but they could hear the rumble of its engine and smell its diesel exhaust. It was for real.

Dumping their bikes at the taxi stand, the boys barged into the dim terminal and tripped over a bunch of people kneeling on the floor, rudely interrupting the murmur of prayers.

Ray went sprawling over a bearded old man. "Whoa, shit, sorry!"

Out of nowhere, a snarling, monstrous creature with yellow eyes and huge fangs appeared, driving the boys into a corner. It was a large mandrill baboon.

One of the worshippers called, "Don! Down, down!"

The baboon reluctantly backed off, and an old man came forward—the man Ray had tripped over. He was wearing a robe and sandals, and had a long gray beard, like some biblical patriarch. Eyes adjusting, the boys could see other old men in robes as well.

*Moguls,* Ray thought, remembering what Miska had said. *Resurrected Moguls.*

There were maybe a hundred people in the room, and hundreds more in a long line leading to the mall.

"Who are you?" the man asked.

The boys were speechless, spellbound by the sight of so many human beings out in the open. What's more, they appeared totally defenseless—no face protection, no body armor, no weapons of any kind. And there were *women* among them. The women all wore similar winged bonnets, and were corralled in a small group separate from the men.

Finding his bearings, Todd said, "I'm Todd Holmes, and this is Ray Despineau. We want to join you."

"Are you . . . anointed?"

"Anointed?"

"Sealed with the Blessed Sacrament."

"The Sacrament, right! No, um, I don't think so. We just got stranded here because our ship was attacked while we were foraging for supplies. It left without us."

"The Lord Adam gathers the Righteous, Praise Be Upon Him."

"Awesome," Ray said gloomily.

The man asked, "Have you come seeking Miska?"

"Not really," Todd said. "Actually, we're more like running away from him."

"You've seen Miska!"

"Yeah, he was right over in Fox Point. Very weird dude."

*"Todd, shut up,"* Ray said, sotto voce.

"Well, hallelujah! This is surely a sign." The old man called to everyone in earshot, "Brothers, the Lord Adam has sent us two guides in our search for the Evil One. They are the seal on our Covenant! The Oracle has spoken true!"

Amid the hallelujahs and amens, Ray asked, "Sorry, what's this Covenant?"

"It is Man's truce with Eve. After the Blue Apocalypse, Man had no Covenant, and in his zeal to avenge Adam, he offended the Goddess Eve. She summoned Her Blue Furies to visit the Sons of Adam with plagues wherever they took refuge, driving them first out of Providence, then out of Valhalla. For thirty days and thirty nights, the Apostle Chace led the Adamites through the wilderness, praying for a sign, their numbers dwindling as the imps of Miska stole their souls. Until finally their sufferings were rewarded: They witnessed the Resurrection of the Prophet—the Prophet Jim! The first Resurrection of many, including my own!"

"Jim?"

"Jim saved us! Jim anointed us against the Hellions, that now we may walk freely upon the land!"

"Wow—how do we get in on that?"

"You must submit to be Sanctified."

"Definitely. We submit."

"Kneel down."

The boys knelt.

"Now close your eyes and open your mouths."

Trading a wary glance with Ray, Todd asked, "Why?"

"Just do it!"

Taking a deep breath, the boys closed their eyes and opened wide. They flinched as something cold was sprayed in their throats, a bitter-tasting mist. Gagging, they tried to talk and found that they couldn't—their mouths wouldn't work. The deadness rushed through their bloodstreams and instantly soaked their brains, killing all their senses, stopping their hearts, but before they could panic, they passed out.

# CHAPTER **EIGHT**

## TODD HOLMES

Perhaps it was the sight of those women that caused Todd Holmes to dream of his own mother. Awake, he blocked her completely out of his mind. He knew the term for it: "post-traumatic stress syndrome," but he always thought that was just something that happened to soldiers in wartime. Now, in his sleep, he remembered all.

"You must really think I'm dumb. Boy oh boy, you must really take me for a dummy."

"Huh?"

"Listen, if you hate me so much, why don't you just go live with him? I'll tell you why: because he wouldn't put up with you. You think he wants that responsibility? Don't bet on it."

"What are you talking about, Mom?"

"What am I talking about? That's a good one. Oh, that's funny. Fun-ee." Her voice warped like a pane of glass just before it broke. "Don't play dumb with me. You've been seeing him behind my back. Oh my God, how could you, how could you?"

"Seeing who?"

"Your father!"

"Why shouldn't I?"

"Why?" She laughed. "You of all people ask why. Oh, that is funny, after all we've been through together because of that man. Who do you think keeps a roof over our heads? Who do you think has worked and slaved away to keep us out of the gutter? Not him! He couldn't care less! And now you stab me in the back! My own son! I can't believe it, I can *not* believe it. Oh my God!" At once she seemed far away, lost and weeping in hurt reverie. "What did I ever do to deserve this?" she sniffled. "What did I ever do?"

"Nothing," Todd said. "It's not always about you."

She returned to him, resentful eyes brimming, "You want to know how I found out? Oh, you'll love this one. He came by yesterday, the bum, looking for forgiveness. He actually had the nerve to ask if he could take you to the plant with him! I couldn't believe it!"

Unable to listen to any more, Todd made for the door, but his mother jerked him back by his dreadlocks. That wasn't the worst; when she was really mad, she twisted his piercings.

"Ow! Mom!"

"Where do you think you're going?"

"Out!"

"Oh no, you don't. I know what you're up to: You think you can just go cry to him, and the two of you can commiserate about what a horrible bitch I am, what a miserable, controlling harpy. Well, I'm through playing bad cop. Go ahead." She released Todd, giving his head a shove. "You go! Go right ahead, buddy-boy. But don't think you're coming back here, uh-uh. If you leave now, you better plan on staying with him for good. It's about time he got a turn being the parent. Go ahead. See how fast he takes you in. Go right ahead, fine by me."

Todd hesitated, took a few steps toward the door, and wavered. "I can't believe you're doing this, Mom."

"Join the club."

Looking at his mother, so resolute and red-faced, Todd was unexpectedly alarmed. This was no bluff—she meant it. She was prepared to let him go and perhaps never return.

All at once, he knew he couldn't take another step; things had gone too far already. Though he hated his mother for the ultimatum, the humiliation, he understood in his heart that the blame was not really hers but his father's, for all the lies and empty promises. If Todd truly trusted his dad, he'd have been out that door without a backward glance. He'd be gone so fast, your head would spin. Much as he wished that could be so, the truth was that his old man remained an unknown quantity. And not really so unknown—the man was simply not trustworthy.

Todd shut himself in his room and threw himself face-down on the bed, sobbing curses and slamming his fists into the pillows.

Shaking her head, his mother finished dressing and went out.

All afternoon Todd stayed in bed, curled against the on-slaught of grief like a rolled-up pangolin, his fevered still-ness punctuated by fits of hysterical rage. He fantasized at great length about suicide, making specific, elaborate plans and composing various versions of his suicide note. It was hard to strike the right tone. Apologetic? Accusatory? Sad and profound? Snide and angry? Brief and pithy, or a de-tailed manifesto? He couldn't decide. Eventually, with eve-ning coming on and the apartment submerged in gloom, Todd fell asleep.

At midnight, he was awakened from a deep slumber by people running up and down the halls, yelling incoherently and slamming doors. A lot of stupid screaming and shout-ing. Down in the streets there was the crackle of fireworks and a crazy profusion of car horns and sirens. It sounded like the whole city was in an uproar.

It took him a second to gather his wits, then he realized, *Oh yeah: New Year's Eve.* The thought that he was missing all the fun made him even more depressed, and Todd dis-gustedly covered his head with a couch cushion and fell instantly back asleep.

A few hours later, just after 4:00 A.M., he was awakened again.

At first he wasn't sure what it was that had disturbed him. He was fully awake and clearheaded, staring up at patterns of light reflected on the ceiling. It was quiet now, the urgent sounds of the city muted to a faraway din.

Then he heard it again: a metallic rattling from the front door. It was the doorknob—someone out in the hallway was twisting it, trying to get in. Not just turning the knob, but jerking and yanking at it, as if stubbornly refusing to accept that the door was locked. Todd could see the shadow of the person's feet through the crack underneath.

He sat up in alarm. Was someone trying to break in? His father maybe, come to sneak him out? He glanced across the room to his mom's bed, intending to wake her, but the bed was still made up—she hadn't even been home. This was perplexing, so unlike her, but Todd reminded himself it was New Year's—perhaps she had been invited to a party after work. Again, very unlikely, but it gave him the fleeting hope that it must be her at the door, tired—surely not drunk—and fumbling for her keys.

Hesitantly, he called out, "Mom?"

In reply to his voice, something like a load of bricks slammed into the door, crunching the frame and shaking the whole apartment. Then came a frenzied, whinnying scream, a shrill eruption of nonsense syllables that made Todd shrivel inside his skin. Far worse than nails on a chalkboard, the weird voice made an arcing live wire out of Todd's every hair follicle and nerve ending. He almost pissed his pants.

A pause.

Todd slowly got up, trembling hard. Listening. He could no longer see the foot-shadows under the door.

What was THAT?

He had never heard such a voice in his life; nor could he imagine what would cause a person to sound like that. He couldn't even tell if it was a man or a woman. It terrified him to think it was someone who needed help, who was grievously injured, dying or bleeding to death on his doorstep. That's what the voice evoked: catastrophic pain . . . or was it laughter? No, it was something more savage—demanding, not pleading—an animalistic keen that resonated in the most primitive part of Todd's being and triggered a similarly primal response: to flee.

But he had nowhere to go. As the thing outside started jiggling and wrenching at the doorknob again, the confines of the tiny apartment took on the dimensions of a cage, a death trap. Todd picked up the phone and tapped 911. The line was busy—could they do that? He delicately hung up, trying not to clatter the phone with his shaking hand.

Okay . . . I'll just wait for it to go away. Someone else in the building must have heard that jibbering outburst—any such disturbance usually caused their Filipino landlady to go ballistic. Never before had Todd so eagerly awaited one of Mrs. Mazola's tirades. But she didn't come. No one came. The building was dead silent.

Suddenly, there was a sound he did recognize: the familiar homely jingle of his mother's key ring! Oh my God— was it her outside the door? But that scream . . . ? The thought was too baffling to contemplate. Before he could stop himself, Todd crossed to the door and listened, heart pounding. Yes, those were definitely her keys . . . but why was it taking her so long? He started crying with terror and despair, unable to comprehend how it could be her who had made that noise. What was wrong with her? He wasn't sure he could bear to know.

"Mom?" he whispered, his lips touching the cracked paint.

There was no answer except that idiot jingling. It was taking much longer than it should to unlock the door, as if the person outside was deeply, moronically engrossed in those keys. That was enough; he had to do something. Todd connected the security chain, gingerly turned the bolt, and opened the door a crack . . .

And slammed it shut again.

And screamed.

The thing out there—that demonic blue hag that some-how resembled his mother—lunged against the door, barely too late. It screeched furiously, and Todd could make out some of the garbled words this time:

"—HEEETODDEEOHHTODDEEMYTOD-DEESWEETBABYOHBABEEEEE—"

"Mom, no!" he cried, as the thing hit the door again, split-ting the frame. Once more, and it would give.

Chest heaving, he ran for the bathroom and locked him-self in. As he stood there listening, his gaze was fixed on his own reflection in the mirror: a wiry, wild-eyed boy, skin deathly pale and etched with runic black vines, whose blue eyes stared back at him under an overhanging shock of blond dreadlocks, as if awaiting some cue.

His eyes were drawn past the mirror to the air vent beside the toilet. This was an old building, an old hotel converted to apartments, and instead of a window in the bathroom there was an air shaft covered with a cruddy metal grate. While sitting on the toilet, Todd often heard the intimate sounds of other tenants using their bathrooms, a bit of voyeurism that he found endlessly, disgustingly fascinating. There was also something distinctly creepy about it, that barely visible dark shaft in which anything could be hiding and peeping back at him. Sometimes when he went to the bathroom late at night, he envisioned a weird, spidery man who lived behind the grate, scuttling up and down the shaft or huddling only inches away as Todd sat on the toilet. Mr. Green.

He heard the outer door crash open. The fearsome thing that had been his mother entered the apartment like a vio-lent wind, upending furniture and tearing everything apart as it ransacked the place looking for him.

Todd opened the medicine cabinet. On the bottom was a

plastic margarine tub full of tweezers and toenail clippers, and there was also a small multipurpose tool with pliers and a screwdriver. Using the screwdriver, he knelt on the toilet lid and went to work on the screws securing the air-shaft grate. Musty warmed air blew in his face. At first he almost gave up—the screws were old, tight and thickly painted over—but he stuck with it and suddenly the yellow enamel cracked off like candy coating. The first screw turned.

The thing outside grabbed the knob and slammed into the bathroom door.

Todd flinched, fumbled, then got the screw off. The second screw was easier, and the third and fourth didn't have to be removed at all—he found he could pry the grate open without touching them.

He stuck his head into the shaft and looked down. It was gross, black with greasy lint, utterly dark and forbidding. Not to mention deep—their apartment was up on the third floor.

The bathroom door was warping, cracking, sending splinters of wood bouncing off the walls. Any second it would give, and that would be it—there was no place left to hide. A hideously mangled blue arm snaked through a hole in the plywood and thrashed around in the close space, straining for him. It could just touch, its fingertips grazing his shirt.

Ducking and dodging, Todd grabbed an armload of towels off the shelf and stuffed them down the chute. He did the same with the towels on the racks, then with the thick, shaggy bathmat. Finally, he climbed up on the toilet lid and squirmed feet first into the tight shaft until he was completely inside, painfully dangling by his armpits.

The bathroom door smashed inward.

Todd let go.

It was over very quickly: a brief plummet down a furry chimney, then his body slammed through something soft with a loud, concussive bang—it was his towels on a sheet-metal panel that collapsed beneath him and tumbled him into the basement.

Todd came to his senses in a pile of gallon jugs of used fryer oil. The wind had been knocked out of him, and he was covered with sticky black fluff, but he was not in pain. Later, he would feel it. He had bottomed out in the big main heating duct that fed the building, the force of his impact popping all its metal rivets and collapsing the duct like a cardboard box. Beside him, the ancient furnace was shuddering, squealing as if mortally wounded, its flame snuffed out. The basement was filling with the stink of gas.

Though still stunned, Todd forced himself to move; he didn't want to see what might follow him down that chute. He was nearly up the stairs when the gas exploded.

The force of it hurled him out of the basement like a powerful shove. He picked himself up, shrieking, "Help! Help!" as he ran down the building's back corridor. He was facing an array of doorways: the restaurant kitchen, the utility room, the stairway to the apartments, the fire exit. He was surprised to see the exit door wide open to the back alley, and a trail of odd debris—shoes and torn clothing— strewn across the floor. That door was never supposed to be left open; Mrs. Mazola was a fanatic about that, just as she was about any kind of mess in her building. But Todd didn't have time to think about Mrs. Mazola—all he saw was the open door to the outside.

As he rushed for it, something flew out of the stairwell and knocked him down. Crazy whipcord arms skinnier than his own wrapped around his neck, and a gaping, ravenous fish mouth sought his. In the sickly, strobing fluorescents, Todd recognized the overpowering perfume of his tiny landlady, Mrs. Mazola.

If he had been caught completely off guard, Todd would have had no chance against the rabid attack, but his blood was already running so high with adrenaline that his own panicked reflexes bordered on the supernatural.

Screaming, he dove with his clinging attacker straight into the sharp steel edge of the doorjamb, using it as a wedge to pry them apart. Already he could feel his thoughts blurring from the lack of oxygen. He tried to say, *Lady, quit it!* but no words would come out. The woman showed no signs of slacking, and Todd kept frantically thrusting her against the metal door flange as if trying to saw off an unwanted Siamese twin. The sharp edge gashed Mrs. Mazola's purpled face and arm to the bone, smearing inky black blood all over Todd and the wall . . . but she just wouldn't let go.

In a final, extreme feat of desperation, Todd lugged her over to the big industrial fire extinguisher. Todd and his buddies often dared each other to shoot this thing off in the alley, but they had never gone through with it. They were too terrified of the wrath of his crazy landlady. Little had they known!

Blacking out, barely able to think another second, Todd yanked out the extinguisher's safety pin, grabbed the rubber hose, and rammed its nozzle down Mrs. Mazola's yawning black gullet. Then he squeezed the handle.

The result was instantaneous—and spectacular: She broke off in a backward somersault, vomiting incredible billows of white chemical dust all over the room and vanishing in the cloud.

Without looking back, Todd scrambled clear and bolted through the red fire door to the alley.

# CHAPTER **NINE**

## INQUISITION

"**C**an I trust you boys to behave?"

Todd and Ray warily nodded, squinting up at the bright blur of their interrogator. The light in their faces was blinding. Averting their eyes, they could see they were in a fancy public restroom with gold fixtures and black marble tile. Their butts ached from sitting on the hard, cold floor.

The man was wearing a peculiar helmet, a tall black tube with flat sides, crimped in back like a rudder fin, with a cross-shaped hole in front for him to see through. He asked, "What exactly are you two trying to do?"

"Join you," Todd said. His tongue felt like a dead slug.

"Why is that?"

"We don't want to end up like those blue freaks out there."

"You say you came from a ship. What was the name of this ship?"

"It didn't have a name. It was a decommissioned nuclear submarine."

"Who else was on this submarine?"

"A lot of people. You want a list?"

"Was the Demon Lulu on the submarine with you?"

"Lulu? You mean Lulu Pangloss? What about her?"

"You know her!"

"We did. Until she became a Xombie."

"You are minions of the Blue Fury! Admit it!"

"Sir, the last we heard of Lulu was that she was going ashore. We never saw her after that."

"Liar! You are spies of hers! Why else would you have come ashore?"

"We were short of supplies, so the crew sent us out for more."

"Weren't you worried about Hellions?"

"Hellions?"

"Xombies. Exes. Maenads."

"We couldn't see any from the boat. We thought the coast was clear. We were wrong."

"Why would you assume the coast was clear?"

"We were desperate."

"Or was it that your Mistress sent you to infiltrate and undermine our holy mission?"

Ray said, "That would be so cool. But no."

"Liar! You are agents of evil, slaves and supplicants of the Shevil!"

"The what?"

"The She-Devil!"

Todd said, "That's *bullshit*, man, *bullshit*. For one thing, Lulu was just a messed-up chick, not some kind of . . . Shevil. For another, we had no idea you even existed, or we would have tried to contact you. Why else would we have been desperate enough to go ashore? We had no weapons, nothing. We saw almost forty of our friends get killed, either by Xombies or by Reapers, so you can go fuck yourself!"

*"Todd,"* Ray hinted through his teeth.

"I'm cool, I'm cool."

At Todd's outburst, their interrogator mellowed his tone. "Perhaps you are telling the truth. Or perhaps not—we will see. I just have a few more questions, and I suggest you answer truthfully because you will be judged. Not by me, but by the Lord Adam, Blessings Be Upon Him."

"My bad. Go ahead."

"Do you repent your sins?"

"Definitely!"

"Have you rejoiced in the company of homosexuals?"

"What?"

"I assume you are repenting being Sodomites and sexual deviants?"

"That's not really—"

"There's no need to lie. We have signed affidavits testifying to your perversions at Thule."

"*Thule!* Are you kidding? We were *prisoners* of those motherfuckers!"

"That's immaterial," the man said mildly. "Are you sexually attracted to each other?"

"*No!*"

"So you are free of sin?"

"No—just not that one."

"Are you prepared to take a vow of chastity from this day forth?"

Sensing closure, both boys jumped at it. "Hell yeah."

"Do you love America?"

"Of course."

"Are you true patriots? Would you die for your country?"

"Yeah . . . probably."

"Then why aren't you dead, like so many other patriots?"

"Why aren't *you*?"

"Because I have a sacred duty to perform. Answer the question!"

"Well . . . same here."

"Which is better: the Prophet Jim or the Apostle Chace?"

"Uh, Jim?"

"Both are equal in the eyes of the Lord! Do you believe in the Resurrection of the Moguls?"

"Oh, absolutely."

"Are you prepared to swear loyalty to the Lord Adam, the Lord's Prophet Jim, the Lord's Apostle Chace, and all the Living Saints of the Adamites?"

"Uh—sure."

"What is His purpose in revealing Himself at this time?"

"Who?"

"The Prophet Jim."

"I . . . don't know."

"You haven't witnessed His deeds?"

"I don't think so . . . Have we, Ray?"

"No."

"Are you prepared to swear undying allegiance to the Living God, that ye may serve Him as instruments of Miska's final destruction? Are ye prepared to don the mantle of the Sons of Adam?"

"Sure."

"And if any man among us should fall short, or betray the trust placed in him, or otherwise desecrate this sacred oath, do you swear to uphold the penalties for such conduct, even if those penalties be imposed upon you or your dearest loved ones?"

"What are the penalties?"

"Hard labor. Scourging of the flesh. Castration. Purification by fire. In that order."

"Wow. And, just out of curiosity, what's the alternative to joining?"

"Purification."

"Right. I guess we're in!"

"Then welcome, brothers! Welcome and rejoice!"


After the debriefing, Todd and Ray were released from their bonds but left locked in the windowless restroom. Many hours went by, perhaps days—they had no way of telling except by their increasingly ravenous hunger. They had ample water from the tap, but no food or privacy. They took turns sleeping on the hard tile floor.

By the time the door burst in, they had no strength left to resist. They didn't want to. "What took you so long?" Ray asked, as a man hogtied him and put a bag over his head.

They were carried up a dead escalator to a deserted Italian restaurant on the next floor. When the door of the restaurant closed behind them, it suddenly became very quiet. Their captors sat them down and removed their hoods. Todd sneezed, and a man said, "God bless you."

"Thanks," he said.

The restaurant was cleaned out. It was just a large carpeted room with floor-to-ceiling tinted windows overlooking the street. Sepia daylight filtered in. The only furnishings were the banquet chairs on which they sat, and a small table between them.

On that table was a feast beyond their wildest imagining: a platter of cold cuts, pickled vegetables, crackers, dried fruit, and two cans of cold apple juice.

As they ravenously dug in, the door opened, and someone entered the room—a tall bald man with a limp. He was very grave and very pale, wearing steel-rimmed glasses and a dark robe. He looked like some kind of Orthodox priest. Then Ray had a second look and dropped his spoon.

"Uncle *Jim*?" he said. He clapped his mouth shut, thinking, *Shut up, idiot!*

"Uncle?" Todd said.

"More like a family friend."

The man turned ominous, rearing up over Ray like Nosferatu.

"I know you," he intoned.

Ray nodded, shrinking in his seat. "You're not dead."

"Reports of my death have been greatly exaggerated. What are you two doing here?"

Ray was speechless, so Todd intervened: "We came back here after you . . . left the ship. I'm Todd Holmes, sir. My father was your shop foreman—Larry Holmes?"

"I know Larry," Sandoval said.

"He died, sir." Todd almost said, *Same as you.*

Sandoval's eyes flicked from Todd to Ray and back. "The submarine. Is it here?"

"No. It was, but it's gone. It was attacked by these Reaper dudes and pulled out. We came ashore to forage for supplies, so we got stranded."

"Alice Langhorne, was she on board?"

"Yes."

"How is she?"

"We don't know."

"What about the rest of them? Lulu Pangloss?"

"Lulu's a Xombie," Ray said.

"A Xombie. How?"

Todd jumped in. "A bunch of people got turned into Xombies at Thule, but Dr. Langhorne figured out a way to keep them under control using Lulu's blood."

"I bet she did," Sandoval said thoughtfully. "I just bet she did. What was that you said about Reapers?"

"They attacked the boat. We saw it all from India Point."

"Saw what?"

"Uh—that's a good question. Something really . . . weird . . . came out of the boat and got 'em. That's why we didn't try to get back aboard."

"I see . . ."

"What happens to us now?"

"You'll be taken to Indoctrination," the man said. "There's a whole process for new disciples, you'll see. Everybody has to go through it."

"How long does it take?"

"Just a few days; it's like a crash course."

"A crash course in what?"

"Good citizenship."

# CHAPTER **TEN**

## SANDOVAL

Having literally been run over by a truck, James Sandoval was half-frozen and already half-dead when Fred Cowper's headless body strangled him. Cowper wasn't doing so well either, having been mangled by a monkey and beheaded by Lulu Pangloss. They froze solid like that, a pair of vandalized statues from a forgotten war memorial. The dead monkey lay frozen a short distance away.

Over the following weeks, the sagging Mogul dome overhead was ripped away by storms, and the weird tableau of Sandoval and Cowper became drifted with snow and collected wind-driven icicles on its leeward side—just another strange formation on the frozen sea. But then the sea began to thaw. Spring was coming earlier and earlier every year; seas that had once been frozen in May were now navigable. The sun beat down, and soon the thick white mantle on the Davis Straight cracked loose and started to move. More storms came, bringing rain and waves that fractured the ice into huge floes, herding them into sun-warmed waters farther south.

On one of these floes, an iceberg the size of six city blocks, Sandoval and Cowper came back to life.

"Oh my God," Sandoval said, or rather tried to say—his throat was still crushed in Cowper's grip. The choking was not what bothered him; it was the feel of Cowper's alien flesh. "Get . . . off . . . me!"

Voice or no voice, Cowper's headless corpse seemed to understand him. Having no more business to transact, it willingly pulled free, though their blue skin had bonded and required some nasty-looking tearing to separate.

*Where am I?* Sandoval wondered, staring with black eyes over the vast expanse of ice-strewn ocean. There was no land in sight. *What am I?* But he already knew the answer to the latter question—it was no mystery. Good thing, because he could hardly expect any answers from Fred Cowper. Looking at that ridiculous headless figure in its bloodstained hospital gown, then down at his own blue hands, Sandoval thought, *I'm a Xombie—great.*

As he came to this unbelievable conclusion, he suddenly realized he wasn't the only one waking to a strange new destiny: The baboon that had kept him company in his last moments of life was apparently going to keep him company in the afterlife as well.

It lived.

They drifted for days, weeks, partially refreezing every night and thawing again in the sun. Cowper barely moved, facing south like a gnarled tree. The broken-necked baboon paced around the floe's rim, occasionally staring at Sandoval with its head cocked quizzically to one side, as if to ask, "Am I dreaming?" *I know the feeling, buddy,* Sandoval thought. His crushed legs caused him no pain, but they prevented him from walking, so he took great interest in their healing process: the splintered bones softening like putty, and his newly prehensile muscle tissues kneading them back into shape—a shape he could actually control if he wanted to. Long and fast, or short and strong—or something else altogether? He was afraid to mess with the original design too much, lest he screw it up and never get it back the way it was. But the possibilities of this newly plastic body fascinated him.

All around him, he sensed life, an awesome profusion of microscopic organisms that made the sea look like a living nebula, an animated horoscope of swimming, drifting, dancing celestial bodies, all eating or being eaten. The life was thickest on the bottom, illuminating the topography, so that at night Sandoval felt as though he were flying high above a radiant red desert. He would have gladly walked across that desert to the distant shore of Canada, except he knew there were a lot of crabs down there, and crabs ate Xombies. Miska had designed them to.

By day there were seals, birds, whales, an occasional polar bear. But even the hungriest bear could make nothing of Sandoval, Cowper, or the baboon—they had no smell, no warmth, no presence. They weren't living flesh, and they weren't carrion. They were about as palatable as clay.

Then Sandoval remembered his pen. It was a special pen, a laser pointer with a GPS beacon, designed to direct aerial fire on ground targets. A powerful tool for playing God. But Sandoval no longer had any desire to play God; he just wanted to reach dry land. So he turned on the beacon and waited. And while he waited he remembered.

The chairman of the board, James Sandoval, was not surprised by sounds of gunfire filtering into the briefing room. He was already despondent over the shooting of a civilian employee at the company picnic though it had been far from unexpected: Bob Martino was a union organizer and chronic loudmouth from way back. Still, a terrible threshold had been crossed. Things could only get worse from here on out.

Sandoval and the NavSea leadership were sitting around the big conference table, watching a live video feed from the security cameras at the fence line, less than a mile away, where things were going downhill fast.

*"Everyone off the fence!"* the guards shouted, sounding like harried gym teachers. *"Pull back, pull back!"*

They were leaderless, rudderless, shocked by the sudden death of Security Chief Beau Reynolds, who had gotten blown up in a freak explosion while standing on his observation platform like a half-assed Douglas MacArthur.

Sandoval panned the closed-circuit cameras as guards were snatched off the scaffolds and abandoned the fence, retreating before the horror that they had dreaded and drilled for, but for which no one could ever be truly prepared. Perhaps some were even relieved that the waiting was over.

The main gate was on fire, its bright glow in the evening mist silhouetting a scene of desperate flight. Shots sputtered like strings of firecrackers all along the perimeter, and men could be heard shouting hysterically for ammo, for reinforcements, for God Almighty.

Whatever was outside the fence was mostly hidden by plastic slats threaded through the wires, but the crashing chain link gave clear indication of multiple climbers, a sound like a stirred-up monkey cage. White phosphorous and burning magnesium fluoresced brightly in the fog, strobing, and it was possible to see scores of flaming shadow puppets scrambling up the barrier.

Two figures stood apart from the confusion, looking weirdly out of place: a skinny old man in golf slacks and a dark-haired little girl in a green velvet party dress.

"Holy hell," said Commander Harvey Coombs, staring at the monitor. "Is that Fred Cowper?"

"It is indeed," said Sandoval. "I don't know what he thinks he's doing bringing that girl in here. Figures he'd pick a time like this to show up."

"We could use his experience. He served on the original 726, didn't he?"

"Yeah. Put in his twenty in the Navy, then did a full term here. He's one of the real old-timers. Looks like he's taking us up on our offer."

"A little late. Can we get him, you think?"

"Well . . . it's pretty hairy down there. I'd have to say no, and the girl is completely out of the question. It's just too late—he had his chance a month ago and blew it. In a matter of minutes, that post will be completely overrun, and after that the compound is wide open. It's critical that you men get to the boat right now . . . or you never will."

Sandoval had a pang of regret saying this. At one time he had really hoped to get Cowper for this run. The man was a maverick, a hard case who knew subs inside and out and could be counted on to get the job done, red tape be damned. Rough around the edges, sure. A bit of a crank. Some people couldn't stand him, especially those in the upper echelons of military/industrial middle management, but to Sandoval, that was the highest recommendation of all.

At least most of the executive committee was safely aboard the rescue ship to Diego Garcia—that was a load off his mind. His adopted nephew, Ray, had made it to the compound in one piece, though Ray's sister had not—another good woman lost to the plague. And his ex-wife, Alice, had landed in Thule weeks ago to head up the science team. Sandoval had hoped to be away by now himself, but endless last-minute delays kept piling up until he was a whole day behind schedule.

From the sound of it, things would have to be accelerated a bit.

"Gentlemen," he said, gathering up his things and breaking the hush in the room. "The corporation wishes to thank you for your efforts in securing the enormous volume of classified material stored at this facility. By your efforts over the past weeks, you have safeguarded the cream of naval war-fighting technology, as well as the very building blocks of American civilization, assuring that they will neither fall into the wrong hands nor be lost to future generations. Without your work, it would be impossible to do what I now propose we all do: get the hell out of here."

There were hasty handshakes and good-byes all around. A sense of imminent death was in the air, but no one wanted to be the first to run, to show fear, and Jim found himself repeating, "We've done all we can, we've done all we can," until finally it was just him and Harvey Coombs.

"Come on, Mr. Sandoval, time to close up shop."

"You go ahead and make ready to cast off. I'll be right behind you."

"You know I can't do that, sir. We don't sail without you."

"I have one more small errand to run, and it's my eyes only. Don't worry, Harvey, I'm not going to blow my brains out or anything. But I do need a few more minutes before I can get down to the dock."

"Then I'll accompany you."

"You will not. Your business is running that boat, getting it safely out of here, and nothing can jeopardize that—not even me. So you worry about your job and let me worry about mine. That's an executive order, Commander."

"You're out of your mind if you think I'm leaving you out here all alone."

"I appreciate your concern, but you're interfering with both our duties. Until I'm aboard that boat, I am not your responsibility."

"I could take you under armed guard."

"But you won't." Sandoval opened his coat, revealing a nickel-plated .357 Magnum in a shoulder holster.

Coombs shook his head. "Jesus Christ. I hope you know what the hell you're doing." He turned on his heel and left.

Sandoval called after him, "Thanks, Harv."

There was a lull in the shooting, then an explosion that rattled the blinds.

*Huh. Better hurry.*

Instead, Jim dawdled, picking up a heavy pewter model of the proposed Hawaii-class boat and turning it over in his hands. It would've been a beautiful thing, a marvel for the ages, but it was a dream never to be realized. In spite of all they'd done to preserve its essence for posterity, Sandoval was poignantly aware that it would never be more than this shiny little paperweight—a trillion-dollar toy.

He thought of a book he had read as a child, about a carved toy canoe set afloat in a stream that made its way to the Great Lakes and finally out to sea. There was something terribly sad about it: The boy who made the canoe would never know how its journey ended, if it went a mile or a thousand miles—he just gave it the first push.

There was a radio telephone on the conference table, and Jim picked up the receiver. "I'm on my way, Mr. Velocek," he said.

"Yes, sir."

Sandoval pushed the model over with a bump and went to the door, turning off the lights as he left the room.

Walking downstairs and out the rear exit, he took a golf cart through deserted machine shops full of massive lathes, drills, and other steel-milling equipment. He found his Caddy in the east loading dock and gratefully sank into its deep upholstery one last time, reveling in its lush, amniotic suspension.

Jim could live in that car; he loved his things and hated to leave them. Having been born poor and come to wealth in his late teens, he never lost his deep need for material validation. In that way, both MoCo and the SPAM program reflected his packrat mentality: you *can* take it with you. *Having known both abject poverty and absolute luxury,* Sandoval liked to say, *I prefer luxury.*

He started the engine and pulled onto the service road.

Outside, the shooting had stopped, and a muffled calm descended with the fog.

*Isolated pockets, isolated pockets, isolated pockets . . .*

Sandoval caught himself muttering and put a stop to it. Those words had been cropping up in his thoughts too often, like an insipid tune he couldn't stop humming. He supposed it was some kind of post-traumatic stress thing, and wondered if worse was to come. Bitter-cold pragmatist though he was, he knew he hadn't yet really faced THE END OF THE WORLD, any more than he had faced his daughter's suicide, and he wondered if it was even possible to come to terms with such a thing. Short of dropping dead from grief, what could be an appropriate reaction? And he had to put up a brave front, lest his own horror demoralize his subordinates.

Most of the people at the plant had been rather sheltered from the terrible events of the past month. The remote point of land occupied by the submarine compound was not on any map and was screened from prying eyes by miles of restricted Navy property. It was a rare "isolated pocket"—a place the Maenad plague had not penetrated. Its convenient desolation was the sole reason for their survival, but it also created a false sense of security. Most of them had never even seen a so-called "Xombie."

Well, now they would. Oh yes.

As he passed through the deserted inner checkpoint and turned away from the direction of the submarine pen, Sandoval was a bit surprised to see that Coombs had really taken him at his word—they had gone ahead to the boat and left him alone. That was easier than expected; maybe they were glad to get rid of him. But why should that be surprising? They had military duties to perform, a ship to make ready, a crucial mission to undertake. Jim Sandoval was ballast, deadweight. He was a civilian and, from their point of view, the worst kind of civilian: a civilian you had to kiss up to. By bailing out, he was probably doing them a favor.

How many other residual pockets of humanity were out there? Jim wondered. Hundreds? Thousands? The corporation had obviously benefited from isolation and dumb luck, and he knew of a few other such organized hideaways from

the epidemic, but that was no indication of how many survivors there might be among the general population. The
independents, the rogue elements. Because, ultimately, they
would be the backbone of any new civilization.

Sandoval's own experience had not been hopeful. He'd
been in touch with Washington for the better part of January, discussing contingencies and implementing the Family-
to-Work Plan, just so the illusion could be sustained that the
company was keeping up its contractual commitments to
the Navy, but after martial law was announced, it became
harder and harder to get anyone on the horn. When he did,
they urged him to "sit tight" and "hold the fort," as if all he
needed was a little bucking up.

The NavSea team on the factory premises, led by Commander Harvey Coombs, became a paranoid clique that
transferred its base of operations to the boat and didn't want
to share whatever information was coming over the submarine's communications array. But, apparently, they hadn't
had any better luck than Sandoval at calling in the cavalry
because Coombs soon turned up, hat in hand, stressing the
need for cooperation . . . especially in regard to the Plan. As
keeper of the Plan, Jim Sandoval held all the cards and held
them close to his vest. One thing that was clear to both of
them was that their deadlines and employee morale issues
were small potatoes in the larger scheme of things.

Jim counted as victories his ability to persuade the rank
and file that a gutted nuclear submarine could be a godsend
to them and their male offspring—a big steel safety net—as
well as to finagle extra security and a sea convoy for routine
supplies.

But in doing these things, he had the inescapable feeling
that he was engaged in something shady, that the resources
he was diverting to one neutered SSBN (or an SSGN, as the
Navy had permitted him to call it, though the bellyful of
guided cruise missiles it was supposed to carry would never

be delivered) might be more desperately needed elsewhere. Who was he to decide who lived and who died? Even using the submarine's S8G reactor to supply power to the local grid could be interpreted as a wasteful extravagance, lighting a few suburbs while the rest of human civilization went dark.

By mid-January, everything had really shut down. Sandoval received a last official instruction: to compile all the available records of the Agent X epidemic into one report, a sort of doomsday scrapbook, and preserve it for posterity as an essential part of the boat's cargo. A message in a bottle. Everything had happened so fast, there was no other official record, no history. Anyone still alive was to participate in this final archive and add their own perspective on the disaster. Officially, it was called *The Maenad Project*. Jim dubbed it *The Apocalypticon*.

At first, Sandoval looked upon this ridiculous assignment as truly the last nail in the coffin—who exactly did they think was going to take time out from the struggle for survival to participate in this scavenger hunt? And who would be around to read it?

But during the long nights in limbo, he began to find the idea strangely compelling: that he was at the center of extraordinary events that deserved to be memorialized. It had never occurred to him that all this sad, ugly scrabble for crumbs could be shaped into something coherent . . . and even majestic. That it only required a historian who could do it justice, a writer who could really milk the situation for all the poetry and pathos it was worth. A writer who could immortalize *him*, James Sandoval, as a keeper of the flame of civilization. A prophet for a new age.

He thought of the Emma Lazarus poem on the Statue of Liberty: "Give me your tired, your poor, your huddled masses yearning to breath free . . ." Yes! That was *exactly* the kind of writing this situation called for. Unfortunately,

Sandoval knew, he wasn't that writer. And unless by some extraordinary accident he found another Emma Lazarus with the requisite skills to enshrine in poetry or prose such an eternal testament to the unquenchable power of the human spirit, the project would have to languish. Sandoval had other things to worry about.

That was the beginning of the true "isolated pockets" phase of the plague, when all commerce, all movement, seemed to grind to a halt like film jamming in an old movie projector. Telephone, radio, satellite, and computer networks folded simultaneously, leaving an ominous silence that was all too easy to fill in with raging paranoia. Sandoval's people were reduced to using shortwave radio over the submarine's transmitter, but without functioning relays or a direct line to SOSUS, this was a feeble candle in the darkness.

Delegations of volunteer fact finders were sent out and never heard from again. They lost half the men this way, and nearly all the company vehicles. The tidbits of news they did hear were all bad:

Population centers worldwide were saturated with Maenad Cytosis and Xombie psychosis, cities rupturing outward like virus-infected cells to spread waves of raving maniacs across the remnants of civilization. Canada was being bombed. Long lists of expired "safe zones" were broadcast, but even while still operational, these were nothing but tracts of remote countryside where truckloads of uninfected females were dumped—huge, open-air refugee farms that resembled POW camps, surrounded by watchtowers and silver briars of razor ribbon. No warm school gymnasiums, cozy church basements, dry armories and civil defense shelters loaded with blankets and hot coffee and donuts. It was all mass hysteria and sudden death. Death at *best*.

Especially in those early days, Sandoval received all kinds of conflicting instructions from an assortment of increasingly incoherent provisional leaders—those who would talk to him at all—raving about EMP detonations, satellite warfare, alien invaders over Kansas, and the ever-popular Rapture. He knew one man in particular who was making great hay with the religious angle, a former media Mogul named Chace Dixon, who begged him for help he had no power to send. It had been days now since he last bothered tuning in.

In the end, the last acting NATO commander—some third-tier lieutenant in the French Navy—decided that humanity's last, best chance was to set up a nautical sanctuary in Chesapeake Bay. This cockeyed optimist ordered every survivor to report to Norfolk, where he and his staff were supposedly following orders from the president of the United States—the *dead* president—to guard some kind of secret project called Xanadu.

It was all nuts. Yet even Sandoval wasn't immune to these fantasies. He often pictured a simple, nautical existence for the dregs of mankind, coming ashore only when necessary to forage, the way old-time mariners approached uncharted coasts, maybe finding a tropical island somewhere to settle down. Live out your years on fish and coconuts. Swim every day and get a really deep tan. No bills to pay—in fact, forget all about the pain in the ass that was Western Civilization. It was more trouble than it was worth, anyway.

All very delightful, except that Sandoval knew there were precious few island havens. Islands were the first things to go because there was nowhere to run when your women came after you. Most of the islands he knew of were either embattled fortresses or Xombie-infested charnel houses. That such daydreams had taken the place of serious planning was perhaps the clearest possible indication of THE END OF THE WORLD.

Harvey Coombs himself had recommended going to Norfolk in search of whatever seaborne military forces still existed. Sandoval didn't have the heart to tell him that their real mission was in the opposite direction.

The helicopter landing pad was at the extreme northern tip of the compound, a barren patch of dirt overlooking the

upper reaches of Narragansett Bay. As Sandoval pulled
up, the fog was so thick he could barely see the black Bell
JetRanger. But the pilot saw his headlights and came running to meet the car.

"Can we fly in this?" Sandoval asked.

"Oh yeah, no prob. With GPS, it's no sweat, and we'll be
flying above the muck anyway—it's just ground fog. Hang
tight for a second while I finish my preflight."

"You're the boss." Sandoval locked himself in the car
and plugged in some music. He already owed his life to Stan
Velocek several times over, and was accustomed to doing
whatever the retired aviator told him to do. As both his personal pilot and bodyguard, Stan went everywhere with him,
and the first thing Jim had done when he arrived at the plant
was to make sure the man would be well taken care of.

Good thing, too. If it wasn't for Stan, he would never
have survived the expedition to Brown University. None of
the other two hundred men who went out there ever made it
back to the plant. Jim could still picture that line of company
vans and trucks leaving the gate like a military convoy, full
of heroic working stiffs—solemn-faced shipfitters and tank
rats who had been stirring up revolution and were placated
with an offer to seek out lost loved ones outside the gates:
all the mothers, sisters, and daughters who hadn't even been
infected when they abandoned them and took shelter in the
submarine compound.

They didn't find anyone . . . but at least Jim found what
he was looking for: Miska's Tonic.

Well, maybe not *the* Tonic, the fabled magic bullet—Uri
Miska had either been lying about that or destroyed all traces
of his work. But Sandoval did get a preliminary version of
CORE: Miska's Cognition-Retention Enzyme.

Though CORE was neither a cure nor a true vaccine, it
was a reasonable stopgap, a suitable substitute that Sandoval could sell to his Mogul partners. Snake oil. It was cer-

tainly the closest he ever intended to let those bastards come
to being gods. There wasn't much, just a residue on a test
sample, but with this they could theoretically make more . . .
as much more as they needed.

His ex-wife, Alice Langhorne, PhD, had told him where
to find it. Alice could be a pain in the ass, but she usually
came through when it counted. She had hidden the sample
in her office high atop the monolithic Brown Science Labo-
ratory, and when they got there, it was just where she said,
in the back of the fridge. A copy of Miska's hard drive was
there, too—good girl!

While he was at it, Sandoval would have liked to take
another slight detour and visit his father at the Xibalba
annex—Miska's underground hideaway—but it was just
too dangerous. He knew where it was, but he had never
been inside, and this was not the time to figure it out. Good
old Piers Alaric was certainly not going anywhere.

As it was, the lab building almost killed him. It was fortunate that Alice's directions were so good—there was not
a second to spare. One would think the Xombies had been
expecting them.

The infernal creatures stayed out of sight until everyone
was inside the tower, just hid there until the very last man
filed up that dark stairwell, passing floor after empty floor.
Then, *pow!*—they sprang the trap. It was a damned massacre. Grabbing the precious serum sample, Sandoval ran
to the roof like a cornered rat . . . and there was Stan Velocek with the helicopter, hand outstretched like some angel
from heaven.

Jim watched now as the man darted around the helicopter, a picture of cool competence, scanning every direction
for signs of danger, combat shotgun at the ready. Removing
the anchor lines, he did a quick visual inspection of the
engine and tail rotor before starting it up.

Sandoval was glad he wouldn't have to ride with Coombs

and the other Navy men in that broken-down hulk of a submarine. What a nightmare that would have been. Considering the working conditions at the plant, it would be a miracle if that thing ever made it out of Narragansett Bay.

From the very beginning, he had intended to take the chopper to the desolate island airstrip where his private 757 was waiting, but he wasn't about to leave anything up to chance. It was vitally important to have a backup escape plan, just in case Velocek realized there was nothing stopping him from taking the whirlybird for himself. But the pilot didn't disappoint; Jim should have known he was as good as gold.

Thumbs-up—the helicopter was ready. As Sandoval stepped out of the car, something flickered at the edge of his peripheral vision: a pale shape rushing through the fog. It was so silent and quick that at first he thought it was something in his eye, a bit of fuzz or his mind playing tricks, and even when he looked at it full on, he could scarcely believe it was happening—because that's how these things got you. Then it jumped on the copter.

It was a grotesque salamander of a woman, naked, muddy, and mottled blue-black from the sea. As Sandoval watched, the slippery creature clawed at the copter's bubble canopy, trying to get at the man inside. Velocek tried shooting at it through the small side port and almost lost his gun; he just couldn't get a good angle. In a second, it was going to rip the door right off the cockpit.

Waving at Sandoval to stay put, the pilot strapped himself in and throttled up for liftoff—obviously he was going to try to shake the thing loose. Knowing what a daredevil Stan was, Sandoval had no doubt the man could do it . . . it just made him a little uncomfortable to be left sitting here in the dark watching his ride take off without him. Knowing more of those things could appear any second. He clutched his pistol with both hands and half cocked the hammer. *Hurry up, Stan . . .*

The helicopter rose into the air, wobbling as it strained against the unequal weight. It was a light, wasplike craft, a four-seater converted to two for the sake of a reserve fuel tank, fast and highly maneuverable, whose expert pilot knew how to handle unusual loads.

With the creature beating on his window, Velocek gunned forward and broke hard to the right. He was using centrifugal force to dislodge the thing, and it nearly worked, but instead of being shaken loose, the Maenad merely lost its footing, both legs swinging up into the rotor blades. With a sound like a weed whacker hitting a clump, its feet went spinning free into the sky.

Still holding on, the thing shoved the ragged ends of its shins into the warped edge of the cockpit door, using the exposed bones as wedges to pry open the flimsy latch. It burrowed in like a parasite, a giant tick, its every heinous fiber digging at that weak spot. The Perspex window cracked, then shattered as the Xombie lunged through.

Straight into both barrels of Velocek's shotgun.

The blast sheared off most of the Xombie's head, slinging bone and brain matter far out over the bay. Cropped to its nostrils, the creature toppled backward, scrambling for a handhold as it spilled the last of its brains out the open goblet of its skull . . . then recovered as if from a bad step. Spurting black goo out the exposed pits of its sinuses, it came at the pilot with renewed vigor.

Velocek fired again, into its chest. At the same time, he pulled hard out of his dive and yawed right, creating intense g-forces that caused both the creature and the canopy door to be ripped loose, vanishing into thin air like a magic trick.

Grinning with relief—*Gotcha!*—Stan Velocek leveled his aircraft and barely had time to blink as a huge white cylinder loomed out of the fog. Then he and the helicopter ceased to exist.

Jim Sandoval had lost sight of the chopper, but he tried to stay calm, knowing the pilot would put down and collect him at the first opportunity. Stan was reliable if anyone was. Then, from somewhere back in the factory complex, came an eruption of yellow light, followed by a sickening thud that jarred the car. It was an exploding chemical silo.

*What the hell's that?* Sandoval thought. And then: *Oh shit.*

Time for plan B.

Racing back to the wharf at top speed, cursing and pounding the steering wheel as he drove, Sandoval came upon something blocking the road and barely had time to hit his brakes.

*What the—?*

A mass of ghostly people materialized out of the thick gloom; he nearly plowed right into them. *Xombies!* No, not Xombies—kids! Hundreds of teenage boys crossing the compound on foot, with adults from the factory herding them like a flock of sheep.

Trundling amid the crowd like a parade float was a large construction vehicle, the Sallie, a specialized flat-top crawler used to move hundred-ton sections of the submarine. Now its dance-hall-sized freight bed was loaded with teenagers dangling their legs off, like a truck hauling migrant workers to the fields. The rolling behemoth was heading slowly but implacably toward the Fitting Bay and, just beyond, the gates to the wharf.

That wasn't good . . . not good at all.

Working up the nerve to toot his horn, Sandoval watched in agonized frustration as the mob closed ranks on him. A sneering overweight boy pounded the car's hood while the rest scowled at him with the dull effrontery of a bunch of hooligans, shielding their faces from the Cadillac's headlights.

They were after the boat. The rebellious idiots were storming the submarine—*his* submarine. It was unbelievable . . . or maybe not so unbelievable. This was exactly the kind of thing he had been hoping to avoid all these weeks, and now here he was, caught up in a revolt, prevented from getting to the boat himself.

They were armed, too, not with guns but with the even more alarming weapons of angry villagers: hammers, clubs, makeshift blades, and bludgeons of all sorts. Sandoval had a gun, but it would be worse than useless against a mob like this. If he wasn't careful, this could turn into a bloodbath—*his* blood.

These were the folks he had dropped the bomb on only yesterday, serving up the bad news with barbecued chicken and a side of coleslaw. Apparently, they weren't taking it well. According to plan, they should've all been under lockdown until force withdrawal was complete. Until the boat was gone.

So much for the plan.

Sandoval saw the shop foreman Larry Holmes coming over at a fast trot, dangerously clutching a big hammer. Jim didn't want to find out what these people would do if they got their hands on him. Gun or no gun, he put the car in reverse and backed away as fast as he could until the fog shielded him once more, then stopped and turned off his headlights. Sitting in the dark, he could still make out the shadowy crowd limned by the orange caution lights of the Sallie.

*Shit.* There was just no way past them.

Directly ahead, so close and yet so unattainable, were the big cranes of the yard, which had recently been used to pull all the ballistic missile tubes out of the boat and line them up in neat rows on the ground. And before that, the missiles themselves, yanked like so many bad teeth by the watchful representatives of the Strategic Air Command. That had been a new experience for Sandoval—he had always secretly regretted not joining the Air Force, thinking his vertigo had condemned him to an alliance with the less sophisticated, less *lordly* of the two services. And those pompous SAC bastards had proved him right, hoisting their precious missiles like somber priests removing idols from a defiled temple. God, he had envied them. The civilian sector could never hold a candle to that kind of self-importance: the fate of the world in your hands.

As the crowd started to thin, Jim cautiously nudged his car forward. All the people passing him now were adults, his formerly dutiful employees, everybody hustling the slowpokes along. The fearful way they were glancing backward toward the main gate made Jim nervous about sitting still for too long.

Someone rapped hard on the driver's side window, causing Sandoval to jump. He turned to find himself staring at Gus DeLuca from the machine shop. The man's jowly mug was sweaty and flushed, but not hostile. DeLuca appeared taken aback to find himself face-to-face with the company CEO.

Smiling apologetically, DeLuca shouted a muffled, "Uh, sir? Mr. Sandoval, sir?"

Damn. Jim rolled down his window a crack, saying with false cordiality, "Well, howdy there, Gus. What's this all about? You know, these people are heading into a restricted—"

He was interrupted by a length of steel pipe smashing his passenger window. Peppered with glass, Sandoval cringed, then felt himself yanked bodily out of the car.

"Sorry, Jim, we need the ride," said Gus as he wrestled him to the ground. "I'll explain later."

Lying there on the damp pavement, Sandoval looked around at his attackers: DeLuca, Holmes, Big Ed Albemarle. "Take me with you," he said. "Let me talk to Coombs— you'll never get through without me. I can help you."

Ignoring him, DeLuca shouted, "Holmes, you're up! Take the car and deliver our terms. Honk if they're amenable to discussion."

More urgently, Sandoval said, "I'm telling you, let me talk to them. You can't negotiate. They have orders to shoot to kill."

Gus looked at the others as if to ask, *What do you think?*

"Take him along," someone said—Sandoval realized it was Fred Cowper. So Cowper had made it after all! Hell, this was all probably his idea. The old man had aged a lot since his retirement party, but he was clearly as cantankerous as ever.

Cowper said, "Gus, you and Ed ride shotgun."

They shoved Sandoval into the passenger seat and piled in behind him. "Say the wrong thing, and none of us gets out alive," Albemarle said.

As the car skirted the crowd and caught up to the rolling platform, Sandoval's attention was suddenly drawn to a blurry figure running alongside. At first he assumed it was someone else from the crowd trying to catch their attention, but then he heard shouting and noticed that the adults were banding together and throwing the smaller kids up onto the crawler's deck. Everyone was pointing at the Cadillac with terrified expressions on their faces.

A hand grabbed hold of Sandoval's window frame, making him jump. He whipped around to see a vision so awful that his mind couldn't absorb it. The sight hit him like a physical blow, a rabbit punch that knocked all the air out of him.

The thing was an obscene caricature of a beautiful young woman, her perfect teeth gleaming Pepsodent white in a tautly grinning purple face, with a gaping crater in her skull through which the remaining brain matter was visible, undulating like a wrinkled scrotum. The living matter seemed to be reaching out of her head for him.

Before Sandoval had time to react to the shock, the woman seized the car with both hands and vaulted up like a circus rider mounting a galloping horse. He drew breath to shout, *Look out!* But before he could get the words out, two long legs slithered in through the broken window, and her whole naked body landed on his lap. He could see right through her heart.

Pandemonium broke out in the car.

Gus DeLuca spun the wheel, and suddenly there was a utility pole in the headlights. They were only moving at about 15 mph, but the car slammed hard, deploying its air bags, and everyone dove, screaming, out the doors. Sandoval tumbled to the ground with the woman wrapped around him, her nimble and ridiculously strong arms crushing his windpipe while her neck strained to force that crazed suckerfish mouth over his. Her exposed brain licked his forehead like a sticky tongue.

*Help me!* he tried to shout, head twisting wildly to avoid her questing mouth. *Somebody help!* He couldn't reach the gun; his arms were clamped tight by her cold, naked thighs. Sandoval could feel himself blacking out.

Then by some miracle he was free, doubled over on his side and retching in pain. It was Gus DeLuca and Big Ed Albemarle: They had brained the thing with the heavy hammers they used in the factory—they were *still* braining it. It had no brains left to brain.

*"X marks the spot,"* DeLuca crowed.

"Die . . . die . . . die . . ." muttered Albemarle, his denim coveralls speckling with inky blood as they pounded the writhing thing into the ground.

Stepping back to rest his arm, Gus DeLuca said, "Ed, we gotta go." The parade had moved on, and they were alone in the fog. The Cadillac was steaming from its crumpled hood, totaled.

"What about *him*?" He pointed to Sandoval.

An eruption of gunfire and screams rattled the gloom, then a rockslide of trampling feet that was the sound of mass panic. An amplified voice said, "HALT. YOU ARE IN A RESTRICTED AREA."

"Fuck him and the car he rode in on," said DeLuca. "We gotta get down there."

They left him.

In the distance, Sandoval could hear a chorus of voices begging to be let on the boat. He knew there wasn't much chance of them ever getting past the Marines posted there. It was the end of the line for all of them, himself included.

He could picture the scene: the dockyard full of empty missile tubes, the dead hulk of the Sallie blocking the road, its driver shot dead in the front cab and terrified boys pouring off the crawler's deck like panicked wildebeests entering a crocodile-infested river.

They were pinned down on the broad tarmac between the submarine's gangway—the "brow"—and the terraced lawn that was the site of yesterday's dockside picnic. Bob Martino's blood would still be there in the grass for anyone who cared to look. The boat would still be there, too, though not for long, its speckled mast array looming in the dark as if suspended in midair. Beneath that, the railed gantry would fade into black nothingness, a bridge to nowhere.

How did those poor saps think they were going to escape when the man who owned the submarine factory could not? Did they imagine they could appeal to pity? Lay claim to human dignity, decency, or justice? At this late hour, when the coin of mercy was a debased slug not even fit to steal a gumball? When the sleep of death itself had become a luxury? How dare they be so stupid—Jim Sandoval damned them for their pride.

Resigned, lying there in the dirt, he could only shake his head as the shooting resumed. It would all be over soon.

Something slippery touched his hand.

He jumped up to see the ruined Maenad coming toward him. She was just a quivering pulp on the ground, roadkill, but she was still alive, still moving. Not fast, but faster by the second. Most incredibly, he still sensed that same wild ea-

gerness as before, emanating from these smashed remains—
pure, frenzied lust at the sight of him. As he watched, the
mincemeat of her mangled flesh was knitting back together,
not quite *healing* but gathering itself into sturdier form. The
sound it made was awful.

There was an explosive crash down at the wharf. Still
staring in horror, Sandoval thought, *What the hell are they
doing now?* The shooting abruptly stopped. and the thinly
officious voice of Harvey Coombs came over a loudspeaker:

"FRED, THIS IS COMMANDER COOMBS. I DON'T
KNOW WHAT YOU THINK YOU'RE DOING, BUT IN
MY BOOK IT'S TREASON. YOU ARE INTERFERING
WITH CRITICAL NAVAL OPERATIONS."

Jim listened, snorting incredulously as the amplified
voice of Fred Cowper, USN (Ret.), replied, "LET ME AND
ALL THESE PEOPLE ON BOARD, THEN PUT US
ASHORE SOMEPLACE HALFWAY SECURE!"

Was this a joke? Fred talked as if *he* was calling the
shots. As if he and a ragtag bunch of hardhats and teenage
boys were the ones holding the aces.

Which, Sandoval suddenly realized, they just might be.

With dawning wonder, he understood why they had
brought the Sallie vehicle on their little crusade: The massive
freight hauler wasn't just to give the kids a lift. In its sheer
bulk, it was the only weapon they had capable of sinking a
nuclear submarine. What he was hearing down there was the
ultimate game of chicken.

*Demolition derby,* Sandoval thought, not without admi-
ration. *Fred, you old bastard!*

As he stood there shaking his head, the raveled Maenad
rose to its feet and lurched toward him. At the same time, he
could see movement in the fog: several odd-looking people running for the wharf. Not people—*Xombies*. Lots more
Xombies, attracted by the light and commotion.

It was going to be a hell of a fight. Feeling reanimated

himself, Jim knew he had to get down there, too . . . but obviously he'd never make it on foot. Dodging the gropes of that mangled Hellion, he sprinted toward the nearest available vehicle, an electric cart by the tool shed.

He wouldn't miss this for the world.

# CHAPTER **ELEVEN**

## THE MOSH PIT

Todd and Ray were sworn in as disciples of the Prophet Jim.

It was a strange process, requiring them first to stuff themselves with rich foods like cheese, cured meats, and canned fruitcake, then to become violently ill for three days. Purged to the point of dehydration and delirium, they were forced to confess their sins and desires at the end of a red-hot poker. After declaring their total fealty to the approved pantheon of gods and prophets, they were stripped to the waist—their revealed torsos covered with cross-shaped welts—and doused in freezing water almost to the point of drowning. Finally, they were allowed to sleep. For years, it seemed.

When they awoke, it was to gentle voices, soft robes, and delicious bread and soup.

Then the praying began. Prayers before meals, after meals, before bed, upon waking, and randomly throughout the day, religious obeisance required before and after engaging in any activity, however trivial, a constant, compulsive drone of gratitude and contrition.

Time blurred. Reality warped.

*"Yoo-hoo.* Wake up, sleepyhead. I'd like to show you something."

Ray awoke to find a man's face staring at him, inches away. It was a bulbous, boyish face, the face of a middle-aged schoolboy with hair sleeked back like a sumo. It took Ray a second to remember where he was: in his new quarters on the fourth floor of the Westin Hotel. Todd's room was down the hall. The hotel was less luxurious than it had been formerly, having no heat, running water, electricity, working elevators, or room service, but it still looked pretty snazzy. Most of the disciples were bivouacked next door in the Providence Place Mall, camped out on the floor of Macy's or Old Navy, and taking their meals in the Food Court.

"Who the fuck are you?" Ray asked in alarm.

"Whoa. Hey. Easy there, big fella. It's only little ol' me, Chace Dixon."

The name didn't immediately register. *"What are you doing in my room?"*

"Ray, I know it's been a while, but come on. Don't you recognize me?"

*Oh shit.* Ray hurriedly braided the frayed ends of his wits. Chace Dixon. Media Mogul and associate of Jim Sandoval. He owned an apartment in Jim's building, and Ray had met him a few times in passing. What the hell was *he* doing here?

Then it hit him. Ray said, "Are *you* the Apostle Chace?"

"Did you just realize that? I love it! I was just thinking about you, and thought I'd drop by and say hello."

"Hello . . . and good-bye." Ray rolled over to face the wall.

Dixon sat down on the edge of the bed. "Ray, do you believe in miracles?"

"Not really."

"I love that! *Thank* you. If only more people around here were so honest! Yet you must admit it's a strange coincidence that you and I should meet each other again, here on the far side of the Apocalypse. One might even call it fate."

"This is ridiculous."

"Of course it is! It's totally nuts. But then that's pretty much the definition of a miracle."

"Or mental illness."

"This from someone who claims to have seen Elvis."

"Yeah, but I know it wasn't really Elvis—it was Uri Miska."

"I wouldn't say that too loud—some people around here wouldn't take kindly to it."

"Why not?"

"I mean these Elvis visitations have inspired a bit of a cult. It's a time of miracles and wonders; people are primed to believe in anything, including Elvis. They don't want to think he's an imposter."

"But you know he is."

"Let's just say it's part of my job description to promote miracles and wonders."

"Have you even seen him?"

"Seen him?" Dixon said. "We shot him."

"You what? *Shot* him?"

"Yes indeedy. After what happened to us last time we were in this town, my sentries are on a hair trigger; they shoot anything that moves. One of them put a twelve-gauge shotgun load in Elvis's chest. Blew a hole you could have stuck your fist through, but it had no effect on him. He just kind of shook it off, and said, *'Don't do that, man.'* Then he was gone. I ordered the men not to report anything until I could get to the bottom of it. Thanks to you and your friend, I think we have."

"Miska thinks you're threatening the survival of the human race by spreading immunity to the Xombies. He says some kind of Armageddon is coming that only Xombies can survive."

"And what do you think?"

"I think Miska's probably crazy."

"Put your shoes on," Dixon said, getting up off the bed. "I'd like to show you something."

He led Ray through a dark parking garage that connected the hotel to the Convention Center. The latter was a large, glass-faced building resembling an airport terminal. Unlike the mall or the hotel, there were very few people around.

As they walked, Dixon said, "It's not as if I was ever that pious before Agent X. I believed in God, but organized religion was a tool of manipulation, a way to control the masses. I thought it was purely psychological, but then I had never had any real evidence to the contrary."

Leading at a brisk pace, Dixon took Ray down a utility corridor to a heavy double door marked EMERGENCY EXIT—ALARM WILL SOUND.

In a hushed voice, he said, "We call this the Mosh Pit."

He unbolted the door and pulled it open. On the other side was a dim balcony overlooking a huge convention hall full of people. Not people—Xombies. Thousands of eerily quiet Exes, all staring up at them. Even fifty feet above that sea of blue faces, Ray felt panic squeeze his guts like a big cold hand.

"What are they all doing here?" he asked.

"They're locked in."

"Why?"

"Can't live with 'em, can't kill 'em. Originally, we intended to burn the whole thing down, but then we realized it wasn't necessary. They can't get out. It's like storing nuclear waste. Out of sight, out of mind."

"How'd they all get here in the first place?"

"Some are Red Cross workers and National Guard who tried to set up a safe zone during the outbreak. The rest are poor suckers who made the mistake of taking shelter here. I figure there are around twenty or thirty thousand of them altogether. Once the disease got loose among them, it was all over—we locked the doors and barricaded them shut. It's terrible, I know, but at least they're not suffering."

"Not suffering? It looks like Auschwitz down there."

"If these things suffered, they'd be dead by now. They've been in here almost four months without food or water. Do you smell any rot or decay? No. They don't die; they don't feel pain. In the early days, we wasted a lot of ammo on them before we realized they don't stay dead, either whole or in pieces. Good thing, too, because now we have a big supply of Hellions for the Prophet to convert. He does a few every Sunday."

"Convert how?"

"They are Sealed with the Sacrament, just as you were."

"If you say so. Listen, this is freaking me out—can we go?"

"In a minute. I want you to see something first."

"What?"

"Here, put this on." He handed Ray a safety harness and donned one himself.

To the right of the balcony was a metal ladder up to the roof beams. Dixon checked Ray's harness, and together they climbed up there, clipping onto a safety line as they followed the steel beams to an electric winch in the middle of the ceiling. Attached to the winch was a large hook intended to hoist heavy stage lights or other equipment. With a thumbs-up, Dixon affixed the hook to Ray's harness and pushed the boy off the edge.

*"Whoa, hey, shit!"* Flailing wildly, Ray swung out into space. Then Dixon pressed the DOWN button.

"Stop!" Ray shrieked. "What are you *doing*?" The Xombies rustled at the sound of his voice, swaying like a field of reeds in the wind.

Dixon ignored his cries. As Ray slowly descended, the blue masses cleared an opening for him, a bare atoll in that sea of yearning faces. Ray screamed for help, sobbing, begging, trying to climb the wire, anything, but there was no escape.

The Xombies stared upward, intent on his progress . . .

though not nearly as frenzied as he would have expected. In fact, they looked a little bored, as though they had been through this routine many times and didn't have the energy. Perhaps it was too easy for them, no challenge—why should they have to work for it? Scrunching his body into a fetus-shaped kernel of anticipation, Ray dropped right into their midst.

They made no move to touch him. In fact, they dismissed him entirely, turning all their attention back on Chace Dixon.

*Oh my God.*

Dixon called down, "Pretty neat, huh?"

"What the hell is going on?"

"Hold that thought." He hit a wall switch, and the winch raised Ray to the catwalk. In a moment, both men were out of their harnesses and back on the balcony. "Not bad, huh?"

"What does this mean? How did you do that?"

"Not so crazy now, am I?"

"How are you controlling them?"

"I'm not controlling them—God is."

"What do you mean by that?"

"I mean this is all real, Ray. Blind faith no longer required. I wanted to demonstrate to you that the Lord really is on our side if we choose to serve Him. There really are angels and demons waging a war between Heaven and Hell, and it's up to us to choose sides. You're not dealing with deluded religious nuts. This is not like the Grammy Awards or the Super Bowl, where the winner thanks God and everybody rolls his eyes because it's such bull. This is for real, an actual miracle. As long as you're with us, you are Hellion-proof."

Ray was still in shock; he could barely stand. Voice quaking, he asked, "H-how?"

"The Prophet has interceded on your behalf. You've been through the purification ceremony, been anointed with the blood of the lamb; now your sins are forgiven."

"But that's all just symbolism. How can that make a difference?"

"There are no symbols anymore, no empty ceremonies. That's what I'm trying to tell you, Ray! Everything is exactly what it seems."

He took Ray back outside and chained the doors.

# CHAPTER **TWELVE**

## CONVOCATION

The next day an assembly was announced, and the dazed new recruits joined a parade of soldiers marching up to the State House lawn. They were handed paper scrolls and symbolic scourging rods. Men congratulated Todd and Ray and welcomed them into the family—a euphoric experience after their ordeal.

Entering the capitol grounds, they noticed that all the trees had been cut down for firewood. An artificial grove of X-shaped steel frames had been erected, and dozens of laborers were dismantling old military barricades, building new wooden bleachers, and digging pit latrines around the perimeter. The workers were filthy, exhausted, and demoralized from being jeered at all day and pelted with trash.

"Oh shit," Todd said. "What is this, a giant hazing? I am definitely not feeling this."

"More new arrivals?" asked the supervising Adamite, a former Army Ranger named Sheldon Barnstable.

His fellow cleric, a former bank manager named Lester Mead, said, "Yeah—they're the guys who came in riding bikes."

"Bikes! Are you for real?"

"I saw it myself."

"No shit." To Todd and Ray, he asked, "Where did you guys come from?"

"Fox Point."

"What were you doing there?"

Todd said, "Talking to Elvis."

"You should be down on your knees thanking Adam that we found you before the Hellions did."

"Oh, we are," said Ray.

Lester Mead said, "I just want to go on the record as saying I think it's kind of uncool that you guys have special privileges over those of us who have been in the Adams since before the Tribs."

"We do?"

"Oh yeah. I have your orders right here. No ditches for you boys; you've both been bumped up to custodial detail at the hotel. That requires clearance from the top. Looks like you're even quartered there—sweet gig! Pays to have friends in high places, I guess."

"That's great," Todd said. "Can we go?"

"You're to report as soon as convocation is dismissed." The man lowered his voice. "You know, this is not going to make you very popular around here. Little friendly advice? If I were you, I'd request billeting with the other acolytes. The Prophet will be better off having more experienced guys change His sheets, and you'll have a chance to learn the ropes. It would be a gesture of solidarity."

"I don't think so," Todd said brightly. "But thanks!"

"Your funeral," said Barnstable.

The men gathered on the hillside under the capitol. At the bottom of the field was a fenced compound containing rows of RVs, a combination trailer park and concentration camp. Laundry lines hung between the trailers, and women young and old could be seen washing clothes in tubs. A few of them were waving or calling to men they knew, their brothers, husbands, fathers, or sons. The men furtively waved or pretended not to hear them—others whistled or mocked.

Todd asked, "I don't get it. If women are no threat, why are they still being quarantined?"

"They're an endangered species," Captain Barnstable explained. "They have to be protected."

"You mean from Xombies?"

Barnstable looked at him as if he was stupid. "From *us*. We worked too hard to find these; we can't take any chances of losing them. Especially the Evians."

"Evians?"

"Daughters of Eve. Brides of the Prophet."

Ray started to react, but Todd stepped on his foot.

"What's with the trailers?" Todd asked. "Aren't there enough empty buildings to house everybody?"

"Trailers are easier to police and maintain. And transport, of course."

*"Jesus."* Ray erupted. "You're treating women like animals in a zoo. They're human beings."

"Watch your language, punk. I'm letting you off with a warning this time because you're new, but we don't blaspheme around here. Next time, the penalty is scourging. And for your information, treating men and women equally is what brought down the whole human race."

Shaking his head, Ray opened his scroll. It read:

### WHO IS THE RISEN PROPHET?

As an acolyte of the RISEN PROPHET JIM SANDO-VAL, you may well wonder, "Who is this PROPHET of OUR LORD?" The answer is simple: Born of a virgin, the PROPHET witnessed his mother's struggles in the face of creeping socialism and the decline of American values. Early on, He developed an interest in politics, believing the System could be changed from within . . . but He soon learned the System was Rigged. Witnessing the corruption in Washington, the PROPHET realized it was impossible to run for higher office and remain Pure, so He quit the gutter of politics and devoted His attention to the Mogul Foundation, a nonprofit organization dedi-

cated to supporting Real American Values. The PROPH-
ET's wisdom was revealed in the choice of His first
APOSTLE, CHACE DIXON, as the Voice of MoFo. The
CHACE formula of high-energy talk and Apocalyptic
prediction was a hit with millions of listeners worldwide,
and CHACE's interfaith ministry quickly expanded to
include a publishing wing, a high-traffic Web site, and a
cable TV show broadcast in over twenty countries, with
corresponding outreach programs and affiliated churches,
all dedicated to the Bible's teachings that all ailments can
be cured by prayer, and that atheists, witches, socialists,
and homosexuals are abominations in the eyes of the
LORD. There were many who called CHACE a crack-
pot, who derided his prophesies as nothing more than the
ravings of a "shock jock." Soon the world would learn
that CHASE DIXON was a LIVING SAINT, whose
words were all too true . . . but for most it would be too
late. They would join THE ACCURSED, possessed by
Miska and damned to roam the land for eternity. As followers of OUR LORD ADAM, we have been spared
this fate! ADAM has shown us His favor by bestowing
upon us the RISEN PROPHET JIM and the APOSTLE
CHACE, hallowed be Their names. Thanks to these
LIVING SAINTS, we need not fear either DEATH or
UNDEATH, knowing that when that glorious day comes,
our bodies will return to the Earth, and our Souls will
be released to HEAVEN'S EVERLASTING PEACE.
GLORY, GLORY, HALLELUJAH!

"Anything good?" Todd asked.
"Same old, same old," said Ray.
Suddenly a voice yelled, "The Prophet! Prophet on deck!"
"Holy shit, here we go," muttered Barnstable.
The disciples jostled each other into loose ranks. From
around the hill, a large group of bicycles appeared, their rid-
ers humming Beethoven's "Ode to Joy." They all wore gray

robes and tall, cylindrical helmets. Gliding in their midst was a dramatic figure on a gold-ornamented chariot. With his boots and riding breeches and trailing white scarf, he looked like an old-time aviator. The flying motif extended to his electric scooter, which sported a figurehead of an angel with spread wings.

He was the Prophet James Sandoval.

Ray remembered his reaction when Sandoval first told him and Todd the news of his holy title:

*"You?"*

*"Absolutely. Don't act so surprised—it's not as if I haven't performed my share of miracles."*

*"What miracles?"*

*"Saving all these people, for one thing. Before I came along they were like you, hiding out in ships and underground bunkers and sewers—you name it. Enter the Prophet James Sandoval, patron saint of radical Fundamentalist militias, and now the world is their oyster. Yours, too, for that matter. You may be aware of my considerable public holdings, including that submarine plant that was so dear to all of us. I actually have much bigger stakes in more obscure commodities, and the connections to move them. It's an industry that thrives the more society breaks down—my partners and I call it our rainy-day fund. Women have always been a staple of this black market, but their value dropped to nothing after Agent X. Any that didn't become Xombies were killed by fearful men, and the few that survive are still shunned or shot on sight. But not by us—not anymore. Thanks to me, we have no more Xombie problem, and thus no more need to hate or fear women. In fact, women are now our most precious resource, so we are gathering as many as we can find."*

Ray asked, *"How many have you found?"*

*"Not nearly enough. Maenads are incredibly hard to catch now that we're immune to them, so the women we have are mostly elderly survivors or very young girls. The*

*girls at least offer some hope for the future, but in the mean-
time, they're a logistical nightmare. Part of the problem
is I'm dealing with a lot of men who are still reliving the
Xombie Apocalypse. A lot of these guys probably never
liked women to begin with, and now all they want to do
is kill them. I thought with a little forward progress we
could start toning down the macho bullshit, but it hasn't
worked out that way. God's approval has only made them
more fanatical."*

Todd asked, "Excuse me, Mr. Sandoval, but I don't understand how you survived in the first place. I could have
sworn I saw you get killed at Thule. Weren't you run over
by a tank?"

Sandoval sighed. "It's a long story, son. Suffice it to say
I had unfinished business, and I never shirk when it comes
to business."

"What kind of business?"

"What kind of business do you think? I'm here to save
the world."

As the Prophet's entourage approached the clearing, a
larger group swept in from the street on the opposite side,
chanting and spreading incense. The chant sounded like
Coolio's "Gangsta's Paradise." These men were not on
bicycles but on in-line skates, identical with their scythe-
bladed hockey sticks and black hooded sweatshirts—a mob
of street hockey Grim Reapers. Rolling among them was
another vehicle liberated from mall security, an electric cart
with a small freight bed, on which a huge gold crucifix
stood like an uprooted tree. Ray recognized its driver as the
Apostle Chace Dixon. The Living Saint.

After his recent encounter with Dixon, Ray had ransacked his memory for what he knew about the man. There
wasn't much. He knew Dixon had been incredibly wealthy—
which his followers took as the surest sign of God's approval. His success had drawn the mighty to him, particularly
those who were less interested in the meek inheriting the

Earth than in Congress repealing the inheritance tax. Oh, they had tithed richly for *that* gospel, and Dixon was only too happy to give it to them. His pulpit had aimed squarely at a certain breed of militantly prosperous Christian who was ready to ditch fuddy-duddy traditions of charity for a dose of stronger dope—and Chace was just the doctor to write the prescription.

The two groups met in the middle.

"Welcome, Your Greatness, welcome," Dixon said grandly, assuming the role of host as he bowed before Sandoval.

Sandoval impatiently gestured for him to rise, saying, "Thanks, Dix."

Hopping lightly up to the microphone, Dixon said, "Thank *you*, O Holy One." Was there perhaps just the slightest tinge of sarcasm in his voice? Gesturing toward the marble dome of the State House, he indicated the gold statue on its summit and addressed the assembly: "Divine Providence! Since the founder of this city was a clergyman, I feel that at long last it is time to raise a cross atop our capitol. The glorious unification of church and state has finally been achieved—hallelujah!"

Sandoval said, "What about the statue that's already up there?"

"Hah! The Independent Man?"

"The Independent Man, yes."

"What a monstrosity. That's what you want representing your state: a big gold sociopath with a spear."

"As opposed to a big fat sociopath with a cross?"

Turning red, Chace pretended he hadn't heard, saying, "I always hated that thing; it looks like a kitschy lamp. Not to mention, it's a contradiction in terms: an iconic iconoclast. So absurd! Most human beings are dependent by nature—it's not a bad thing. Hey, that's why civilization was invented, folks, in case you didn't know. Let's have everybody be a loner, good idea. See how many bridges and tunnels that gets you. But that's exactly the kind of liberal thinking that brought down the whole country, the whole world."

Facing the crowd, Chace shouted, "Hey, gang! How we all doin'?" This was one of his most popular catchphrases, and the audience responded with customary enthusiasm. When the noise abated, he said, "Everybody doing good? Fantastic. Nice *day*. Speaking of which, has anybody noticed anything . . . unusual?"

He was answered by cheers and applause.

"That's right. We are standing in the open, under the clear blue sky. Can you believe this? Barely a month ago, we were desperate scavengers, barricaded inside that mall. Then we were visited by an Angel of our Lord Adam, who told us to go north and seek the Prophet Jim. Now we return from our journey in triumph, the Prophet at our side, to stand outdoors in the light of day! With no high walls protecting us, no armored convoys, no weapons. And listen! What do you hear? Nothing. Nothing but sweet, sweet silence." He paused. "Ladies and gentlemen. I am here to tell you that this land . . . *is our land*!"

Someone handed him a guitar and he broke into a slightly pitchy rendition of the Woody Guthrie song. But the crowd went wild. Everyone sang along, even Todd and Ray, and when it was over, the cheering and victory chants went on for ten minutes.

Finally, Chace called for quiet. Grave-faced, he said, "But there is a threat."

A chill swept the audience. He nodded slowly, panning his cold gaze across the crowd.

When the suspense had built enough, he continued, "Yes, it has just come to my attention that there is a threat to our mission of salvation and purification. Eighteen days ago we received transmissions from a substantial party of survivors in Washington, DC." The crowd gasped. "Yes.

Apparently they have established a Godless, socialistic society called Xanadu. And they are recruiting more heathens by the minute!"

This caused a tremendous stir.

Breaking through the hubbub, he bellowed, "Should we tolerate this new Gomorrah in the heart of our nation's capital?"

Amid the confusion, a number of voices cried, "No!"

"No? Not even if it means committing ourselves fully to an attack against entrenched human beings—not just demons?"

A smaller number, harder to hear over the growing opposition: "No!"

"Then that is what I propose we do!"

The majority turned against him, roaring their displeasure. Dixon shouted them down: "*Not* just because I believe we have superior firepower and the Lord on our side, but because we have reason to believe that this other group has already invaded our lines and is engaged in a campaign of spying and subversion!"

Now any stray sounds of protest were buried in an avalanche of gung ho fury. Dixon bellowed, "I'm speaking of the disappearances! I am speaking of the mysterious thefts and sabotage! This may be the Enemy we have been waiting for—the secular army of Satan! Yes, we must engage them, not to destroy them but to save their souls! And once we have conquered them, we will add their arms to our Lord's arsenal. At long last we will be able to put an end to the corruption of our land by socialists and subversives and the so-called liberal elite! At long last we will avenge the victims of Waco and Ruby Ridge and Oklahoma City and 9/11—all precursors to the ultimate atrocity of Agent X! It's time to end the terror, once and for all! It's time to send a message to Mecca and Moscow and Washington, DC! Hallelujah! Thank you, Adam! Amen!"

Standing on the sidelines, James Sandoval raised his hands, and the crowd immediately fell silent, urgently shushing each other. Voices whispered, "Let the Prophet speak!"

In a soft voice, he said, "Greetings, my friends. So nice to see you all here. I would like to welcome the new recruits among you, but first I must make a special announcement. This is important." He paused, as if searching for the right words. "I blame myself for this, for allowing things to go so far. It shouldn't have happened; I'm sorry. Chace, I apologize to you most of all, since I obviously should have been more clear with you from the beginning. I wasn't, and now I have no choice but to do this in front of all these good folks. Here it is:

"There will be no crusade against our fellow man. Not happening. Not now, not next week or next year, not ever. That's not what we're here for. Chace, these people don't need an Ayatollah, they need a Gandhi, and you're not it. You're not even close. I only wish I could have prevented you from burning all those poor women. Believe me, I'm sorry as hell about that—the thought of it makes me physically sick. But I failed them, I failed you, and most of all I failed God . . . and for my sins I died. But the Lord gave me a second chance. He raised me from the dead, and He said, 'Hold on a minute, Jim. I have a job for you.' That doesn't make me Jesus, and it doesn't make you the Pope, okay? You're just a guy who used to work for me, but now you're fired. You understand? You're fired."

Before Sandoval even finished speaking, Chace yelled, "I don't have to listen to this! You wouldn't even be alive if not for me! You'd still be a half-frozen Xombie up in fucking Canada! You're no prophet! You don't speak for Adam; I don't think you even believe in Him! I renounce you!" To the crowd, he shouted, "Attention everyone! This man has just revealed himself as a false prophet, a phony! He must be one of *them*! Yes, he is a spy, sent to infiltrate and corrupt us! Do not believe him! Do not obey him!"

The assembly dissolved into a riot of accusations and counteraccusations. The extremists of both sides wanted to fight it out then and there, but since most of the troops weren't sure which side they were on, the brawl was postponed. Dixon and Sandoval stormed from the field, followed by their core supporters. Dixon had clearly gained a few.

Todd, Ray, and the other disciples were dismissed.

# CHAPTER **THIRTEEN**

## COUP

" **J**esus, that was scary," Ray said. "I think I pissed my pants."

"Did you?" Todd asked.

"*No.* But I would kill for a shower."

Hours had passed since the big schism, and still there were no arrests, no statements from either the Prophet or the Apostle, no fallout of any kind. The whole complex seemed to be holding its breath.

After finishing their cleaning duties at the hotel, Todd and Ray crossed the glass Skybridge to the mall. Below the bridge, they could see long rows of abandoned Humvees and other military vehicles leading up and down the highway ramps. Roads were impassable now, but across the field was the Amtrak station, with very irregular service to Boston and points north. Nothing was better for morale than the sound of a train whistle—it was an advertisement for civilization. Like Todd and Ray, many of the men had been lured in by that sound.

The mall was even busier than the hotel, full of holy warriors eating, sleeping, and doing religious devotions. It smelled like a school cafeteria. Men were gathered at the mall's central atrium, an oval space rising two floors to the ceiling skylights. A bank of windows overlooked Waterplace Park, formerly a summertime attraction with gondolas and mimes, now a debris-choked concrete pond. To the far left was the fenced field below the State House—the women's camp. Men crowded the windows as if watching a show.

Ascending to the Food Court on the top floor, Todd and Ray sat down to a dinner of "stew"—what the cooks called stew. It was a lot of random canned things poured into a pot and heated together—in this case tomatoes, green beans, beets, tuna fish, and hominy. It actually wasn't that terrible, but Ray had no appetite.

As they finished and prepared to leave, they were joined by Captain Barnstable, who took them aside, and said, "I have a message for you guys." He looked shaken and preoccupied. As if coming to a difficult decision, he asked, "Did you say you talked to Elvis?"

The boys were wary. Todd said, "We haven't seen him lately, if that's what you're asking."

Barnstable leaned close and palmed Ray a folded square of toilet paper, "This is from the Prophet to all of us. He asked me to show it to you. I suppose that must mean he thinks you can be trusted."

"How do we know you can?"

"Just read it, then eat it." Barnstable walked away.

The note read:

This is Jim Sandoval, your Prophet. An assassination attempt has been made on my life, and I have reluctantly accepted an offer of sanctuary by the Evians. They do this in full knowledge that it is a breach of their inviolate status, but know it is imperative that we prevent Chace Dixon and his followers from committing a heinous crime in the name of our Lord Adam. As most of you already know, Dixon intends to wage war on the innocent human beings at our nation's capital. What you may not know is that he has a nuclear missile at his disposal and is gathering a trainload of other heavy weapons. That train is being outfitted as a war machine, an engine of destruction, and within days or weeks, it will begin its terrible journey south. We must not allow this. I hereby authorize any and all resistance against Chace Dixon and his supporters.

"What the hell, man," Todd said despondently. "Figures we'd find ourselves in the middle of a fuckin' jihad." He noticed the intensity of Ray's expression, and said, "Don't sweat it so hard, man. This shit has nothing to do with us."

"Todd, I've gotta try and break Sandoval out of there."

"Huh?"

"You know how I called him 'uncle' before? Well, the truth is, he's been more like a father to me. He took me and my sister in when we had no place else to go, and he's the only family I have left now."

"Are we talking about the same guy here? This is Chairman Sandoval."

"Yes."

"How come you never told me about this?"

"I never told anyone. He swore me to secrecy so I'd be allowed on board the boat with the rest of you. Truth is, I was too messed up after the death of my sister to talk much about anything. But if it weren't for Uncle Jim, I would've never known about the sub. He saved my life. I have to at least try to return the favor. But I'll understand if you don't want to take the risk."

Todd was offended. "Screw you, man. Of course I'm going to help you, that's not the issue. Do you even have any idea what you're going to do?"

"No. But I'm thinking we need to create some kind of diversion, like what happened with the Reapers. Then, in all the confusion, I sneak into the women's camp and smuggle Jim out."

"Assuming he even wants to go. We don't know what

he's got going on in there. We could get ourselves into deep shit for nothing."

Ray nodded. "No, you're right. I really need to talk to him first."

"Oh, is that all? And just how, exactly, do you plan on getting in there?"

"Maybe I'll dress up as a woman."

"Yeah." Todd looked him over skeptically. "Good luck with that."

# CHAPTER **FOURTEEN**

## RAY AND BRENDA

**W**hen Agent X hit, Ray Despineau and his big sister, Brenda, were on the road.

It was midnight, New Year's Eve, and Brenda had a splitting headache. They had been trapped in traffic for more than nine hours, all routes south inexplicably blocked by police and armed troops. Through sheer gall, their driver had managed to bully his way to an off-ramp, but the situation was no better on the streets below. They should have been at the plant by nightfall; Uncle Jim would not be pleased.

"Happy fucking New Year," muttered their burly limo driver, Apollo, knowing the axe would fall heaviest on him. He was desperate for a toilet break but was punishing himself with the discomfort. His passengers had overcome their own aversion to peeing in plastic cups from the minibar and dumping it out the windows.

"It's okay, Apollo," Brenda said. "It's not your fault. There was no way of knowing the roads would be blocked off like this."

"I knew we shoulda had a police escort, a big official motorcade. But the bastards wouldn't give it to us, and now I see why: They were all pulling fucking traffic duty. Goddamn flagmen. This is bullshit."

Suddenly, everything went crazy: a lunatic orchestra of car horns, sirens, alarms, people screaming and yelling—

and gunfire. The amount of racket was astounding even for midnight on New Year's Eve. But very quickly, Ray, Brenda, and Apollo knew something else was going on.

Car crashes! Ray could hear a ridiculous smashing and screeching of tires up on I-95, just a never-ending pileup, hundreds of cars in a row—*crash, boom, bash!* Their own car was underneath the highway, near the I-195 interchange, so this was all happening right over their heads. Glass rained down, and Ray could see fires up there and hear blood-curdling screams . . . and then *people* started falling! Just jumping over the highway barrier and slamming into the street below like sacks of potatoes.

Drivers started pouring out of their cars, wondering what the hell was going on. Cops screamed at them to get back inside their vehicles. Others just went crazy, hitting the gas and crashing into the traffic around them, like mad bumper cars. As Ray watched, an ambulance swerved into the opposing lane, busted through the line of cars, flew off the road, and hit a freeway pylon—*kabam!*

All this was bad enough, but what freaked him out the most was when everybody started *fighting* all of a sudden. Wherever he looked, there were these weird struggles going on: people trying to either kill or kiss one another—it was hard to tell which. But in either case, they were going at it like crazed wildcats, men and women both.

Some of them—a lot of them—looked oddly blue. Blue women ran in from all over, jumping out of cars, tearing their clothes off, and running naked down the road. They all had the same freaky black eyes, shark eyes, and they just swept in from out of nowhere like sharks joining a great big feeding frenzy. Only instead of eating you, they . . . *kissed* you. Kissed you and killed you and sucked the living breath right out of your body. Then you came back as one of *them*.

Ray saw it happening more and more, everywhere he looked. Clothes were shredded; blood was shed, blood both red and black. But one after another, the normal folk were

taken down, even the toughest-looking dudes turning into
two-legged blue sharks, adding their fevered lust to the
frenzy. Crazy was winning, the night overthrown by eye-
popping, blue-in-the-face, hysterical lunacy.

The horrible spectacle was not lost on Apollo. He said,
"Belt yourselves in and hold tight."

"What are you doing?" Brenda asked.

"Getting us the fuck out of here." He shifted into reverse
and stomped on the gas.

The limo was a customized 4x4 Escalade, armor-plated
and with bulletproof windows and tires that wouldn't go flat
even with big holes in them. Apollo drove it like a bat out
of Hell even in normal circumstances—he was a retired
Secret Service agent, picking up extra change providing
personal security for Sandoval's "family"—so all at once,
they were plowing clear of the mess, making a U-turn, and
flying around car wrecks and fight scenes like a star quarterback running for a touchdown. The northbound lane
was much less congested, but now they were going in the
wrong direction, heading back into the city. A number of
other cars were right behind them, piggybacking on the
SUV's momentum.

"Stop!" Brenda shouted. "Where are we going?"

"Sorry, Miss Despineau, but I'm taking you two back
home, if we can even make it. It's the safest place right now.
I'm sure Mr. Sandoval would agree."

Just ahead, Ray could see the lights and big, reassuring
office towers of downtown Providence. All that still looked
so normal he started to let himself collapse, flipping out
from the horrible things he had just witnessed . . . until they
started getting closer. Then he could see the smoke and hear
the noise, even with the windows rolled up.

*Oh God . . . oh no, please . . .*

Downtown Providence was a living Hell. All the unfortunate people who had come downtown to join the First
Night celebration were discovering it was their Last Night,

or in most cases their Last Minute. They were everywhere, running or being chased, and wherever Ray looked, the blue freaks were gaining.

Right away it was obvious that the limo was not getting anywhere near their high-rise condo complex because the main intersection was jammed with all kinds of police and emergency vehicles. But there weren't too many cops around—just lots of Ex-cops. People kept jumping on the car and beating on the windows, and Apollo kept having to swerve around or speed up and hit the brakes to throw them off. It was making Ray nauseous. Apollo also ran over a few folks, which really pushed Ray over the edge because he couldn't even run over a squirrel without feeling bad about it.

So Ray was screaming, *"Stop! Stop!"* and Brenda was babbling, "It's okay, it's okay," and everybody all around them was going nuts, but Apollo . . . Apollo was a damn rock. He knew exactly where he was going and soon found a little alleyway straight into the city.

The streets were surprisingly empty inside, which was maybe not so surprising since it was a holiday and all the offices were closed, but now Apollo could really hit it, and before Ray knew what was happening, they were shooting down a ramp into Sandoval's underground parking garage. The big steel gate came down like a medieval portcullis.

"Awesome," Ray moaned.

At least they were safe for the moment. Riverdale Residences was a high-security building for a very exclusive clientele. Nobody could get in or out without an electronic passkey, and each unit had its own private floor and key code. No solicitors.

Brenda threw her BlackBerry down, and cried, "It's dead! Everything's dead! I can't stay here! Darryl is probably freaking out—I have to go get him!" Darryl was Brenda's miniature schnauzer. She had dropped him at the kennel earlier that morning.

"Don't you fuckin' *dare* go anywhere," Ray said.

"I have to! I have to get Darryl!"

"Everybody calm down," Apollo commanded. "Let's don't get ahead of ourselves."

Modulating his voice, Ray said, "Brenda, Darryl would want you to be safe, wouldn't he? It doesn't do him any good to have you rush out there and get yourself killed."

"It's staying here in this zoo that's going to get us all killed! We need to get out of here!"

Apollo said, "No, this is the safest place to be until help arrives. This building is like a bank vault, and we have everything we need for now. Whatever's happening out there will probably take care of itself by morning. We just have to sit tight."

They sat . . . and listened.

All night long, they heard sounds of war: glass breaking, shooting, screams, car alarms, explosions. They smelled gun smoke, burnt rubber, burning gasoline, and burning flesh. TV and radio provided only loose scraps of bad news, worse news, and finally no news. All they had to do was look out the window to see the world coming apart at the seams: towers of smoke and raging fires all over the city.

"Oh my God," Brenda said, shutting the curtains against the horror. "Oh my God, there's no chance. There's just no chance. What are we going to *do*?"

"Whatever we have to," said Apollo. "For now, all we can do is wait."

"Wait for what? For those things to crawl in here and get us in our sleep?"

"No. They can't get in here. This building is hermetically sealed. It's allergy-proof, hurricane-proof, and crime-proof. It's designed for paranoid corporate hotshots like your uncle. Trust me, the security is total. I helped set it up."

By dawn, things went quiet. Except for an occasional spasm of violence, the odd scream or shooting, there was very little that broke the peace for the next few days. But there was no escape either—blue people were everywhere.

"We have to get out of here," Brenda wearily persisted.

Ray wasn't ready to quit. After the initial shock had passed, he found a deep reserve of stone-cold determination. He hadn't survived this long just to give in to the blues.

Apollo said, "There's food for another week, maybe two if we ration it out. That's enough time for this whole thing to blow over. There must be people in charge who are working on this problem. We just have to give them time to do it."

"Don't count on it," Brenda said.

They tried contacting other people in the building, buzzing all the units from the lobby, but either there was no one home or no one wanted company. It was a very select membership, Moguls Only: politicians, religious leaders, business magnates, all of them living incognito, privacy being one of the building's premium selling points. Odd that they would have all left town at once. But it was just as well: Ray had nothing to offer them but tea and sympathy—and the tea was running low.

The cavalry finally arrived.

It started with a promising sound: the tinkling of an ice-cream truck. How wonderful it was to hear such familiar, friendly music—it sounded like summer. Looking down from the balcony, they watched as the truck passed directly below, towing a trailer full of caged women.

"What the hell is that?" Apollo asked.

From what Ray could see, the women were clearly not Xombies. If it was true that the plague mainly struck women, as the Emergency Broadcast had implied, then why were these not infected? Perhaps they were being kept in the cage for their own safety . . . although it certainly didn't look like that. It looked more like some kind of twisted freak show with Xombies as the prime audience.

As the truck reached the far end of the street, it released the trailer and sped away. Brenda and Apollo argued about what to do, but there was really nothing to be done because the Xombies were there, swarming over the cage like maggots. Screaming, Brenda covered her ears and fled from the window, and Apollo dragged Ray away as well, so they all missed the brilliant explosion that followed.

There was nothing left to console them. It was all too obvious what was going on and what that meant for the future of the human race. No women, no babies, in which case this really was the end of everything.

When the fires died down, the loudspeakers started up:

"THIS IS A MESSAGE TO ALL LOYAL AMERICANS: YOU ARE CALLED UPON TO JOIN IN THE FIGHT AGAINST EVIL. JOIN OUR VICTORIOUS CAMPAIGN, AND HELP BANISH THE SCOURGE OF AGENT X. HAVE NO FEAR—THE HELLIONS ARE ON THE RUN. COME FORTH AND STAND WITH US. WE ARE YOUR FRIENDS, AND WE BRING GOOD NEWS. THE WORST IS OVER. SHARE OUR FOOD, MEDICINE, FELLOW-SHIP, AND SAFE REFUGE. COME FORTH, COME FORTH, ALL YE FAITHFUL. THE HOLY AVENGERS OF ADAM WANT YOU."

"What the hell's the Avengers of Adam?" asked Brenda.

"Sounds like a comic book," said Ray.

The crusaders were systematically searching the city and arresting any survivors. What was remarkable was the sudden absence of Xombies; the city was temporarily free of ghouls. And there were surprisingly many human holdouts, quick-thinking folks who had hidden in attics, basements, and bomb shelters—mostly men, but also a few women. With brusque efficiency, the soldiers bagged their captives and drove them away, sealing off each building as it was cleared. There was not much resistance. Brenda had no interest in joining those refugees, and Ray and Apollo were in full agreement with her.

Day after day, hour after hour, they kept waiting for help to arrive, some legitimate entity of the U.S. government, like the National Guard, or perhaps the Red Cross. The Boy

Scouts of America—*anything*. Panic set in as it became clear that nothing was going to happen in time to save them: The Holy Avengers of Adam were starting on their block. Very soon, the lobby's heavy security doors would be broken down, the building would be invaded, and they would be dragged outside to join the prisoners on those trucks . . . bound for whatever fate the HAA had in store.

"We have to get you out of here," Apollo said at last.

"Thank God," Brenda said. "I'm about ready to join the Xombies at this point."

"That's the trouble—there's no place to go. Even if we got past those whack jobs, we'd just be running right smack into an even bigger problem. I'm sure the countryside is still crawling."

"Out of the frying pan and into the fire," commented Ray, dishing out scrambled eggs.

"Maybe not," Apollo said. "Not if we can get to Sandoval's defense plant like we were originally supposed to."

"A little late for that, don't you think? It's way down in South County, and the roads will be even more impassable than they were before. Not to mention, the place has probably been overrun."

"I doubt it. The whole plant can be closed off like a fortress in the event of emergency. These guys have specific security requirements just in case of attacks by terrorist hit squads, chemical attacks, even nuclear war. I'm beginning to think it was no accident that Sandoval wanted you there when he did."

"What are you saying? That he had advance warning of the plague? If he knew about it, why wouldn't he tell us? I mean, I sure as hell wouldn't have been late!"

"Maybe he didn't know for sure. Maybe he called in all the families just in case."

Ray and Brenda processed this, being familiar with the eccentricities of their "Uncle Jim." He was not their real uncle but a very wealthy older man who had taken them in when Brenda was a teenager stuck raising her baby brother because their mother had flown the coop. He gave them a place to live and a generous allowance, but beyond that, they rarely saw him, which was perhaps the biggest gift of all. He expected nothing, he asked for nothing . . . until the day he asked them to show up at the plant. He even sent a car.

*Shit.* There was a long pause as minds hardened against hope tried to process this remote possibility. Then Brenda said, "All right. Sure. Yes. Let's go!"


The city was quiet at night—quiet and dark and bitter cold. In that deep silence, any noise would have been loud, and this was a loud noise to begin with: the rumble of an electronic garage door. Pulled by a chain drive, heavy steel slats were raised and wrapped around a rotating drum, making an almighty racket. Even before the door was all the way up, a huge black SUV blazed through and up the exit ramp.

Barreling in zigzags down the empty streets, the car met no obstacles, no opposition from living or dead. It was just too cold. Hurtling down an alley, the vehicle slowed as it approached a glowing tarpaulin at the end—a big tent blocking the way. Shadows could be seen moving inside, sentries roused by the sound of approaching vehicles.

"Guards!" Brenda yelled. "Go back, go back!"

"I'm trying!" Apollo said. "We're blocked from behind."

Ray and Brenda craned their necks, horrified to see a large vehicle coming up fast. It was not an ordinary truck but an armored riot vehicle stenciled with daggerlike crucifixes dripping blood. A six-wheeled Deathmobile.

"Then go forward!" Brenda cried.

"You got it." Apollo hit the gas and plowed through the canvas wall. There was a burst of orange embers as the Escalade struck a flaming trash barrel, then a violent crash that caused the air bags to deploy. A loud alarm started going off.

"Shi-i-it," Ray said, pushing away the air bag and feeling his nose for blood.

They had struck a concrete barricade. The force of the crash had knocked one of the blocks over and dragged it under the car for a good ten feet.

Apollo shouted, "Get out! Get out now!"

As they abandoned the car, a blaze of tracer fire erupted from the approaching vehicle, cutting through the Escalade's armor plating as if it were sliced provolone. Windows blew out, tires exploded, and Apollo grunted as he was shot to pieces. Ray braced himself to die, but miraculously no bullet struck him. His sister, however, was hit.

"Brenda! Oh shit!" He dove to help her, propping her upright against the concrete slab as though it were a chaise. Her face was pale and her eyes very bright, but she didn't seem to be in pain. Her injury was hidden somewhere under her clothes, just a spreading dark stain running down her side. "Can you walk? We gotta go!"

Apologetically, she said, "I don't think I can, Ray. You have to go without me."

"No way! You're coming, if I have to carry you!" He tried to pick her up, but she cried out in sudden agony, shaking her head no. He hurriedly let her down, his sleeves soaked with her steaming-hot blood. He didn't know what to do. His bare hands had touched the enormous rip in her flesh, feeling the slimy tissue hanging out, and he shuddered in terror and grief. Brenda was dying. His big sister was dying. The sister who was his only relative in the world, who had been as much a mother as a sister to him, and whom he had never imagined living without . . . because without her, he was totally and utterly alone.

The Deathmobile pulled up to the barricade, and several men got out. They were matter-of-fact about the destruction they had wrought, no strangers to killing. One of them had a flamethrower. "All right, kid," he said. "Step away from the body so we can purify the area."

"Fuck off," Ray said.

"Yeah, yeah. Brother Matt, come get this kid, will you?"

"You got it, chief." Brother Matt stepped over the barricade and raised his boot to kick Ray off Brenda, but before he could deliver the blow, his body jerked rigid and he made a strangled noise from the back of his throat. His eyes bulged and his tongue popped out, and all of a sudden his torso twisted apart at the waist.

Apollo rose into the light. He was a shot-up wreck, an animated blue monstrosity, but a Xombie was still a Xombie, and his big hands gleamed red, clutching pieces of Brother Matt's severed spine.

The other men opened fire, but even before they pulled the triggers, more Xombies materialized out of thin air, literally falling upon them from windows overlooking the street. In an instant, every man was down. Their radios crackled with anxious queries.

Brenda touched Ray's hand. Her fingers were ice-cold. "Go, honey," she said. It took her great effort to say it, and she didn't have much left. "Please."

Not knowing what he was doing, Ray crawled away from her. He would later realize he never kissed her good-bye, never told her he loved her, and this would torment him during the long voyage on the submarine. There was a wine store a few feet away, and he went inside. The Xombies didn't seem to notice. Ray walked through the store and out the back door into an alley. No one saw him; no one followed. A few blocks away, he found a motor scooter lying on its side. It was a nice Vespa, just abandoned, with the keys still in it.

It started right up.

# CHAPTER **FIFTEEN**

## GULAG

Todd pushed the hooded prisoner in front of him, trying to look brusque as he approached the sentries. The two Brethren sat in a huge riot vehicle, the Deathmobile, one at the wheel and the other manning a rooftop machine gun. The gunner trained his weapon on the approaching pair.

"State your business," he called.

"This woman just surrendered to me outside. She says the Hellions won't touch her."

The driver sat up. "No shit? You know, there's a bounty on Munies. If she's for real, you get a promotion. Where's your incident report?"

"Right here."

The man barely glanced at the paper. "Why haven't I seen you before?"

"I'm new. I've been assigned to the hotel."

"You're not one of those guys who rode in on bikes?"

"That's right."

"*Cool.* And you weren't even anointed? No protection at all?"

"No. Can we get through this?"

"Be done in a sec. Whose side are you on, the Prophet or the Apostle?"

"The Prophet."

"Bad idea, if you ask me. Odds are with the Living

Saint, two to one. This is one horse race you want to be sure to bet on the favorite."

"Amen to that, brother."

The man at the gun seemed to be studying the prisoner closely.

Todd suddenly felt very stupid to think this plan could work. Sneaking a dress, a wig, and some cosmetics from the mall stores, Todd had watched as Ray tried to create a look that was feminine without being overly fussy—apocalypse chic. "That'll work, that'll work," Todd kept muttering doubtfully. It was all a bad joke. At best, Ray looked like a soot-smudged female impersonator.

But it seemed to be good enough. The guard gave the okay, and Ray was allowed through the gate of the compound and released from his bonds. Todd was dismissed.

*Peace, bro,* he thought.

Unhooded, Ray found himself standing alongside a row of portable toilets. Straight ahead were ranks of brand-new recreational vehicles, dozens of them, with an open space in the center. In that clearing, he could see a group of women sitting at several picnic tables, playing cards.

Before Agent X, Ray had come here every Fourth of July. It was nice: Bands played and people brought beach chairs to watch fireworks over the State House. With the trailers and fences and huddled figures, it now looked more like a gulag.

The group at the table waved him over. There were about ten of them, anonymous figures with scarves wrapped around their heads. They looked like old homeless ladies, bundled in whatever the men supplied them with from Nordstrom's, Macy's, or Bed, Bath & Beyond. Heart hammering, Ray started over to them, wondering how he was going to pull this off.

From off to the side, a man's voice called, "Ray . . . ? Oh my God, is that you?"

"Uncle Jim!" Ray said.

He rushed to embrace the man and was held off by a warning look. In a low voice, Sandoval said, "No touchee. It's the rules." Looking askance at Ray, he asked, "What the hell are you wearing?"

Now it was Ray's turn to lower his voice. "I know, I'm a girl, just go along with it. Call me Raven."

"Raven. Right. Right, of course. What are you doing in here?"

"I came to see you. I had Todd pretend to arrest me."

"You jackass! Don't you realize there's about to be a holy war? Dixon's people are crazy!"

"Why do you think I came? I got your note—are you okay?"

"I'm all right, considering some nutball tried to stick a knife in me. I'm fine. You really shouldn't have come in here."

"I had to do *something*."

"I know." Sandoval spoke urgently in Ray's ear: "Listen, if things go the way I'm hoping, we won't have to be in here much longer anyway."

"Why? What's going on?"

"You'll see. Just play it cool."

The women were fascinated and suspicious. "Who's this, Jim?" one of them called. "You never told us you had a girlfriend on the outside. Why don't you introduce us? And maybe fetch her a drink. She looks like she needs it."

"She's not my girlfriend, Chandra," Sandoval said. "She's my . . . niece. Raven."

The woman looked unconvinced. "Raven. Really. Well, it's quite the jolly little family reunion, isn't it? What a fortunate coincidence that you both survived the plague!"

"Not such a coincidence. Raven and I both escaped on the submarine."

"Oh, is that submarine of yours back in town?"

"Just long enough to drop her off, apparently."

Ray said, "That's right. They didn't want any women on board, so they put me ashore."

"Well, that's just terrible. You're certainly welcome with us."

"Thank you."

"Now there's just one thing. As you can see, dear, most of us here are old enough to be your mother . . . or even your grandmother. That suggests that you have an unusual resistance to Agent X for someone your age. You can bear children—possibly *immune* children. This places you in a very select minority. Has Jim explained to you what that means?"

"Uh, well—"

Sandoval jumped in, steering Ray away toward a table of sandwiches and drinks. "All right, all right! Get your minds out of the gutter!"

The women cackled in their wake.

"Fucking biddies." Sandoval poured Ray a glass of lemonade. "Unbelievable."

The sound of women's laughter almost made Ray weep. Taking a bite of a ham sandwich, he asked, "What did you mean when you said we might not be in here much longer?"

"My people are staging a coup against Chace. If all goes as planned, by this time tomorrow, we'll all be set free."

Ray swallowed. "Are you sure? It looked to me like Chace has the popular vote."

"They've just known him longer; he's a celebrity. People always like a charismatic yokel, but they'll jump ship as soon as he stumbles. Which he already has. He thinks they're all fired up for this war on Washington, but I guarantee you that most of them will bail out at the first opportunity."

"What if he kills you first?"

"He doesn't dare kill me."

"Why not?"

"Because these women won't permit it. They remember

what these nuts did to them during the Agent X panic. Female survivors were almost exterminated. They're not about to let that happen again."

"But if Chace has all the weapons you mentioned, what's to stop him from just marching in here and doing whatever the hell he wants? These women are helpless prisoners."

"Are they?"

"What do you mean?"

"Well, look around you. Who's out there in the city doing all the grunt work, and who's in here on the lawn, playing cards and drinking Margaritas?"

"I . . . don't get it. Are you saying these women are somehow in charge?"

Sandoval grinned.

"But how?" Ray asked.

"Because the Evians hold the Sacrament. They are the Munies—the truly immune, not just resistant to Agent X infection, but actually *counterinfectious*, able to neutralize Xombies. Make them human. In fact, Xombies shun them—I hear you've experienced this yourself at one of Chace's little demonstrations. Well, it's a tincture of immune blood that makes it possible. That's how I was restored to my humanity . . . and how we will eventually restore the whole human race."

"Oh my God."

"At present, however, that goal of Xombie salvation is limited by the small number of available donors. The immunizing effect of the blood serum is temporary, which means there has to be a reliable supply. The living come first, and obviously the supply of vaccine can only increase if the number of Immunes increases. That means having immune babies—as many as possible, preferably females."

"Hence your harem."

"Now don't jump to conclusions. I haven't touched those girls. In fact, I can't touch them—nobody can. Not without their full consent."

"Why not?"

"You'll see. As a presumed Immune, you'll be staying with them."

"I still don't understand what's to stop Dixon from marching in here and taking charge of the whole operation. Making the Immunes his slaves."

"It's all under control, trust me. Do you think I wouldn't have it covered?"

"You? How could I doubt?"

"Damn straight."

They talked for hours about old times, until the sun fell below the mall. A blustery wind kicked up, and the women stowed their cards and went inside their trailers. Finally, Sandoval said, "Phew, I hate to let you go, but I can tell you're beat. Come on, I'll take you to your trailer."

"Can't I stay with you?"

"I wish. The others would never stand for it. No, you have to bunk with the Evians. Don't worry—you'll like them. They're some of the nicer people in camp."

He took Ray to a fence within the fence—a smaller enclosure containing a single trailer. The gate was locked shut, but Sandoval waved at the camera, and they were buzzed in. He sighed. "Well, this is as far as I go."

"Really? You can't even just introduce me?"

Sandoval shook his head no, choked up with emotion. "But I'm really glad to see you, Ray. I should kick your butt for risking your fool neck like this, but I'm grateful you came. "

"Me too."

They hugged, clinching tightly. A nearby woman's voice shrieked, "Get a room!" and they hurriedly broke apart.

As the fence shut between them, Sandoval called, "Don't you worry, everything's going to be all right!"

Ray went up the short walk and knocked on the trailer. When he looked back, Jim Sandoval was gone.

The door opened, releasing a torrent of music—Fiona

Apple's "Criminal." A sour-faced young woman stood in the doorway, looking Ray up and down. She was wearing what looked like an orange life vest over a peasant skirt, army boots, and an oversized knit hat with dangling earflaps. "Who're you?" she asked.

"Hi. Sorry to bother you. My name is Ray Despineau— uh, Raven."

The woman ignored his outstretched hand. "What do you want?"

"I guess I'm staying here tonight."

"Why?"

"Because I'm immune. So they say."

"Oh. Great. Well, c'mon in. I'm Fran." The woman stood aside to let him pass.

"Hi, Fran. Nice to meet you."

"Seriously?"

Ray stepped into a very cluttered room. Heaps of clothing, shoes, games, books, magazines, cookware, food garbage, and all manner of random electronic paraphernalia were scattered on the floor or piled on the furniture. The music was very loud. For a second, he didn't realize there were people hidden amid the mess: two teenage girls, both wearing life vests similar to Fran's. One girl was on the couch, and the other sprawled on the carpet. All three were pale to the point of translucence, with dark circles under their eyes. *Cancer ward,* Ray thought.

He introduced himself again.

"I'm Ashleigh," said the one on the couch, who was decorating her huge artificial nails.

The one on the floor was reading an art magazine called *Hi Fructose*. She said, "Deena."

"Hi, Ashleigh and Deena. Looks like I'm gonna be staying with you guys."

"We heard," said Ashleigh. "You can have Wanda's room. It's the one in the middle."

"Thanks," Ray said, "but doesn't Wanda need it?"

"Not anymore. Shit happens." Ashleigh went back to her nails.

Deena said, "Hey, is it true that Michael Jackson is back from the dead?"

"That's such bullshit, man," scoffed Ashleigh.

Deena said, "You're the one who thinks Elvis is still alive!"

"Elvis is *totally* still alive—I *saw* him, bitch."

"Why should Elvis come back and not Michael Jackson?"

"Dude, if you have to ask that, there's nothing I can do for you."

"Why? Michael Jackson probably sold more records in his lifetime than—"

"Stop—just stop it. Elvis is a *classic*, do you get it? He's the King, the original."

"You always do this." Deena turned to Ray. "She always does this. Do *you* think Michael Jackson's back?"

"Anything's possible," Ray said.

He went and found the empty bedroom. The dead girl's things were still there, the bed unmade. A picture of Jesus was taped to the wall. As he stood looking at it, something moved under the wadded-up bedding, something not human. Part of its shin was exposed: pink gooseflesh with black hair. With a howl, it suddenly jumped off the bed and raced through his legs and into the hall. Ray half shrieked before realizing it was a dog, a very ugly, piebald mutt.

Ray jumped as someone touched him on the shoulder. It was Fran. "Sorry," she said, "but I almost forgot to give you this. I'll help you put it on." It was one of the orange life vests.

"What is that?" he asked.

"About ten pounds of Thermite with a C-4 chaser."

*"What?"*

"Don't freak out, it's actually very stable . . . unless you trigger the detonator by pulling this tab. Then you have five seconds to say your prayers. C'mon, don't you want to be in control of your own destiny?" She helped him put the vest on and secure its fasteners. Aside from the bomb itself, Ray was nervous that Fran might take notice of his lack of cleavage, which he had concealed with padding, but she politely took no notice.

Finishing up, Fran said, "Now, the only time you really want to take this off is when you're taking a shower or during our designated sleep periods. Everybody sleeps at different times so we don't have to sleep in these things—it's too uncomfortable. Now that you're here, we'll have to readjust to a four-way schedule, but it's cool. Well, that's about it. If you need anything, I'm right in the next room."

Ray closed the door and wept.


Later, over dinner, they talked some more. Canned food had been dropped off at the gate, and Fran heated it on the propane stove. Ashleigh said grace.

"So what do you girls make of all this?" Ray asked as they ate.

"You sound like my mom," said Ashleigh.

Deena affected a robotic grin, and squawked, *"'What do you girls make of all this?'"*

"Just wondering," Ray said.

"Are you a man?" asked Deena.

He almost choked. "Why do you say that?"

"I don't know. Just something about you."

"Does it help you to hurt my feelings, Deena?" he asked.

"Kind of, yeah."

"It really does," said Ashleigh.

"Now, girls . . ." Fran said.

Ray said, "If I was a man, I wouldn't be in here, would I? The only reason you're all here is because you can still bear children, right? Without that, there's no other hope for mankind."

"Like Eve," Ashleigh said.

"I thought Eve was a dirty word around here."

Fran said, "Depends on who you talk to. We've been hearing rumors that Eve may be getting a reprieve. You wouldn't happen to know anything about that, would you, Raven?"

"Maybe so."

All attention turned to Ray. Deena said, "Oooh. Sounds like she does know something."

"Just that a lot of people are fed up with the God Squad out there. You girls may want to start thinking about where you're going to spend your golden years."

Ashleigh bristled at the words "God Squad." "You're an *unbeliever*."

Rolling her eyes, Fran interrupted, "Where else is there to go?"

Ray said, "They say there's some kind of refugee base down around Washington, DC. Supposedly it's pretty nice. They're calling it Xanadu."

"How do you know that?"

"Just rumors. But that Dixon character is prepared to go to war against it, so *he* obviously believes it's true."

Ashleigh erupted. "Well, he is the Living Saint, so he must have a good reason."

"I wouldn't count on it," Ray said.

"How dare you! He's doing God's work, and if you could see how he suffers to obey our Savior's will, you would keep your stupid mouth shut!"

"I saw his men killing women, Ashleigh."

"You saw them *saving* women! You saw women being sent to Paradise rather than eternal torment. It's a blessing! Women bear the burden of God's anger, and it is our duty and our privilege to sacrifice ourselves for the good of Man! It is the only way to expunge ourselves of Eve's sin."

"You can't be serious."

"I will not stand here and have godless witches like you tell me what—"

Fran stepped in. "Okay, that's enough, Ashleigh. This

kind of thing gets us nowhere, so let's just all agree to dis-
agree and move on.

They finished eating in silence.


Ray was awakened by someone banging on the door of
the trailer. When he tried to get up, he almost fainted from
a rush of dizziness and nausea. His left arm hurt, and when
he rubbed it he found a bandage in the crook of his elbow.
The whole thing felt bruised. Dragging himself into the
hall, he heard Fran answering the front door.

"What is it, Elaine?" Fran asked, yawning.

"There's someone outside the fence asking to talk to a
Raven Despineau."

"*Outside?* Who?"

"I don't know; I've never seen him before. A new guard.
He says he's a friend of hers."

"What's going on?" Ray asked.

"Someone wants you outside. A *man.*"

Deena and Ashleigh now appeared. "What the hell's
going on?" Deena asked.

"Some man outside is asking for *her.*"

The girls were very intrigued.

Shivering with cold and fright, Ray put on his vest and
shoes and wrapped a comforter around his shoulders, then
he and the others trooped along the frosty path to the main
gate. The girls whispered among themselves. The moon was
bright, silvering the State House dome on their right and
downtown on their left. Straight ahead, the shopping mall
was a high, dark cliff. As they entered its shadow, no one
spoke, their breaths puffing from their hoods like empty
thought balloons. There was someone at the fence, just a
hooded black shape.

Goaded ahead by the others, Ray walked the last fifty
feet alone. "I'm Raven Despineau," he said warily. "What
do you want?"

"Ray? It's me, Todd!"

"Todd! Thank God. What's going on?"

"I can't talk long. Did you find Sandoval?"

"Yes."

"Did he tell you what's going on?"

"He said there was going to be a rebellion against Dixon."

"That's right. There's going to be a surprise attack on Chace Central, and Barnstable want us to run our diversion to draw Chace's disciples into a trap."

"When is it all happening?"

"Sometime before dawn. All the Prophet's forces are involved, so just be ready to pitch in as soon as the gate goes down. Everybody's pretty high on this plan, but I just want to let you know that if the whole thing falls apart, and it looks like we're about to eat major dirt, I'm busting you out of here, and we're running for it."

"Running where?"

"I thought we'd head south, see if we can give a heads-up to those people at Xanadu."

"How are you planning on us getting there? The roads are impassable."

"Same way we got here—by bike."

"Oh, Jesus. All right, is that it?"

"That's it. Just go inside and wait for my signal."

"What's the signal?"

"You'll know it, trust me." Then Todd was gone.


Ray went back to the others and explained the situation.

Fran and Deena were excited, but Ashleigh was silent. The one named Elaine, an older, heavyset woman with the title of Night Matron, said, "Even if this guy's telling you the truth, which I doubt, we would be fools to do what he says. We have a good thing going here, everything we need, and I'm not about to just abandon it for some wild-goose chase. We wouldn't last five minutes out there on our own. This isn't a prison; these fences were put up to protect us! You Munies might not care about that, but the rest of us do."

"Oh, I agree," Ray said. "It's a stupid idea."

*"What?"* Fran exploded. "Are you serious? You're the one who said we were going to get the hell away from here, and now you're just going to wimp out like that?"

"I'm sorry, Fran. I was just daydreaming; I didn't think anyone would take it seriously. Of course we can't leave."

"That's fucked up, dude," said Deena.

Elaine said, "Girls, you should listen to the advice of your new roommate. It's a nice fantasy, but the truth is, a man will say anything to get into your pants."

*"Men,"* Ray said, shaking his head.

*"Men,"* Elaine agreed.

"Elaine, do you by any chance happen to know my uncle Jim?"

"Of course I know the Prophet. He's the one who asked me to come get you."

"Oh . . . cool. Well, say hello to him for me, would you? And please tell him that Barnstable says hello."

"I certainly will."

Elaine returned them to their trailer. As soon as she was gone, Ray jumped into action.

"All right, ladies," he said, rifling through the kitchen drawers, "we have to arm ourselves and be ready to fight our way out of here. I need your help—move!"

"What are you talking about?" Ashleigh asked.

"Obviously, nobody's going to help us, so we have to help ourselves."

Disconcerted by the abrupt mood swing, the three were wary of believing anything Ray said, but Fran and Deena reluctantly went along with it. Ashleigh sulked, praying for their souls.

The trailer held very little in the way of weapons, so Ray hoped no one would dare interfere with them as long as they were wearing their vests. And since Xombies couldn't touch them either, they should be able to simply walk out of the compound once the electrified outer fence was down. As the hours passed, exhaustion set in, and they dozed.

They were awakened by a burst of gunfire, then a series of explosions.

"Shit, it's time," Ray cried. "Everybody up, it's time!"

Throwing a mattress over the inner fence, they boosted each other over and hurried to the main gate. All the other women were out and about, chattering anxiously, but there was no sign of Sandoval. Along the street, generators chugged into action; electric wires fizzed; sirens blared. Spotlights swept the field and beamed across the dome of the State House. From inside the building there were muffled alarms and gunfire. For a moment, the shooting increased . . . then just as quickly it petered out. Skate-troopers zipped purposefully up and down the street, then simultaneously changed direction as their radios crackled instructions to report for an emergency security inspection. As they skated away, they killed the generators, leaving silence and dark in their wake.

Ray and the girls waited by the fence, shivering. It seemed to get colder as the sun came up.

"Is that it?" Fran asked.

"I think that's it," Ray said miserably.

"Damn."

Deena said, "Well, let's go inside, I'm freezing."

"You go ahead," Ray said. "I'm going to wait a few more minutes."

Fran and Deena left, leaving Ray alone with Ashleigh.

"There's no need to wait for me," Ray told her, trying to control his voice. If Barnstable's coup had failed, then Todd was probably dead . . . and Sandoval would be next. "Go back inside. I just have to give it a little while longer."

"There's no point," said Ashleigh.

"You never know."

"No, I do know. Your scheme didn't work because I warned them about it."

"What?" Ray's brain fumbled for purchase. "What are you talking about?"

Ashleigh held up a small walkie-talkie. "I told them—with this! I told them, and I'm glad I told them! Yes! That's right! Because those men are trying to do the Lord's work, and it's our job to help them, not sell them out to Miska!"

"Oh my God . . ."

"You might well pray for Eve's mercy, because you'll have none from me!"

"Oh my God, you crazy bitch . . ."

Ray felt boiling-hot tears running down his frozen face, and before he knew what he was doing he slapped the girl. The instant he did it, he regretted it. Ray had never hit a girl in his life, and hitting a misguided teenager was just wrong. But there was no taking it back.

Ashleigh immediately returned the blow, clawing Ray's cheek with her long, painted nails and attacking like a wild-cat. Stunned by the furious assault, he fell back, ducking and dodging the girl's clawed hands. Ashleigh was clearly experienced at catfighting, a natural street brawler. Ray hadn't been in a fight since grade school, and he didn't want to be in one now, but the girl was all over him, punching and scratching and kicking as hard as she could—which was *very hard*.

"Stop it, stop it!" Ray cried, defending his eyes from those sharp nails.

Ashleigh drove even harder, her baby-doll features twisted into a mask of rage, spittle flying from her mouth. The left side of her face was bright red from his slap. In panic, Ray suddenly realized that no one was going to save him; that if he surrendered or showed weakness, this maniac might kill him, so he started fighting back with all his might. Pinwheeling his arms, he landed a lucky blow to the girl's jaw—*crack!*—and just like that, Ashleigh went down.

She went down hard, looking pitiful and frail, just a kid really. Ray knelt to help her and found she wasn't breathing. *Oh God,* he thought. *Not this. Please not this.*

"Help!" he cried. "Somebody help! We need medical attention here—it's an emergency! Anybody, please help!"

No one seemed to hear, and Ray decided to try CPR. He remembered there was some song you could use to time chest compressions—was it "Stayin' Alive"? Suddenly, something hit him like a wrecking ball. The force knocked him a good ten feet. Stunned, he looked back to see a strange figure straddling Ashleigh's helpless body.

It was the girls' dog—the ugly pig-dog.

Only now the animal looked almost human. It had human hands and a childish human face, its skin mottled pink and black, and its eyes two dark marbles. Those bulging, manic eyes fixed on Ray, and he shrank in horror to realize he was alone, unarmed, and trapped in a fence with this grotesque hybrid monstrosity.

But the thing was not interested in him. As he watched, it cradled Ashleigh's limp body in its hands and leaned down as if to kiss her. To Ray's horror, it *did* kiss her, the dreaded Xombie kiss. Black demon lips cupped pink human ones and proceeded to suck face . . . but then something unusual happened:

Instead of collapsing, Ashleigh's chest swelled with air. At once the girl coughed to life, not as a hellish Maenad but as a normal human female. Her attacker let her go and spit something on the ground: Ashleigh's bubble gum. The creature had saved her from choking.

Having done its good deed, the dog-thing now came for Ray. From its maniacal face, he knew there was no such benevolence in store for him, and he scrambled to escape, slip-sliding on the dewy grass. *Dead I'm dead I'm so dead.*

Just before the weird thing reached him, a pinpoint of red light skittered across its body, and it started coming apart. Ray hit the ground, thinking, *Snipers!* Whatever that laser sight touched magically exploded as if spring-loaded. Chunks flew from the dog-boy's head and torso; its legs snapped like twigs. As the creature went down, incendiaries pelted the grass, flaring white-hot. It writhed in the fire, curling backward and inside out as it tried to flee its own burning flesh.

Suddenly a voice yelled, "Come on!" and a hand jerked Ray to his feet. It was Todd. He ran for the main gate, pulling Ray with him. There was an EMT vehicle there, a gleaming white ambulance with Sandoval at the wheel. He was holding a laser pointer.

"Wait!" Ray cried. "I have to get Ashleigh!"

"You can't!"

"Yes!" Ray yanked free and ran to Ashleigh. She was sitting with her head down, hugging her legs. As gently yet urgently as he could, Ray said, "Ashleigh, we're leaving now. Come on, get up."

"No," she said dully.

Suddenly, dozens of men began pouring out of the State House as if roused by an alarm. They rounded the building and took shooting positions on the hillside, preparing to unleash a hail of death upon the field. Ray knew he was as good as dead, trapped in plain sight.

"Ashleigh, please!"

"No! Stop!"

The guards were well drilled, adjusting their gun sights for perfect accuracy. They didn't want to waste any ammunition—that stuff didn't grow on trees. As they focused all their attention on their targets, they didn't notice the earth itself rising around them.

A profusion of weird black spores uncoiled from the mud, spreading and growing, branching outward to form a web of vines that encompassed the entire hill.

For weeks the black sludge had been migrating underground, creeping through soil and pipes and groundwater as it converged on the capitol. This living tar was the pure Maenad essence—the boiled-down lees from a million cooked Xombies. Impervious to fire, these tough, long-chain fibers formed wormlike tendrils, exaggerated fingers tipped with rudimentary sense organs that spread faster than the most pernicious weed.

The snipers were oblivious to the wild activity around their feet. As the strands of dark matter proliferated, they also thickened and toughened, pulsing from within with vital juices. Fat globules formed at their junctions, splitting open like fibrous gourds to release vertical shoots that expanded to resemble hideous giant mushrooms, vaguely humanoid blobs that rose amid the oblivious snipers and jostled them for space.

Some of the men began noticing that they had been infiltrated by a second army, a gray, faceless corps, but before they could speak, the net contracted and engulfed them. Such contractions were happening all over the field, *shloop! shloop! shloop!* like coral polyps snapping shut, until the siege became evident to all, and wholesale panic broke out.

Scores of men disappeared, and for a moment the State House lawn was a garden of heaving human pumpkins, fast turning from red to blue. Then the vines relaxed, and all the new Xombies emerged.

Witnessing this, Ray said, "Ashleigh, come *on*." He tried to bodily lift her, but she was like a rag doll, deadweight. Todd joined him, and together they picked her up. As they carried her toward the truck, Ashleigh suddenly looked at Ray with clear eyes. Her expression was so challenging that he searched for some cause . . . and instantly found it. She had torn the fail-safe tab from her vest. The detonator cord was in her fist; all she had to do was pull.

The instant she knew he saw, Ashleigh yanked the cord. Ray dropped her, and screamed, "TODD! RUN!"

Taken by surprise, Todd was slow to react, but this time

Ray grabbed *him*, and together they bolted for the gate. They could hear Ashleigh laughing behind them, her voice cut short as the entire face of the mall turned white and a wave of scorching heat blasted their backs. Blinding fireballs rained down on the truck as Todd and Ray dove for cover inside. Fran and Deena were waiting; they hauled the boys up and slapped out their burning clothes as the truck lurched into motion.

*"Woo-hooo!"* Sandoval howled. "I loves me some fireworks!"

**PART III**

Chesapeake

# CHAPTER **SIXTEEN**

## POWWOW

I rode in a pickup truck squeezed between Alice Langhorne and Ed Albemarle. Alice was driving. Bobby Rubio sat on my lap. The back of the truck was full of Xombies, crammed together like sharecroppers during the dust bowl. All of us were dirty and torn.

Leaving Loveville behind, we left with it the last of our humanity. All that remained was a vestigial sense of loss, as if we had awakened from a beautiful dream. A dream America that never existed except in childhood fantasies, now blown threadbare. The human world was gone; all that was left was an incantatory kick.

As we passed a weathered flag on a car dealer's pole, a low, gruff voice started singing, *"Oh-h say can you see, by the dawn's early light . . ."*

It was Albemarle. Big Ed Albemarle, who had barely begun to speak since his Resurrection as a Xombie, was singing.

For a moment we just listened, the lines of our faces traced in grime. Then, softly, tentatively, we sang along. After a minute or so, the feeling passed, and we stopped.

The submarine was just as we had left it. We took her back to blue water and dove deep, licking our wounds. We stayed down there a long time, months perhaps, wrapped in darkness and silence. Then we heard something that woke us up: the throbbing of human hearts. A reservoir of hot blood suspended in the cold sea.

It was another submarine, passing right over our heads. Not the French boat. This was an American submarine—Virginia-class.

There was no discussion; we had to get them. As the crew set about surfacing the boat, the senior officers dressed in the most official-looking costumes they could find. Donning his never-worn admiral regalia, Coombs went to the bridge and turned on the ULF secure channel:

"Attention, Virginia: This is a message for Commander Arnold Parminter, from Admiral Harvey Coombs. We are at the rendezvous point, awaiting contact."

There was no reply. Coombs was reluctant to repeat the message, not wanting to raise undue suspicion. It was a risk to broadcast his position at all, which in ordinary circumstances would have been a serious breach of operational security—just as answering his message would be. Submariners were trained to be cautious; they didn't call it the Silent Service for nothing. But circumstances had changed—times were desperate, human voices scarce. One might reasonably expect a slight relaxation of military formality.

Finally, a wary voice cut through the static: "Sorry, Admiral, we're having a bit of a debate here about protocol. Please identify your boat again?"

"My boat has no official identity because it was decommissioned and secretly refitted for a classified operation known as SPAM—Sensitive Personnel and Materials. The SPAM mission no longer exists, but we are still custodians of the cargo, which includes several hundred tons of food and other basic provisions."

"And why are you sharing this information with us?"

"You're Americans. You and your vessel are a vital strategic resource. It's our duty to assist you in any way we can."

"What is it you want from us?"

"Nothing at all, other than whatever information you can provide us in locating other survivors like yourselves, either military or civilian. Anyone we can help, or who can help us. We are very much in need of a submarine port facility where we can overhaul our vessel."

"Join the club. From our experience, all shore facilities are . . . unsafe."

"Then we need to talk about that."

There was a pause, and Phil Tran whispered, "They've locked torpedoes on our radio signal."

Coombs said, "Be aware that if you fire on us, we will fire back. We have torpedoes loaded and preset. But we didn't come here to fight; we would rather join forces with you."

"Sounds like you may need us more than we need you."

"What have you got to lose?"

"Our starry-eyed optimism? Cut the shit, man. We heard the Mogul Cooperative was out of business."

"It is. We are not MoCo."

"And we just have to take your word on that."

"It cuts both ways."

"Life's a bitch, is that it? All right, stand by; I'm giving the order to surface. Here's how it's going to work: Upon visual confirmation of our positions, we will each dispatch a runabout with our executive officers for debriefing. If everything you say checks out, we will then heave to and all have a big powwow together. If not, or you do anything that makes me or my crew nervous, you will be treated as a menace and destroyed. Are these conditions acceptable?"

"Yes."

"Then let's proceed."

The formalities were discharged without incident, and the captains arranged to meet over a celebratory meal in the larger submarine—ours.

Captain Parminter's entourage came with good appetites; they had heard how well their XO was treated during his visit. He had made a full report of the mysterious boat, mentioning that it had undergone extensive modifications at the hands of its largely civilian crew, many of them teenagers, but the Virginia's people still weren't prepared for what they saw when they stepped aboard the USS *No-Name*.

"Oh my God," said Parminter, shaking his head.

The exterior of the ship, its matte black anechoic skin, was spray painted with colorful graffiti, most conspicuously a garish pirate emblem high up on the fairwater: a grinning skull with two crossed hammers. It looked like a giant tattoo.

Belowdecks, things only got worse. "What is this," Parminter muttered, "The Fun House?" He wasn't exaggerating; the boat was dark and cold, its steel corridors rotten with thick formations of an unusual substance, some sort of blue lichen or moss that was causing all the paint to peel.

"Why?" Coombs asked. "Having fun?"

"What is this stuff?"

"Oh, that? That's . . . mildew."

*"Mildew?"* Parminter would clearly have to have a word with his XO for not including this in his report. He had never seen anything like it in his life. The stuff was velvety to the touch, slightly luminous in the shadows. It smelled strongly of iodine. "My God. Are you serious?" Every metal surface bulged with this organic, fungal padding, turning linear corridors into leviathan guts. The mechanical made flesh.

But his men were starving, and what they saw next shocked them out of their dismay.

The crew's mess had been cleared except for one table. The room was dim, lit by a single lamp, but the men could see a gorgeous table set with a blue linen tablecloth, cloth napkins, expensive silverware, and fine china decorated with the boat's crest.

None of that meant anything to them; what they cared about was the food.

It looked like a fancy luau, a regular Thanksgiving feast,

with enormous gourds serving as tureens, and a whole roast pig garnished with unusually large, glistening vegetables and fruit. In the center was a silver dome, and next to it a platter holding a spectacular arrangement of glossy red steamed crabs layered on a bed of lacy black seaweed. Smaller side platters were filled with mountains of gooseneck barnacles, mussels, oysters, and other hull-dwelling shellfish. There were peculiar sausages and cheeses and a wicker basket piled high with warm, crusty loaves of bread. To accompany the food was a case of fine French champagne—Bollinger—perhaps the last ever to be drunk.

Once the men had all taken their places and the champagne had been poured, Coombs raised a glass: "To the journey."

"To the journey," the guests agreed, eyes fixed on the food. They were dizzy from hunger and lack of oxygen.

"Well, dig in."

The men reached for the feast . . . and the feast reached for them. Crabs became grasping, clawed hands; the roast pig reared up and became a headless human torso, innards flailing; veggies turned to writhing gobbets of flesh; loaves to severed limbs. As the visitors recoiled in panic, they realized they were anchored to their seats by vines of sticky living sinew. They shouted, trying to break free, but the undead tissue was immovable, tough as old tree roots. It covered the mouths of all but Parminter, silencing their screams.

I entered the room, followed by little Bobby Rubio and a few other boys.

"What do you think you're doing?" cried Parminter.

"Saving you, sir," I said.

"What kind of damn freak show is this? Why are you doing this to us?"

"Because we must," I said. "Because we're the only ones who can."

"What the hell are you?"

"Friends."

"Friends my ass. You're using people as fucking live bait!" To Coombs he said, "I see how it is, Harvey: They let you live so you can help them hunt down every last straggler. You rotten bastard, you're a traitor to the human race. And what happens when we're all gone? Have you thought of that? Are they going to just let you sail around the world like this forever? No—then it'll be your turn."

Coombs said, "I've already been converted."

"You're not a Xombie! You're still human!"

"Things are not as black and white as you think. Some of us have found it's better to be . . . flexible."

I nudged Bobby forward, since he looked the least threatening of any of us. A perfectly ordinary little kid.

"Show 'em," I whispered.

Bobby held up his right hand to make a fist. With a crackling sound, the fingers merged together, forming a smooth ball.

"Holy shit!" Parminter said.

The ball now began to expand, swelling larger and larger, pulsating like bubbling porridge. While this was happening, Bobby's face suddenly crumpled inward, withering like a prune, as if his entire head was being sucked into his neck. A moment later, the swollen ball of his hand unfurled into a thing very much like a face. It quickly became Bobby's face—Bobby's whole head. The shrunken bulb that had been his head now divided into five lobes and blossomed into a perfect human hand atop his neck. It waggled its fingers.

I said, "You see?"

Parminter threw up. Eyes full of horror and rage, he turned to Coombs. "How can you let them do this to you? To the human race? They're monsters! You're the captain of a U.S. Navy vessel, for Christ's sake!"

"I'm not the captain," Coombs said.

"What? Then who is?"

"Fred Cowper."

I gave a silent command to the man sitting beside Parminter, Lieutenant Dan Robles. Robles reached across the table to the covered dish in its center, the pièce de résistance. With a reproachful look at me, he lifted its bell.

There was a severed head underneath—a bald blue head that was no longer remotely human but which had once belonged to Captain Fred Cowper, retired. Parminter knew Cowper well; he had trained under him and had the highest regard for the man. Cowper had been an old-school submariner from the early days of the nuclear Navy. The technocrats hated him, but to Parminter he was the real thing, a no-bullshit maverick—the kind of guy you could bet your life on in a tight spot, whatever the cost to the Navy. Or to himself.

Well, it had cost Fred everything this time—everything but his head. But that head was alive, an independent entity with multiple little legs, its huge black eyeballs fixed on Parminter.

"Hiya, Arnie," it croaked.

*"That's not Cowper!"* Parminter objected. "You're not Fred Cowper, you fucking ghoul!"

"I yam what I yam," said Cowper's head.

"You think you're going to get away with this? If my men don't hear from me in the next ten minutes, they will blow you out of the water."

I said, "In ten minutes, you'll understand."

"Understand what? What the fuck am I going to understand? That a bunch of twisted monstrosities have taken over a submarine? That they've learned to play human?"

Cowper's head opened its jagged-toothed mouth and guffawed.

A bit miffed, I said, "No . . . that we are the last hope of Mankind."

"What does that even mean?"

"Life on Earth is going to be wiped out. The only thing that may survive is our kind."

"Malarkey!" Cowper shouted.

Parminter asked me, "How do you know that?"

"We can see it."

"See what?"

"The future. Every person we save is a thread of our human destiny—an irreplaceable piece of genetic memory going back a billion years. A clue to the ultimate puzzle, which we may one day be called upon to solve. There's not going to be any more evolution, no future generations—we're it. The restoration of our species depends upon how many lives we save. Lose one person, and we lose all their stored equity—and that is forever. Eternity is a long time to be cooped up together; we'll want all the company we can get."

"So we're supposed to be grateful, is that it? You think you're actually saving our lives."

"Not exactly. It's more like you're being preserved for future reference. We all are."

"Ah. Sounds pleasant."

"Barrel o' monkeys!" Cowper's head cackled.

"I know it's hard to understand right now, but in a minute you'll see everything."

"I'll see you in Hell, bitch. My boat will nuke us all before it will let you get away with this . . ."

Parminter's voice trailed off as Bobby's upper torso split apart, unfolding like a great, trembling orchid. A glossy blue protuberance shot forward like a chameleon's tongue, flaring wide and engulfing the man's face. He had no time to scream.

The guests left by the first light of dawn, climbing aboard their ship and issuing orders to cast off. The Virginia's XO had already been busy; the work there was done.

# CHAPTER **SEVENTEEN**

## FATHER KNOWS BEST

Bobby came to me after we parted from the other sub. I could tell he wanted to say something, but it made him deeply uncomfortable.

"What is it?" I asked.

"I don't like doing it this way. Why do we have to talk to them so much?"

"To let them know we are not thieves or killers."

"They don't care. It just makes them hate us even more."

"They just don't know. They can't imagine. Could you imagine before you were changed?"

"I don't 'member being changed. I just *was*."

Bobby was our Mystery Boy. He had still never explained to any of us exactly how or when he acquired his unusual abilities. He was brought aboard the boat as a helpless refugee, and forty-eight hours later every human being on board was converted to his peculiar species of ultraplastic, nonspastic, completely human-looking Xombie. If they were even Xombies. As a Maenad myself, one of the ship's original Blue Meanies, I had my doubts.

"Okay," I said. "But you remember before that. Being human."

"Yeah."

"Would you have wanted to be changed?"

Bobby didn't have to think twice. "Yes."

"Well, not everybody feels that way. That's why we try to prepare them."

"But even after we tell them, they're still upset."

"Sure, but they *know*. Knowing is important. You heard the man—they *want* to know."

"They still fight, though."

"Not after the change."

"No, not after the *change*. But why do we have to tell them beforehand? Why can't we just do it and get it over with?"

This was something I had wrestled with myself. I had never been completely convinced that our so-called mission was anything more than wishful thinking. The visions were powerful, yet they could easily be some mass hallucination. It was very possible we were all insane. Just as with the wild Xombies ashore, we had a deep need to convert people, but our more-lucid brains required elaborate justifications for doing so. Or at least mine did.

I said, "I think it's necessary and right to reveal our purpose to those we are about to change. I don't like hiding it as if we're ashamed. If what we're doing is the most important work on the planet, then we should say so."

"Even if it they don't believe us?"

"Even if they don't believe us."

"Okay. Can I ask you something else?"

"Yes."

"You know that head on the table?"

"You mean Fred Cowper."

"Isn't he your father?"

"That's what I thought . . . but I just found out my dad was someone named Despineau."

"Then why is your name Lulu Pangloss?"

"He and my mother were never married. Her name was Grace Pangloss."

"Oh. There was somebody else named Despineau when I was in Providence. A lady."

This was the first time Bobby had ever mentioned Providence. Something very traumatic had happened to him there. Trying not to look overly interested, I said, "A lady named Despineau?"

"Uh-huh. Her first name was Brenda."

Brenda. Brenda *Despineau*. I remembered what Mummy had told me, and wondered if I had just discovered an unknown relative.

"What happened to her?" I asked.

"She got all shot up."

"Shot up? How?"

"There were these guys looking for immune women. They caught her, but Mr. Miska got her out."

"Really," I said. *Immune women.* Well, it made a kind of sense. For a long time I thought I might be immune . . . until I turned into a Xombie. There were rumors of Immunes wandering the landscape, but the thought that some of them might be lost relatives of mine was unexpectedly disturbing. If what we believed was true, then Immunes were inherently doomed. We were helpless to save them. "How do you know all this?"

"I was there."

"Bobby, was Uri Miska the one who changed you?"

"I don't know."

"Were you human before you met him, though?"

"I don't *know*. Shut up!"

"But if Miska changed you, that means he must be a Clear. Maybe the original Clear."

"I don't care! So what?"

I could think of nothing to say to that. So what indeed? It suddenly all seemed so obvious: Of course it had to be Miska. Changing tack, I asked, "So did Miska turn this Brenda woman into a Clear?"

"Yes."

\* \* \*

Thinking about what Bobby had told me, I went to the CO quarters and opened the captain's safe.

"About time," squawked Fred Cowper's head. "I was beginnin' to think you might have forgotten about me."

Cowper's head had developed the ability to form crude words, wheezing like a bagpipe, but he could also actually talk to me without speaking, his voice buzzing inside my head as if broadcast to my brain. All of us on the boat had learned by now that we shared some degree of telepathy, but in most cases it was not as clear, or as consistent, as my connection to Cowper. Otherwise, it would drive us batty—who could tolerate such an inescapable chorus? There was no volume control on thoughts, no on/off switch, hence most Xombies preferred less invasive means of communication. Cowper only did it as a matter of necessity, but even he preferred that I reply aloud.

Since losing his body at Thule, Fred Cowper had learned to function quite well, cinching off the ragged stump of his neck and sprouting a nest of rootlike tendrils with which he could scuttle around like a hermit crab. His mouth had widened to accommodate the enlarged manipulating organ that was his tongue, and this sensitive member was guarded by a phalanx of oversized, jagged teeth.

Cowper's head was somewhat terrifying, but to me he was still Dad—the only dad I ever knew. Angry as I once was at him, I had made peace with the past and now was simply grateful to have him in my eternal life. Whether he really was my father or not, he was a piece of my former humanity, a part of me. A fragment of living memory I clung to like a security blanket. Having found him, I would never lose him again.

"Fred, I need to ask you something. About our past lives."

"I know," he said. "Grace told me she spoke to you."

"She did?"

"Yeah, about me not being your real father. It's true . . .

but that's not all of it. There's something I gotta get off my chest, too."

"You don't have a chest."

"Whatever. There's something I been meaning to tell you."

"What?"

"I know I was never much of a father to you."

"I had no basis for comparison."

"Still, you must've thought I was a real bastard all those years. I felt like one."

"Then why didn't you do something to change it?"

"I was human. Humans are fuckups, and I fucked up big-time. See, there's something else your mother and I never told you."

"What?"

"I'm gay . . . Or rather, I was gay. Now I'm just a head." I stopped. "Excuse me?"

"I shoulda told you while we were both still alive, and it woulda meant something." His black eyes rolled back in his skull, lubricated by their greasy lids; his mouth worked like a gasping fish. "I'm—I'm . . . sorry."

At Fred's unexpected confession, I did something I hadn't done since becoming a Xombie.

I laughed.

"It ain't that funny," he said.

Testing him, I asked, "So if you weren't my father, who was?"

"Another Navy man—a NATO officer named Alaric Despineau. She met him while we were stationed in Europe."

"So she cheated on you?"

"It ain't that simple and you know it. We were all . . . confused. I was at sea for months at a time, which made it easy for me to pretend I had no part in it. Truth was, Grace needed something I couldn't give her. He could."

"You mean children."

"Among other things. I had no understanding at the time

and hung her out to dry. Now I see how she had no choice . . . any more than I did. Biology is a bastard."

"What caused them to break up?"

"Your mother had an unfortunate attraction to men who weren't available. It was her independent streak. Alaric was always away at sea, so Grace was stuck raising you alone. Over time they just drifted apart."

"Who was Brenda?"

He blinked. "Brenda?"

"I just heard of a woman named Brenda Despineau."

He paused a long time. "That was Grace's first child. Your sister."

"Sister. How come I never knew about her?"

"She was a good bit older. At first she helped raise you, but eventually she and your mother had a falling-out. Grace had troubles, as you know. Brenda left home as soon as it was humanly possible . . . and took your brother with her. She woulda taken you, too, if she could have."

A brother now, too. I felt a long-dead nerve throb to life in my skull. "What happened to them?"

He shook his head. "Brenda didn't want my help, or anybody's. She was a real tough cookie. What she really wanted was you, but your mother took you and went on the run. After that, we all lost touch with each other for years. That is, until you and your mother found me."

"You never heard from any of the others? Or bothered looking?"

"Honey, I don't go where I'm not wanted. Just a little fatherly advice."

"You're not my father."

"I can dream, can't I?"

# CHAPTER **EIGHTEEN**

## PETROPOLIS

As we approached the north channel of the great Chesapeake Bay Bridge Tunnel, the hydrophones detected curiously subterranean noises, rushing from one shore to the other. This wasn't the clear swish of boat propellers but a deeper rumble, like bowling balls hurtling through a pipe.

"Traffic," said Phil Tran, listening over the headset.

"Ship traffic?" asked Coombs.

"*Traffic* traffic—there's some heavy machinery passing through the Bridge Tunnel. Big rigs."

"I *told* you so," said Alton Webb. "We should have come here in the first place."

"Hindsight is twenty-twenty." To me, Coombs asked, "Want to take a sighting?"

"A sighting . . . sure."

"Periscope depth." The command flitted through the ship like a dead leaf. Flesh and metal moved fluidly to comply.

"Periscope depth, aye."

"Raise periscope. She's all yours, Lulu."

My stone-cold hands seized stone-cold handles, my stone black eyes drank in daylight. I walked the periscope in a circle, taking a series of pictures, then quickly lowered it.

"Anything to report?"

"Just that bridge causeway, about zero ten degrees. Visibility is bad."

Coombs said, "It's gonna take a miracle to get past that thing."

"What exactly is the Bridge Tunnel?" I asked.

"You've never seen the Chesapeake Bay Bridge Tunnel? It's only one of the engineering wonders of the world: twenty miles of highway crossing the mouth of the Chesapeake, with three elevated bridge segments and two off-shore tunnels. The center bridge is actually out of sight of land and has a rest stop on an artificial island. I'd bet dollars to donuts they've got the north passage netted and probably mined."

"Reapers again?"

"Or somebody more legitimate. Either way, they're bound to not like us."

"So what do you think?"

"You speak for the skipper. What does he think?"

"He thinks we don't have any choice. They're doomed if we leave them like this."

"Concur. So how do you propose we get past their defenses?"

I consulted with Cowper, closing my eyes and putting my hand on my forehead like a cheap psychic communing with spirits. "The captain proposes that we look closer."

"It's risky. We're out of range of their sonar buoys out here, but any closer, and they might ping us."

"We need to know what we're up against."

"Long as we don't find out the hard way. Once they know we're here, we lose all our advantage."

"Oh, not *all* our advantage . . ."

We proceeded south on the surface, the submarine's fairwater silhouetted against the sun as it approached the bay's south entrance. Coombs and Robles climbed up to the bridge cockpit and scanned the sea with binoculars. Neither shore was visible, but the elevated causeway crossed the horizon, abruptly cut short where it dipped underwater—a bridge to nowhere.

Nearing the deep channel, we submerged, running silent right to the mouth of the bay. It was strange to think of that huge tunnel passing beneath us, cars and trucks driving beneath the bottom of the sea. Just beyond rose a strange black tower, jutting into the sky like a gigantic sentinel.

Before we could discuss it, I heard a high-pitched whirring noise from outside the hull. The unmistakable whine of a high-speed propeller.

"What is that?" I demanded.

"Torpedo," said Vic Noteiro. "MK-60. We must have triggered a CAPTOR mine."

"Everybody brace for impact," said Robles.

Before we could brace or do much of anything, a massive shock wave ran the length of the ship, causing floors to buckle and loose objects to go flying. We also went airborne, banging around the works like crash-test dummies, which probably would have killed some of us if we weren't already dead. But everyone just got up and went back to work, leaning right to compensate for a sudden list to port.

"Full reverse," ordered Coombs.

"Full reverse, aye."

"Won't they hear us?" I asked.

"Can't possibly make more noise than we already have. Damage reports."

Phil Tran said, "Looks like we caught a torpedo broadside, port midships, between frames sixty and seventy. Pressure vessel is intact, but there's a breach in the outer hull—we've lost the main port ballast tank. We're also losing hydraulic pressure on the aft port stabilizer. Reactor efficiency is down by sixty percent and still dropping—looks like damage to the fuel rods."

"Any sign of pursuit?"

"Not yet. The mine was probably a stray."

"Just in case, get us below the thermocline and play dead."

"If we go too deep in this shape, we won't have to play dead."

"We have to risk it."

We stabilized the boat as much as was possible at the bottom of the sea. The damage was severe, but not immediately critical; we could still limp along.

Under cover of darkness, we tested the buoyancy and hydraulic controls, surfacing the periscope and slowly cruising the northern Virginia coast, studying the barrier islands at full spectrum and full magnification. We knew from the charts that there were many quaint tourist towns and fishing villages all along these shores, but not a single light was visible. The place looked deserted. It *felt* deserted.

The only aura of human life came from the south entrance to Chesapeake Bay, a dim glow like an untended storm lantern. As we got closer, we could see the glow was coming from a black tower sticking out of the water. It was the giant structure we had seen just before being torpedoed. My thought was, *One if by land, two if by sea.*

"Well, this is it," said Lieutenant Robles. "Looks like somebody's home."

"I recognize that thing," said Alton Webb. "That's Petropolis. What they call a spar platform—some thirty wellheads doing directional drilling. In normal operation, it can pump around sixty thousand barrels of oil a day. What you see there is only the tip of the iceberg; there's a lot more of it underwater, fixed by catenary mooring lines to the bottom."

"Since when is there oil drilling at the mouth of Chesapeake Bay?"

"There isn't. It's been moved here from the Gulf of Mexico."

"Why?"

"Probably to guard the entrance to the bay."

Coombs said, "If there are sentries in that platform, I think we can assume the Chesapeake is being defended. We've already run into one torpedo, it would be foolhardy to go any closer."

"Concur," said Robles. "So what's next?"

Robles and Coombs looked at me, though they were really looking through me to the invisible presence of Fred Cowper.

I said, "We have to get to those guys in the tower."

Coombs was hesitant. "If we do anything to give ourselves away, their defenses will zero right in on us. They're broadcasting on ULF, so we know they intend submarines to hear them. We should be prepared for a trap."

"I doubt they're expecting anyone like us. Besides, we don't have much choice at this point. What else are we here for? If we have to abandon the boat, this is as good a place as any."

"It's your call."

I hated this passive-aggressive stuff. "You guys are the experts. Tell me how we can get aboard that thing."

"My suggestion is we don't go aboard at all but just sink it from a safe distance and move in to collect the sentries."

"Assuming they're not drowned, burned up, or blown to bits."

"Chances are they'll survive, or spontaneously Xombify."

"It's too big a risk."

"Then I think we should forget entering the bay and just go ashore somewhere along the coast, like we did before. Bypass the sea defenses entirely and head overland to DC."

"I have a better idea," I said.


Dead men can't drown. Hence the sea held no terrors for us.

The boys had gotten used to regularly crawling along the boat's great hull, collecting mussels and gooseneck barna-

cles, filling their bags with unearthly delicacies while others trailed at the end of long tethers, spearing bottom fish or
netting crabs and scallops. I, the sole girl, watching from
atop the bridge, my black hair flying in the current as I
mentally ticked off minutes of exposure versus mandatory
items for the menu. It wouldn't do to have the boys freeze
before they could complete the grocery list. It was a novelty
to them, this strange blue harvest; a welcome change from
the sordid grotto of the sub. Despite the darkness and the
cold, they were glad to do it, or maybe *because* of the darkness and cold.

I went to the Big Room, the biggest space in the boat,
which had once held twenty-four nuclear missile tubes. Now
it was packed with mountains of treasure. Not treasure in the
form of gold and jewels (although there was some of that),
but more human-essential valuables such as food, drink, and
medicine. It was a regular Costco down there.

Some months earlier we had plundered these things from
an anchored barge that was the cache of the Reapers. They
didn't need the stuff anymore, and neither did their masters
at MoCo. For that matter, we didn't need it either, but it
came in handy as a lure for hungry refugees.

The Blackpudlians were in there, tuning their instruments.

"You sure it's safe out there?" asked Ringo.

"We're already dead," said Paul. "What more can they
do to us?"

"I don't know. Crush our souls?"

"Our souls are like our bodies, mate, only more so. Like
rubber."

"Rubber soul, my arse," said John. "There's no such thing
as a soul, rubber or otherwise."

"There's filet of sole," mused George.

"I prefer plaice, myself."

"One must have a good sense of plaice."

"I've always known my proper plaice."

"There's a thyme and a plaice for everything."

"Or even a nice bit of halibut."

"The halibut is, we haven't the slightest idea of what we are, what any of this means, or what the risks are in going ashore."

I said, "Don't be afraid. I've been out there, and it's perfectly safe. We're adapted to that world now."

"Lulu's right. Fire with fire, mates."

"Right," I said. "As a wise man once said, 'You can't make an omelet without breaking some eggs.'"

"You hear that, lads? We are the egg men."

# CHAPTER **NINETEEN**

## BRIDGE TUNNEL

Climbing inside the forward escape trunk, I made room for as many guys as would fit, then ordered the inboard hatch shut. The chamber was "full as a nut," as my mother would have said, but it didn't matter; we weren't claustrophobic, and didn't need room to breathe. My only concern was logistical, how to best utilize the available space without touching skin, and we had solved that by wearing fullbody, hooded wet suits.

I backflashed to a pregnant cat I had dissected in biology class, how its unborn kittens fit together as neatly as Escher designs, interlocking yins and yangs. Then I opened a valve and let the water in. It was salty and freezing cold, gushing up powerfully from below.

As brine covered my head, I had the oddest need to scream, recalling a similar experience when I was alive—*Chick is ice-cold*—but then the feeling passed. A few seconds later, the chamber was full. I cranked open the topside hatch, releasing a plume of trapped bubbles.

We set to work. Twenty leagues beneath the sea, three groups of Dreadnauts exited the three hatches and slid down lines to the bottom. To human eyes, the water would have been utterly black and impenetrable, but to Exes it glowed with the muted auras of living creatures. Even plankton had its own light, so that the ocean was full of luminous motes.

Hiking through twilit meadows of eelgrass, with the incoming tide pushing us like a breeze, we made our way up
a wide valley carved in the continental shelf. This was the
mouth of the deepwater channel, the Chesapeake stretch of
the Intracoastal Waterway, connecting Norfolk with An-
napolis and Baltimore in the far upper bay. Up there, it had
been regularly dredged to accommodate shipping, but at this
end it was plenty deep enough for even the largest ships to
pass without risk of hitting the undersea highway tunnel—
which was a good thing, because an Ohio-class submarine
required enormous clearance. Passively drifting on the current, it loomed behind us walkers like a great black zeppe-
lin, weightless as a cloud.

My party followed behind a team led by Alton Webb.
This was a man I had hated and feared in life, and who hated
and feared me. He had abused me, terrorized my friends,
killed my father, and betrayed the entire boat. All this was
irrelevant now, dismissed as pocket change amid the wages
of human ignorance. I could no more hold a grudge from
life than I could blame a trapped animal for biting the hand
that fed it—any more than I could blame myself for my
former human foibles.

No, that wasn't quite true. Blame might be gone, but
guilt was forever. In fact, guilt was the emotional currency
of this new existence—one of the side effects of immortality was an almost frantic selflessness, a deep pity and shame
more potent than Original Sin. This grim empathy was what
kept us working on our common task: to save humanity.
Not in the crude, almost sexual way of wild Xombies but as
a simple matter of conscience.

Alton Webb, bearing a larger burden of shame, was now
perhaps the most humane of all the Dreadnauts, the silent
martyr of the sub, whose devotion to me made him a practical extension of my will. Without his example, I could not
have persuaded the others into continuing the journey after
Providence. I felt guilty about making them feel so guilty—

and round it went, a wheel of never-ending remorse that we all sublimated in duty: duty to the memory of home and country, duty to the ship, duty to each other, and, most intensely, duty to the still-doomed. More than anything else, we lived to save the living.

Before us were fields of sonar buoys, proximity mines, curtains of steel mesh, an obstacle course that no unescorted ship could hope to navigate. *So how do you propose to do it?* Coombs had asked.

*Simple,* I said. *We walk.*

Unlimbering their tools, the blue boys began cutting a wide swath through the barricades. Nearing the drilling rig's anchorage, we could sense humans around us—wisps of life energy like blurred X-rays. Our proximity to them goaded the teams to work faster, Clears and Blues competing for the right to those prizes. The men were drunk on it, desperate to play God. I wanted to say, *Calm down*, but the others were already well ahead of me, bounding up the rocky slope. *Darn it.* Here was the problem with weaning them off my blood; I should have known it wouldn't be so easy.

We reached the spot directly below the oil platform and directly above the tunnel crossing. There was something like a large building on the seafloor, a rusty ziggurat connected by a thick pipeline to the surface. I had brought a device called a Momsen lung, a kind of inflatable life preserver. We had hundreds of them on the sub. Opening the air valve, I instantly became buoyant and shot for the surface.

Emerging between the towering legs of the superstructure, I listened for signs of life, but the thing felt empty. Whoever had been there was gone now.

"Hey!" I shouted. My voice echoed hollowly above the slosh of the waves. There was no answer.

I bled air from my vest and sank back to the bottom. Brushing floating hair out of my face, I checked my GPS display, mentally feeding my coordinates to Cowper's head in the Nav Center, where he typed it out for the crew using his long black tongue.

We came across a sunken ship, a guided-missile frigate. Then a destroyer. A helicopter assault ship. Dozens of smaller vessels. This had been a battleground. Now it was a graveyard.

Signaling the rest of my party to take it slow, I studied the white seabed around us. The bottom appeared to be covered with dead coral, clinking underfoot like bleached bones, and it took me a second to realize it was not coral at all but actual *bones*—human remains. The whole area was a vast killing field. The sheer quantity of bones was remarkable, far more than was accounted for by the sunken wrecks. How did they get there?

Before I could work this out, there was a strange commotion from up front, a lot of yelling inside my head. *Pull back, pull back!* At the same time, a swarm of dim objects, visible only as pale wisps against the bioluminous haze, suddenly swept across the bottom and started fastening onto me with sharp pincers.

They were crabs—millions of crabs. Crabs of all kinds: blue crabs, rock crabs, primitive-looking horseshoe crabs. All of them unusually large and aggressive. Girded with sharp spines and powerful claws, they were hard to get off, hard to kill, and just plain *hard*. Most disturbing of all, they obviously had a taste for Xombies.

*Déjà vu,* I thought, batting at them. Quickly becoming overwhelmed, I ordered, *Retreat!*

I wasn't the only one; all the Dreadnauts were in flight, facing against the tide and dragging bunches of crustaceans from their extremities like bizarre fruit. The frenzied crabs followed, swimming and scuttling over the bottom in a rolling wave.

As the point man, farthest from the ship, Alton Webb had the worst of it, doing what he could to stall the attackers by using his own body as bait, hacking crabs off himself with karate moves. But this was not very effective, and he was quickly enveloped in shrouds of hungry creatures.

My group and I were also covered but not so burdened that we couldn't climb the lines to the boat, shedding our wet suits and some of our flesh to rid ourselves of the sharp-clinging foe, or even biting crabs off each other with our teeth.

Within the ship, Coombs ordered Reverse Slow, causing the great screws to begin resisting the current. It was risky because any sound we made at this range and depth could be noticed by a reasonably alert enemy, but the only other choice was to drift blindly into the defensive lines.

The crabs followed us up the trailing ropes, linking legs and massing by tons to actually put a drag on the submarine. If they reached it, their sheer numbers could block the intake ducts and destabilize the ballast. But the last men to the lines, Alton Webb and Jack Kraus—both of them buried in vicious crustaceans and eroding like sandcastles—realized the danger and simultaneously decided on the last, best course of action:

As one, they pulled out their knives and cut the nylon cords, dropping away from the sub and taking the threat with them. Adding their own bones to the heap.

Once the surviving Dreadnauts were back aboard, crew members armed with bolt cutters and hammers dealt with any persisting crabs. Some of these had actually burrowed into the bodies of their victims, lodging up inside bellies and chest cavities like ironic cancers—the only cancers a Xombie could get—which necessitated the crudest parody of surgery to remove.

Cutting crabs off me, Alice Langhorne asked, "What just happened out there?"

"What does it look like? Crabs! We were attacked by crabs."

"I was worried about something like this. I just didn't expect it to apply so indiscriminately."

"What?" I asked, yanking a small crab off my left earlobe.

"When we were doing risk assessments for MoCo, we realized that Maenads were not deterred by water obstacles. They could easily ford rivers, lakes, and oceans, meaning any kind of moat was useless, and even islands offered only temporary protection. Extreme cold was the only guaranteed defense, which is why the Moguls all came to Thule. But the problem solved itself: It turns out that the ASR morphocyte—Agent X—is able to colonize the bodies of certain invertebrates."

"Shit."

"It does not do this by piggybacking on iron molecules, the way it does in human blood cells. Crabs don't have hemoglobin. Their environment has to be saturated with microbial ASR—pulverized Maenad tissue—so that they absorb it into their bodies and nervous systems. Once this reaches a critical mass, the morphocytes form a rudimentary nerve center that takes control of the host organism, causing it to suddenly develop an insatiable appetite for richer sources of Agent X—such as ourselves."

I erupted. "Why the hell didn't you tell us before we went out there? We just lost three guys!"

"I'm sorry. I'm still getting used to this; my mind is so different than it was when I was alive . . . like a black hole in space. I find it very hard to narrow my focus. To attend."

"Well, you have to. We all have to."

"I'll try to be more careful."

"Screw being careful," I said. "It's time we played hardball."

Keeping well clear of the bay entrance, we headed south until we came to the bottom leg of the causeway, which was basically a long pier connected to the Norfolk shore. The water here was too shallow to dive the boat, but we didn't intend to. Instead, we lined up for an easy shot and fired a spread of four torpedoes at the bridge pylons.

Four plumes of white spray rose to the sky, and a great span of concrete and steel tumbled into the water. Then we just cruised over it.

We were inside Chesapeake Bay.

# CHAPTER **TWENTY**

## FRENCH TOAST

I looked up along the coast. Not far upriver was the sight of the first landing by early settlers of Jamestown—the Pocahontas thing. The Disney musical. As a kid I had liked that cartoon, but my mother despised its cheap sentimentality, its glossing-over of ugly historic events. *Hollywood is bullshit,* she would say. *American history is not pretty.*

Looking at Norfolk, I had to agree. The city was dead, and the Navy base had been a scene of desperate fighting. Waterfront buildings were riddled with bullet holes, windowless from explosions, gutted by fire. A big submarine lay sunk at its moorings, only its radar mast breaking the water. Several vessels had run aground or capsized. Other ships were more or less intact, including an Ohio-class boat suspended on blocks in the vast dry-dock facility. The only one that interested me was the sleek black yacht riding at anchor. I could read its name through the periscope: *La Fantasma*. The yacht was empty; its passengers had come ashore here.

Assembling a shore party to salvage some critically needed items from the dry-docked boat, I consulted Cowper's head about the necessary procedures for stabilizing our vessel.

"I just want to make sure everything is secure before we disembark."

"Sounds like you're not planning on coming back anytime soon."

"It may be a while."

"Good. Because I've had enough of this tub to last me an eternity."

As the engineering team and I entered the dry dock, we could see that we were too late: the other submarine had already been plundered. Hasty scaffolds stood in place, and huge holes had been cut in the vessel's hull, steel carved like blubber and machinery dangling out like entrails from a beached whale. The Reactor Control Operator, Mr. Fisk, could see at once that there was little point in going aboard.

Climbing the ramp out of the dry dock, I began to hear a rhythmic whirring sound from above. It was a thin electronic noise, like a printing teletype. It got louder, and suddenly we could see a strange creature silhouetted against the sky. It was spindly and four-legged, about the size of a deer or large dog, but with boxy saddlebags strapped to its sides.

It had no head.

Even stranger, it had no *presence*, no life energy. As Xombies, we were highly attuned to any aura of life, but this thing was a blank.

I asked, "What is that?"

"I'm not sure," said Julian Noteiro. "I think it's a machine."

Without warning, the weird object erupted in gunfire—a fusillade of metal pellets issuing from where its head should have been. In an instant, half our crew was down, their bodies punched through like cored apples.

Perhaps because Bobby Rubio and I were shorter, we escaped the first volley and jumped over the side of the ramp, clinging by our fingertips. Julian, Sal, and a few other boys did the same, dangling beside us. The bigger men all plummeted to the concrete bottom, shattering limbs and skulls.

Seeking targets, the four-legged robot trotted down the

ramp after them, its pulsing whine echoing in the chamber. As it passed me, I swung my slight body up over the ramp and tried to kick its rear legs out from under it.

But the thing was too fast—with mechanical precision it instantly dodged my kick and fired a side-mounted cannon in my face. It was loaded with metal chaff, a hail of razor-like flakes that would have blasted me to wet spaghetti if Julian wasn't right there, swinging his hammer against the muzzle so that the explosion backfired, rupturing the cannon and knocking the robot off-balance.

Sal DeLuca and Jake Bartholomew used the brief chance to seize the thing and hoist it off its feet, boosting it over the side. Buzzing frantically, trying to stabilize itself in midair, the machine hit the floor and came unsprung like an old clock.

We pulled ourselves together as best we could. In the days and weeks to come, all our injuries would fade away, but for now we mainly had to be mobile enough to walk. To this end, splints were improvised for the worst fractures, and broken heads were tied up with rags and duct tape.

Julian was a mess, his body mangled by shrapnel from the cannon exploding, but he and the crewmen had a bigger concern: the meaning of that killer robot.

"Somebody hadda been remote-controlling that thing," said Cowper's head. "Which means they're still out there."

Coombs agreed. "Sure. But who? And why?"

"Could just be some kind of automated defense system," Dan Robles suggested. "A leftover from the plague."

"No way. That thing was clean, it looked new, which means it musta been maintained by somebody. It's a complicated piece of machinery—it can't just sit outside in the rain for months. I'm telling you, its operators are around here somewhere."

Robles said, "So they just open fire? Some of us look human, yet they fired on all of us indiscriminately, Blues and Clears alike."

Cowper replied, "Some of us are Blue, that's enough. To some poor, scared schmuck, that makes us all suspect. No offense to you Clears, but you don't look all that human."

"I'm not offended," Coombs said, "but I doubt a human could tell the difference."

"You sound offended."

"I'm not. So what's our next move?"

"Somebody's monitoring this place. Which means we either gotta get out of here . . . or we gotta go get 'em."

"I'm not sure we should go off on a wild-goose chase, Fred. That thing could have been operated from anywhere. They could be a thousand miles away for all we know."

"I don't think so."

"That's your prerogative. Mine is to get us out of here in one piece. As it is, some of these guys will be crapping metal for a week."

"Too bad we couldn't trace the radio data link."

"It's still worth trying. We should return to the boat and scan the airwaves."

"Tran already did that when we came in. There was nothing but a lot of interference."

"It wasn't interference driving that robot."

Robles froze. "The boat."

"What?"

"I think I just realized where they might—"

He was interrupted by an explosion. The sound was a deep, ringing gong that registered in our back teeth, and down at the waterfront, a white tower of spray rose far into the air. A pier warped off its concrete pilings and collapsed into the harbor. Almost immediately, there was a second explosion, but very little was visible now through the curtain of mist and falling debris. It took me a moment to realize that our boat was gone—all that was left was a spreading ring of foam.

"Unbelievable," said Dan Robles.

"What?" I asked. "What happened?"

"They sank our boat."

"Who?"

He pointed. *"Them."*

Something was moving beneath the opposite dock slip; the water churned, boiled up, then parted as another submarine broke the surface.

It was the sub we had seen when we first arrived—the ship we thought was wrecked, with only a lonely radar mast to mark its watery grave. It was an easy assumption to make since we hadn't sensed any life aboard. But no—it was very much alive, glowing like a lantern with multiple human candles. The crew had been hiding somehow, playing dead.

At first sight, I thought it was a second Ohio-class boat, but then I realized this vessel was not quite the same as ours. Its sail planes were mounted higher, and the whole thing was shorter and more slender. I had learned a bit about subs these past few months, but this type was new to me.

"What is that?" I asked.

"French boat," Fred's head said. *"Triomphante*-class. Playin' possum, the bastards. I shoulda recognized that Dassault mast, but I was too busy playin' pattycake. S'what I get."

Taking all the time in the world, the foreign sub eased out past the wreckage of ours, heading for the deepwater channel. Men appeared atop the fairwater to pilot the thing out. One of them scanned the shore with binoculars, and when he spotted our party, he gibbered with excitement, motioning the others to look. The one with the greatest air of authority raised his own spyglass. Staring down those lenses, I could almost read the man's mind: *C'est impossible!*

Reaching the channel, the French boat lazily submerged and was soon out of sight.

Over the next few hours, most of our crew trickled ashore. Some chose to remain on board to stabilize the damage, or perhaps because they were trapped and didn't really care. The Blackpudlians probably stayed because they pre-

ferred it that way. Since they could not drown, they simply
went down with the ship and waited for it to settle before
finding a dry compartment in which to practice four-part
harmonies.

Phil Tran was one of the first to appear, looking like
a drowned rat as he slogged up the riverbank. Giving me a
dripping salute, he said, "Lieutenant Tran reporting for
duty, Lulu."

"At ease, Phil," I said. "What happened down there?"

"I picked up a radio transmission coming from the French
boat. We went to battle stations, but they were already lined
up for a shot. It was point-blank: We took two torpedoes
below the waterline. The second one breached the pressure
hull and flooded the missile compartment. She's totally
swamped."

"What now?"

"Well, the enemy seems to have gone, so we have two
choices. We can either ditch the boat or try to salvage it. It's
going to be a big job patching those holes and pumping her
out, but everything we need is right here. And there's another thing . . ."

"What?"

"We actually traced *two* radio transmissions. One was
coming from the French sub—that was the control signal
for the robot. The other was the same ULF signature we
detected off the coast. Xanadu."

"Were you able to pinpoint it?"

"Yes. It's coming from somewhere north of here, say
two hundred miles away. Right in the vicinity of Washington, DC."

The crew went to work. Needing neither rest nor diving
equipment, they scavenged welding equipment from the
Navy yard and quickly sealed the largest holes in the hull.
The job was made easier thanks to the hull plates that had
been conveniently cut from the dry-docked ship.

Once the flooded compartment was airtight, they rigged

up every pump they could find (including a fireboat's water cannon) to drain it. In less than a week, the enormous chamber was sucked dry. But it was a mess. Floating the sub was one thing; making it work was another. Once again, they were able to find much of what they needed in the spare boomer. What they couldn't find, they made, using the steel-milling equipment on base. For some of the men, former shipyard workers, it was almost like old times. All they still needed were some fuel rods to replace the ones that had been damaged, but Mr. Fisk knew of a power reactor up the Chesapeake that was likely to be intact.

"All right," I said. "We need transportation. Everybody spread out and find us a ride. Meet back here in fifteen minutes."

Without a word, we scattered, reconnoitering the base. When we regrouped, it was Julian Noteiro who delivered the report. He had found three vehicles, he said, a convoy capable of carrying the entire party. One was an eighteen-wheel moving van with the word MAYFLOWER on its side; the other two were charter buses. All three needed work to get them running, but our engineers were equal to the task, and in short order we were on board and en route to Washington, DC.

# PART IV
# Xanadu

# CHAPTER **TWENTY-ONE**

## BIG ENTRANCE

"**H**urry up, come on!" Fran had yelled, as Todd and Ray clambered in the rear of the ambulance.

Ray shouted, "We're in, go!"

The truck leaped into gear, making a hard left turn and tossing them around. Todd said, "Well, that was convenient."

"Sit back and leave the driving to us!" Sandoval tossed back a salute.

"How do we get out of here?" Fran asked, quailing as they approached a traffic barrier at high speed—a phalanx of plastic water drums.

Sandoval answered by stomping the accelerator to the floor. As the passengers held tight, the ambulance rammed straight into the drums, bouncing them across the deserted intersection.

Squawking like a radio announcer, Sandoval said, *"Empty water drums—brought to you by your good friends at Slave Labor, Inc. If it's a shitty job, it's gotta be Slave Labor!"*

Keeping up the momentum, he charged over sidewalks and across parking lots, using a GPS device to avoid blocked streets as he raced out of the city. Clearly, the whole route had been painstakingly mapped out ahead of time. James Sandoval didn't leave room for errors.

"What about your people back there?" Ray asked.

Sandoval said, "My crew have been slipping away for the past week, and the few that are left are taking full advantage of this diversion. Don't worry about them; they know how to take care of themselves. We'll all meet later at the rendezvous point."

"What about the Apostle?" Deena asked.

"He's just been cannonized."

Straining up the steep grade of College Hill, Sandoval illegally took the bus tunnel through to the East Side, then hurtled down back streets of formerly expensive residential neighborhoods, swerving around abandoned cars as he crossed a bridge over the Seekonk River. On the other side, he turned left through an oil storage depot and, a moment later, pulled to a stop in a deserted boatyard.

In an ordinary summer, this lot served a small fleet of pleasure craft; now there was only one. Moored at the end of the dock was a striking three-masted yacht. The sight of it almost made Sandoval's four passengers weep with relief.

Picking up the CB microphone, he said, "I'm here, Chandra." There was no reply. "Chandra?"

"What's wrong?" Ray asked.

"Probably nothing. Stay here."

Sandoval got out of the vehicle, taking a shotgun and leaving the engine on. They watched as he walked to the dock ramp, scanning every corner. The whole area appeared to be deserted. Good.

The yacht looked untouched. It was a hell of a thing: a custom-built sixty-foot sloop, lacquered gloss black, with teak decking and ribbed orange sails like dragon's wings. It resembled a futuristic Chinese junk. The elegantly scrolled name on the stern was *La Fantasma*. Ray knew this boat inside and out, having spent the previous summer working on board, transporting it from Sandoval's estate in Venezuela across the Caribbean, then all the way up the East Coast along the Intracoastal Waterway.

Sandoval studied the yacht for another few seconds, then

started down the ramp to the dock. When he reached the middle, cut off from all help, the trap was sprung.

There was a diesel roar, and a huge riot vehicle crashed through the doors of the boathouse and blocked the road. At the same time, dozens of Adamites leaped out of hiding places in the overgrown brush, brandishing automatic weapons and surrounding the ambulance. But they kept their distance, obviously well aware of the girls' explosive vests.

The Apostle Chace appeared.

He rose like a phantom from inside the yacht. It was a deliberately big entrance; he knew he was resplendently silly in his Holy Roman Emperor regalia, replete with towering hat and gold scepter, flanked by hooded bodyguards. But the little folk so adored these exorbitant displays, and Chace was nothing if not a people-pleaser. Savoring the moment, he grandly descended a plank to the dock.

To Sandoval, he said gravely, "*Et tu*, Jimbo? I knew you had to be the ringleader."

"And you the ringmaster."

Addressing the witnesses, Chace said, "Well, as you all can see, it looks like we've had a serpent in our midst, a liar and an imposter! Our friend and ally the Prophet is not what he pretended to be—not a friend, not an ally, and not a prophet. In fact, he isn't a holy man at all, but an *un*holy one! And here he is! Brothers, I'd like you to meet the little man who caused this big fraud: James Sandoval!"

The soldiers erupted in furious boos and catcalls.

"Who is he, you may wonder, and how did he pull the wool over our eyes for so long? I was fooled, too, I admit it! Well, look at him! So aristocratic, so smooth. But we shouldn't be surprised. Satan is a master of deception. That's his MO; he's a scam artist who will masquerade as our fondest desire, tempt us with false idols and false hopes, then stab us in the back. But in the end, liars will always be found out. Even the King of Lies will be exposed. Suffer

not these false prophets, these she-males and Elvis imper-
sonators. Let us drive them into the light of Heavenly justice, just as Christ drove the demon pigs off a cliff!"

Opening a parchment scroll, Dixon put on a pair of reading glasses and declaimed, "James Sandoval, you are all
hereby charged with blasphemy, heresy, and conspiring
against all the Angels, Prophets, and Living Saints, in the
person of Their chosen representative on Earth!"

Sandoval laughed. "You mean you?"

"I am now Prophet and Apostle rolled into one. How
plead ye to these charges?"

"*Ye?* Come on, ye can't be serious."

"Oh, the charges are extremely serious."

"Well, I don't acknowledge your authority, Torquemada.
Go stick that in your hat."

Delightedly, Chace cried, "Guilty! Did you hear that?
Did you all hear that? The accused has freely confessed that
he denies the True Prophet! By rejecting the Apostle of
Adam, he rejects Adam's Word!"

"Adam doesn't give a damn about you," Sandoval said,
"and neither do I."

"Guilty! To deny the authority of Lord Adam's appointed
vassal is to deny Adam Himself, and to deny Adam is to
deny Our Heavenly Father."

"You know what? I'm not really religious, but I seriously
doubt that God needs any help from a bug like you."

"Guilty! The accused admits to opposing Our Lord and
Savior. 'Not really religious,' he says, which is the same
thing as saying he is irreligious, *anti*religious! There is no
middle ground—the Lord accepts no compromise! Therefore, it becomes our solemn duty to save this man from
eternal suffering. To scourge his physical body that he may
repent and be saved."

The guards seized Sandoval and forced him to his knees.
Striking a dramatic pose, Chace cried, "O Heaven bestow
thy Flaming Rod, to smite the Foe of Man . . . and God!"

Chace raised his scepter. It was made from an electric cattle prod: a forked steel bar wrapped in kerosene-soaked rags, with a copper core and an insulated handle. When he flicked the switch, a blue-white spark bounced between the poles, igniting the rod in a wreath of yellow flame. At night the effect was quite spectacular. He swooshed it back and forth a few times for good measure.

"Now, Heathen," he said ominously. "Tremble before the Mighty Scourge of Heaven!"

Sandoval's defiant face twisted away from the burning staff.

That's when the ambulance came to life, popping into gear and lurching forward. Several disciples barely had time to leap aside as the vehicle charged. Gathering force, it smashed through the dockside railing and shot out over the water, landing hard. The hood buckled, and the windshield caved in. In seconds it sank out of sight. No one emerged.

"What the hell was that all about?" Chace asked.

"I think you just lost all your Immunes, buddy."

Dixon's eyes widened with comprehension, then hardened. "That's okay. That's okay. All it means is we have to speed up our train schedule. We have enough doses left for a couple of weeks, and I'm pretty sure there'll be no shortage of Immunes once we get to Xanadu. I'm not worried."

"You should be. Those people will defend themselves, and you're not immune against them."

"They won't be expecting us. We're the Peace Train! We'll come tooting in there like Thomas the Tank Engine, and they'll never know what hit them. The only ones left when it's over will be the Immunes."

"Then I guess you have nothing to worry about."

"You got that right, Jim. But you do." He raised the sizzling torch. "You definitely do."

"I guess I'm caught in a trap," Sandoval said.

"Yes, you are."

"I can't walk out."

"No, you can't."

"You want to know why?"

"Why?"

Out of nowhere, there was a blast of amplified music, and a booming voice sang, "BECAUSE I LOVE YOU TOO MUCH, BABYYYY."

Chace jumped in surprise, craning his neck to find the source. "What the *hell*?"

It was coming from the top of a giant oil tank. There were people up there, a whole rock band. The soldiers hurriedly fell back to see better.

"What is that?" Chace demanded.

Awestruck, one of his men said, "It's the King."

# CHAPTER **TWENTY-TWO**

## FREE CONCERT

The singer's face was partially obscured behind large sunglasses and a glossy black forelock, but the weirdness of that familiar husky voice jerked the heartstrings of all below, as though they were hearing a voice from a tomb. He wore a white suit with bell-bottom pants and a silver-ornamented jacket with an upturned collar. He was frozen in a running stance, only his leg jerking to the drumbeat, and on either side of him were rows of disco-dressed Xombies, all matching his moves with perfect precision.

"No it isn't," Chace said with dawning wonder, climbing the dock ramp. "It's *Miska*."

A series of small pyrotechnic explosions went off, raining showers of cool sparks down on the troops, then the boatyard was filled with the sound of a Hammond organ and electric guitars . . . and suddenly Elvis was moving! He was singing and dancing! The guards started cheering uncontrollably as the long-deceased King rocked above them, his pelvis thrusting and his sexy undead dancers thrusting in sync. The song resumed in an explosion of energy. It was deafening, booming down from a dozen speakers: a command performance of the Elvis classic "Suspicious Minds." And it was beautiful.

Resistance collapsed before this surprise live appearance by one of the greatest entertainers of all time perform-

ing one of his greatest hits. It was insane. It was impossible.
Yet it was *good*. Hardened warriors who hadn't felt such
joy in years gave in to the pure bliss of the moment, grinning uncontrollably as they rocked to the beat and sang
along with the choruses. When the song ended, wild applause broke out, men whistling and howling for an encore.
The ovation was deafening, causing Dixon to shake his
head in wonder.

Elvis called out, "Thank you very much!" then vanished
from the roof. The Xombies scattered with him, abandon-
ing their instruments and costumes like a squad of polter-
geists. Suddenly, it was very quiet.

Gathering his wits, Chace said, "Son of a bitch, my rod's
gone out."

He turned around to deal with Sandoval, but Sandoval
was gone. As Chace's eyes traced the only path the man
could have taken, he was blinded by the sun glaring off the
water . . . a glare that had not been there before. Something
else was missing. His mouth dropped open as he realized
the cheap magician's trick that the Devil had just played
on him.

The yacht had disappeared.


As the EMT vehicle sank, freezing water had galvanized its
stunned passengers to action—air bags or not, that crash
had *hurt*. Trading breaths from an oxygen mask, they waited
until the ambulance was completely flooded, then Ray led
them out the broken windshield. He was a good swimmer,
a champion in summer camp, but the water back then was
never so cold.

Surfacing their heads in the narrow space under the
dock, they could hear loud music starting above.

Ray said, "Okay, this is it—wish me luck."

"Fuck luck," Todd said. "Just hurry, dude, I'm freezing."

Working his way to the end of the dock, Ray took a last

deep breath, then ducked below and swam under the yacht. Its draft was quite shallow for such a large boat, designed for scuba trips on Caribbean reefs. Knowing he was taking a dangerous gamble, he felt his way along the keel to the dive well, praying the external hull panel was still off.

The panel was to cut drag when under sail, but in port it was left open as a convenient latrine for the carpenters since there was no other working toilet. As beautiful as *La Fantasma* looked from the outside, the vessel's interior was still all raw plywood, its planned refurbishing postponed indefinitely by the long work holiday of Agent X.

The dive well was open, a mirrored square under the hull. Crashing his reflection, Ray came up in the dim green light of the well, gasping for air. He was shivering uncontrollably, his nose dripping blood. It was so cold he could see his breath. The second door was just above his head, a watertight hatch into the main hold. It, too, was open. Barely able to feel his extremities, Ray cautiously climbed the ladder and peered above the raised rim. Immediately, he realized there was trouble.

To his left, through the doorway of the galley compartment, he could see a woman's legs—presumably the legs of Sandoval's associate, Chandra Stevens. Her legs were awkwardly splayed as if she were unconscious or dead. There were signs of a struggle and food ransacked from the storage bins. To Ray's right rose the aft companionway, at the top of which were two heavily armed men staring out the portside window. There were many more weapons lying loose all over the cabin: shotguns, pistols, machine guns, rocket launchers, grenades, and multiple cases of ammunition.

Too cold to wait, Ray grabbed a loaded revolver, and said, "P-p-put down your g-guns or I'll shoot."

One of the men spun with his shotgun, and Ray surprised himself by firing first. It was loud and quick: the bullet struck the man in the chest, and he tumbled down the stairs. The second man froze and set down his gun.

"Whoa, whoa," he said. "We're cool, baby, we're cool. Damn, did you just *swim* up in here?"

"What did you assholes do to her?" Ray demanded.

"The doctor lady? Nothing, I swear! She hurt herself resisting so hard—hurt us, too. But we weren't about to kill her; she's too valuable to lose. We just wanted to throw in with y'all since we could obviously use each other's help. Chace is gonna make this his personal flagship, and he needs an experienced crew. I'm Brother Lake Snyder, and that poor bastard was Father Frederick Arnott. But it don't matter now—what matters is obviously you're somebody who can get shit done. We need people like you for the big march on Washington."

Barely listening, Ray knew something had to be done fast, or the people under the dock were going to die of hypothermia. He said, "Okay, take all your weapons off, all of them. You're going for a swim."

"Are you crazy? I can't swim!"

"Do it! Do it now!" He stepped aside to give the man room.

Lake Snyder wavered, then disgustedly shed his arsenal and peered into the green light of the well. "This is ridiculous."

"Get in there, or I'll shoot you!"

"No you won't," said the dead man from the floor.

Turning, Ray felt something hard strike him behind the knees, causing a bright flash of agony. Going down, he thought, *Dummy.* As the men seized and disarmed him, he could see that the man he thought he had killed was wearing a bulletproof vest. Just playing dead—of course.

"You got him, man!" whooped Brother Snyder.

Just as he said this, a woman's face rose out of the dive well behind him. It was one of the Immunes, the one named Fran. Her lips blue with cold, her long hair stringy as wet seaweed, she held the oxygen tank from the ambulance, and

before either man could react, she brought it down like a
sledgehammer on Lake Snyder's head.

"Shit!" cried Father Arnott. He went for his gun, but Ray
kicked him in the face and fought him for it. It was a short
fight: the older man was much bigger and stronger, an experienced warrior, while Ray was just a skinny kid who liked
to dance. As the man broke Ray's grip and knocked him
over, there was a loud bang, and Father Arnott toppled to the
deck with a hole in his head.

"Gotcha," Sandoval said from the top of the stairs.

"What's going on?" Ray asked.

"I just cast us off. We're drifting out with the tide, and in
a minute I'm going to fire up the engines."

"How? Where's Chace?"

"Chace decided to stick around for the encore."

Deena and Todd emerged from the dive well, both shivering uncontrollably. Ray closed the hatch behind them, dog-
ging it tight, then he went to see about Chandra Stevens. He
knew her only slightly as one of Sandoval's many science
connections, along with Alice Langhorne and Uri Miska. In
the aftermath of Agent X, they were a very select group.

Propped in a corner, the gray-haired woman was conscious, her eyes trying to focus. When Ray reached for her
face, she twisted away, moaning.

"Relax, it's okay, I'm just taking the duct tape off your
mouth."

She went limp, nodding.

As gently as possible, he peeled the tape off, and said,
"I'm just going to untie you, okay? Hold still."

"Who are you?"

"A friend. I'm here with Jim Sandoval."

"Jim's here?"

"Yes."

She relaxed and closed her eyes as the engine rumbled
to life.

# CHAPTER **TWENTY-THREE**

## SAILING

Ray Despineau awoke to the smell of coffee. For a long time he just stayed in his bunk, enjoying the thumping motion of the waves, his bleary eyes scanning the familiar bookshelf.

Lots of sailing books: knot tying, navigation, and other basic seamanship. A few old-timey sea stories: *Treasure Island*, *Two Years Before the Mast*, *The Sea-Wolf*, Melville's *White-Jacket* and *Typee*. He had read them all.

He felt pretty good, though his memory of recent events was sketchy. Even not-so-recent events: In the first few minutes of waking, he forgot everything that had happened since New Year's Eve. He blanked out the entire Xombie Apocalypse and imagined he must be aboard Sandoval's boat for a pleasure cruise, perhaps to Bermuda. That would be awesome. Flashes of something unspeakably hideous kept poking through the calm, but he refused to think about it.

He heard snoring from the lower berth and leaned over to see who it was. It was a familiar face, the face of a friend, yet also a face that had no business in that boat. A face that instantly evoked everything they had lived through together for the past six months. Todd Holmes. Todd's ratty, scorched dreadlocks told the whole tale.

* * *

Ray remembered.

He got up and boosted himself out the forward hatch.

It was a beautiful summer day, breezy and cool, with the sun mounted like a diamond in the satin blue sky. Just a hint of chop—it was a crime not to let the spinnaker out. He did so, and the boat leaped forward, heeling steeply as it bounced over the swells.

Jim Sandoval hastily appeared from below, looking weary and overcaffeinated. He had rigged up the auto tiller so he didn't have to man the helm every second. The device was basically a hydraulic piston connected to a GPS, a robot arm that steered the boat in a fixed direction by constantly making small course corrections. But it still required someone to constantly stand watch.

"You're awake," Sandoval said, relieved.

"Yeah, I'm sorry I slept so long. How long was I out?"

"Almost twenty-four hours. I guess you had some catching up to do. We passed New York and New Jersey during the night—you would've thought it was the coast of Borneo. No, Borneo would have more lights. I figured as long as the weather's holding up, we might as well blow past the big metroplex, just to avoid any more refugee situations. We should be around Maryland now."

"Jeez, you should have woken me up so I could take a turn standing watch."

"I know, but you were so zonked out, I didn't have the heart to wake you. Chandra and Fran have been sharing the duty so you guys could sleep."

"Have you seen any other boats?"

"No. We've been staying out of sight of land as much as possible."

"Right . . . definitely." Ray still vividly remembered the sick feeling of being approached by boatloads of desperate refugees while the submarine had sat at anchor. It was not something he ever wanted to repeat.

A surprising number of people had initially survived the plague by taking to the water, but a month in they were all dying of hunger and thirst. Many of the boys camped on the sub's deck wanted to offer what little help they could, but the Navy crewmen were adamant about not letting outsiders anywhere near the boat. Warning shots were fired, leading to a brief gunfight in which the sub crew's superior fire-power and marksmanship quickly knocked out the smaller boat's wheelhouse. Ray would never forget the terrible sight of Xombies running amok aboard that rudderless refugee ship.

*La Fantasma* had quite an arsenal on board, including automatic weapons, long-range sniper rifles, and shoulder-fired missiles. Sandoval had made sure the yacht was well equipped to defend itself. No question the man was a survivor, and an arrogant son of a bitch, but Ray had never been more grateful to have him around.

Sandoval said, "Speaking of which, I'm not sure that spinnaker's such a hot idea. It's a bit . . . grandiose. We don't want to give anybody any ideas."

"Sorry, I'll crank it in."

"No, you may as well leave it up now. We're almost there. How are you feeling?"

"Fine, I think. You look like you could use some sleep. Why don't you crash for a while and let me stand watch?"

"Gladly, but first there's something I need to talk to you about." Sandoval took a small aerosol can out of his coat pocket. "I need a shot of this stuff about every twelve hours, or I'll turn back into a Xombie."

*"What?"*

"It's no big deal. I'm only telling you so you don't let me oversleep and miss a dose. I administered the last one about seven hours ago, so you have to wake me at noon."

"What is it?"

"Just a little pick-me-up. Why do you think Xombies won't touch us? How do you think I came back from the undead? It's because every day we all have a special cocktail—a little Bloody Mary, made with real blood! Immune plasma, that is. It's the simplest kind of oral vaccine: in your case, just a matter of mixing a tiny amount with any beverage, about one part plasma per thirty thousand parts juice or water, however you prefer your sangria."

"That's disgusting."

"It's not as if you can taste it or anything. You've been drinking it all along."

"Oh my God," Ray said. "Are you serious? You turned into a Xombie and back? How?"

"I told you. It's an experimental treatment they're working on at Xanadu."

"What exactly is this Xanadu?"

"It's a private research station in Washington, DC, administered by an industrial consortium that took over the remains of the Mogul Cooperative. They've come up with a method of artificially inducing Agent X in very sick patients."

"Why?"

"It's restorative. The Maenad morphocyte is like a miracle tonic—a real-life Fountain of Youth. The problem is, it starves the body of oxygen, which causes brain damage before the benefits have time to kick in. That's why Xombies are such maniacs. The trick is to actually speed up the rate of infection, and that's where this stuff comes in. Don't touch it! It's loaded with pure poison: two time-release capsules, one containing a cocktail of potassium cyanide and Agent X, the other a dose of antibodies from immune women. They release about five minutes apart. For faster recovery, pure oxygen can be added to purge the body of Agent X. But it's a little traumatic the first time, I gotta say."

Ray asked, "So how many of these Immunes are there?"

"Not many. Most of them were killed off during the hysteria of the Maenad Epidemic. But the ones that do exist are priceless—Xombies won't touch them. In fact, Maenads may actually *protect* them. I found three Immunes by bribing the Coast Guard to screen seaborne refugees for women of that age range. They were glad to hand them over. Chandra and I were trying to transfer them to Xanadu when Chace's men intercepted them. As far as I was concerned, we had no choice but to try to recover them. So I entered into a partnership arrangement with Chace, assuming the role of the Prophet.

"The fish story went that I was a decorated military chaplain who specialized in benedictions for right-wing extremist groups. On the day of the Maenad Epidemic, I graduated from lay priest to Archbishop, having been granted special dispensation to receive the *pallium*—my new insignia of office—from a provisional papal legate rather than from the Pope in Rome. This was easy to arrange through Mogul channels, since the Vatican was in some turmoil, and there were fire sales on high office of every kind, including the Pope. All such titles were up for grabs. Only brute force mattered, and as a charter member of MoCo, I could summon quite a bit.

"I found my soul mate in Apostle Chace, whose public battles against abortion, same-sex marriage, and naked statues were legend. The postapocalyptic truce we arranged between our separate faiths was a model of cooperation that surely guaranteed us both a place at the Lord's right hand."

"It was almost too easy," Sandoval said. "To these guys, everything's a sign from God; they've been expecting this for years."

"Oh, they knew this was coming? Because I wish someone had told me about it."

"Maybe they did, and you weren't listening."

"Now you're scaring me."

"What I mean to say is, I tried to warn you and your sister to get to the submarine plant by midnight. Why didn't you?"

Ray was so shocked it took him a second to speak. "We got hung up in traffic half the night. Maybe you could have tried sending the car a little earlier. Like about a week."

"I depended on you, Ray. And you let me down."

"How did I let *you* down? You let *us* down, you asshole! It's because of you my sister's dead! If you knew that was gonna happen, you could have made absolutely fucking sure we were at that plant. You could have just told us the truth!"

Sandoval nodded, squinting through tears. He cleared his throat. "I know. I'm sorry, Ray."

"Yeah, fuck you! *Fuck* you, man."

As the morning wore on, the wind picked up, sea and sky turning slate gray. Flurries of hail spattered the deck like rice. Everyone else was still asleep, and Ray was basking in the novelty of being alone on the ocean.

He was not a tremendously experienced solo sailor, having only crewed a few pleasure cruises in his life. His father was the real seaman, a lifelong Navy officer who had ultimately estranged himself from the Navy just as he estranged himself from Ray.

Both his parents were products of the postwar era, a fair-weather family who fled from Ray and each other at the time he needed them most. He pitied them their disappointed lives and wondered what had happened to them in the madness of Agent X. Not that he cared much.

Suddenly, Ray realized he was not alone—the immune girl Deena was peering at him from the companionway. "Hey," Ray said.

"Hey," said Deena.

"How are you? Feeling okay?" Ray still found it hard to

believe that Sandoval had not only freed all of them from the Soul Patrol's gulag but delivered them safely to this boat. And acted as though it was nothing unusual.

The girl said, "Your friend Todd is wicked seasick. He's in there throwing up."

"Ech—I'm sorry. You're okay, though?"

"I think so. I'm kind of hungry. Is there any food?"

"Yeah, it's stowed in the compartment under the main cabin. Actually, I'm starved, too. You think you could make us some lunch?"

"Sure, why not?"

"And something hot to drink, tea or coffee."

"Sure. Can I ask you something?"

"No, I'm afraid not."

"Oh . . ."

"I'm *kidding*. What?"

"In those clothes you look kind of . . . butch."

Ray laughed. "That's because I'm a dude."

"Oh. Sorry."

"Hey, I was out of uniform, how were you to know? And Deena?"

"Yeah?"

"I'm really sorry about your friend Ashleigh. I tried to save her."

"It wasn't your fault."

"I know, but still . . ."

She touched his arm. "Hey, man, Ashleigh had problems. After her sister died, she was never the same, so don't take it on yourself. There was nothing anyone could have done."

Ray broke down, and Deena comforted him. "Sorry," he said, pulling himself together. "It's just that I lost my sister, too. Now I really feel like an asshole."

"Join the club," she said. "Listen, I'm going to get us some food. Don't go anywhere."

"Funny. You're very humorous."

Deena was gone a long time. Ray wondered if the girl had blown him off, when she finally appeared with mugs of tea and hot soup, crackers spread with cheese and apple butter, sliced salami, and a selection of cookies and dried fruit.

"Wow, that's what I call service," Ray said. "Did you have any trouble doing all this with the boat rocking?"

"Not really."

As they ate, Chandra and Fran appeared, drawn from their bunks by the smell of soup.

"Nice!" said Chandra, squinting in the sun. "Lemme go make some sandwiches."

It became a picnic. Even Todd was able to take a bit of nourishment between bouts of vomiting. Sandoval remained dead asleep.

As noon rolled around, Ray went below to wake Sandoval. He was annoyed to see that a lot of the yacht's carefully stowed food supplies had been haphazardly unpacked and were now rolling around the cabin. Cans and bottles zigzagged underfoot like small loose cannons. Worst of all, there was a powerful stench of airplane glue—a can of waterproofing sealant had spilled all over the plywood deck.

Cursing, he cleaned up the mess as best he could. As he worked, he began to feel dizzy from the fumes but was determined to muddle through. The swaying of the boat didn't help. Having struggled as long as possible to ignore his rising nausea, he abruptly dropped everything and bolted for the fantail, puking his guts out. When he turned around, Sandoval was standing in the doorway, grinning like blue death.

*"Rayyyy,"* he breathed.

Trying to leap away, Ray was jerked back like a rag doll, pinned face-to-face with the black-eyed horror that had been James Sandoval.

*"Don't be afraid,"* he said. *"I've got you."*

Crushing Ray against the deck, the Xombie pried his resisting jaws apart, stretching its own mouth wide and clamp-

ing onto Ray's in a hellish antithesis of CPR—a kiss of
death. With one suck, he collapsed Ray's lungs. The boy
heaved, convulsing as his rib cage crumpled, then went limp.
Now the creature reversed the action, exhaling with all its
might, inverting its own bronchial tissue into Ray's airway
to flood the dead boy's chest with X-infected blood cells.

Ray died and was born again.

# CHAPTER **TWENTY-FOUR**

## STORM

Sprawled on the aft deck like a corpse, Ray woke up with a bang. His consciousness exploded as his dying brain cells were resurrected by the invading Maenad morphocyte. He was dazzled by the strangeness and beauty of his new world: the plywood cabin transformed into a fairy cave, the sea diamond-bright and seething with energy, the sky awash with ripples of cosmic light, the clouds glowing with ethereal colors. Even by daylight, he could see the invisible tracks of time and space, the ghostly orbits of particles and planets, the rings around the Sun. And amid all these long transits of inanimate matter, the futile blip of human consciousness.

He sprang to his feet.

Todd. Poor doomed Todd. Having just been there, Ray was overwhelmed with pity . . . and dawning comprehension. *Look at this,* he thought, feeling his broken body renew itself. It was nothing. Death was nothing, not anymore. Neither was pain, nor hunger, nor any other yearning of the flesh. He no longer had to tolerate the hopelessness of human existence; he had a choice, he could *do* something about it. Not just for Todd, but for all the miserable human beings still teetering on the brink of death. They didn't have to die! The dread that hung over every living creature could be vanquished. And with that realization came an electric rush of joy, an exultation born of equal parts love, lust, and evangelical ecstasy. He dove back inside to save his friend.

As if having read Ray's mind, the woman named Chandra Stevens was waiting, staring down at him in brazen invitation, her bright inner flame making her clothes a paper lantern. Unable to resist that warmth, Ray tried to speak, to make her understand, but his words came out garbled, a drunken slur. A noise an idiot might make . . . or an animal.

Disdaining the faulty instrument of speech, he leaped like a wild animal, embracing Chandra in a grip of steel and pressing her body against the forward bulkhead, bending her neck back nearly to breaking. She didn't resist, surrendering completely to the kiss, and it was only as Ray sucked the air from her lungs that he realized she had tricked him.

*No!*

The woman was full of pure oxygen, her blood and tissues saturated with it. She had breathed deep from an oxygen tank, hyperventilating like a free diver before descent, then took one last hit and held it. It was no experiment; she knew exactly what she was doing. Behind her, Sandoval's body lay splayed out in the forward compartment, another casualty of her medical expertise.

Ray tried to pull away, but the gas worked too fast, wilting his undead flesh from the inside out, turning his sentient blue-black blood instantly red. That red blood jump-started his heart and hit his brain like a runaway locomotive, knocking him instantly unconscious.


As Ray came back to life, he could hear people talking about him.

"Is there going to be any permanent brain damage?"

"Shouldn't be. We purged him before he was fully saturated. He was only dead a couple of minutes—that's not enough time for oxygen starvation to kill many brain cells."

"Oh my God. What's it like, being a Xombie?"

"It doesn't hurt."

"But don't you still—"

"Son, shut up! I'm already tense enough, all right? Whatever I am, I'm still me, no thanks to this dumb kid. If it weren't for Chandra's quick thinking, you'd all be screwed. Now, we don't have time for this; we have to batten everything down for that front that's coming."

"Yes, sir."

"And make sure you get your dosage. I don't want any more accidents."

"No, sir."

As the others left, Ray heard one remain behind. A soft voice spoke in his ear, "Please get better, Ray. For me." It was Deena.


The hurricane hit.

It was not a true hurricane, merely a minor gale, but none of them had ever been on a small ship in rough seas. Sandoval and Chandra Stevens were unflappable, pretending not to be alarmed by swells that suddenly rose higher than their heads, or by waves breaking over the entire boat, or by the deck heeling over so far it became a steep hill.

But Ray could tell that his elders weren't as confident as they pretended to be: the rabbity look in the Chandra's eyes when the yacht shuddered under tons of whitewater, or Sandoval's anxious silence as the boat struggled to right itself. Jim's green face scared Ray more than the storm itself.

It was impossible to venture above without admitting a deluge into the cabin. Everything belowdecks was awash, and the bilge pump barely kept up. All aboard were soaked to the skin, cold to the bone, dreaming about a hot drink or a hot meal. More than anything, Ray was desperate to go to the bathroom—number two—but the head was a plastic bucket that had to be dumped overboard—a difficult operation under the circumstances. There was no question of opening the dive well. He held it in as long as he could, sweating out the intestinal spasms as he tried to sleep, until finally it was time for his watch.

It was after midnight. The swells were so large that the boat swooped in and out of the canyonlike troughs without much pounding, but the rain and wind were still fierce. Before Sandoval had retired for the night, they had turned off the engine and deployed the sea anchor, so the yacht was dragging along like a small man leashed to a large, eager dog.

As stealthily as possible, Ray left the cockpit and climbed over the starboard rail. Crouching there, hanging on for dear life by one hand, he lowered his pants and jutted his rear end into space.

Before he could let fly, something broke the waves close behind him. Something huge—an enormous black monolith that parted the sea, jutting upward, spreading its wings and casting a blinding white eye upon his bare ass. It was a submarine.

*Aw, shit,* he thought.

# CHAPTER **TWENTY-FIVE**

## MR. DIXON GOES TO WASHINGTON

"This is it, sir! Welcome to Xanadu!"

Looking out the windows of the big helicopter, Air Force 2, James Sandoval could see thousands of people waiting to greet him. A giant banner read, WELCOME CHAIR-MAN SANDOVAL! Flags were flying, bands were playing, children were waving, and hundreds of soldiers stood lined up at attention. Those troops were wearing flamboyant parade uniforms with tall hats, tasseled epaulets, and rows of gold buttons. Their rifles looked like toys.

"Where did all those people come from?" Sandoval asked.

"They're mostly new converts," said his pilot, a jolly Marine aviator named Hapgood Bragg.

"You mean converted Xombies?"

"That's right."

"But they look so . . . normal."

"Of course! We've streamlined the conditioning process. Otherwise, there would be no point."

The helicopter was set down gently, and men came running with a rolling stair platform. At the edge of the landing pad was a group of dignitaries covered with medals and other decorations, the tallest one holding a giant gold key, and a line of women in flowing pastel gowns holding necklaces of flowers. Everyone had formal gloves, cravats, canes, top hats, and other such anachronistic finery, all blowing violently in the helicopter's downdraft. It was ridiculous.

"What is this, the inauguration of Grover Cleveland?"

Sandoval stepped from the chopper as if testing a hot bath, and was immediately swarmed with greeters. One of them was a man he had been told to expect: Kasim Bendis, the mercenary soldier known as Uncle Spam, who had advised the Reapers and was blown to smithereens while hunting Uri Miska. Sandoval had heard that Bendis arrived in Washington a shambling Xombie, little more than a blasted carcass, but clearly that report was old news. The man was completely intact again, a gentleman warrior in full command of his faculties as well as his brigade. He had also jumped several ranks, from major to major general.

"Welcome to Xanadu, Mr. Sandoval," Bendis said.

"Thank you, Kasim. Congratulations on your promotion."

"Yes, sir. Same to you."

Sandoval and Bendis went way back. Long before Agent X, they and Chace Dixon had founded a private security firm that in the heat of 9/11 netted a billion-dollar contract to provide force protection for the U.S. military . . . among other things. Sandoval was the silent partner, supplying capital and global connections, Bendis brought the military expertise, and Chace Dixon handled PR. They called it the Charm School, and it included a Christian men's retreat, a church, a survival-training camp, an airfield, and a weapons range frequented by individuals who did not like to be photographed. The Charm School worked closely with various intelligence agencies as an unofficial recruiting center, just as the seminary recruited from the ranks of ex-servicemen. It was a useful symbiosis, because the seminary was a place in which men were trained to submit their will to God, but it was hardly a place of passive worship. In Chace Dixon's opinion, the assault on traditional values had begun long before Agent X, and men like these had been preparing all their lives to fight it. The Apocalypse came as no surprise to them. Accustomed to railing against government-funded birth control, legal abortion, illegal immigrants, and the election of a socialist, foreign-born Muslim for president, they were amazed it took so long. Yet even as Dixon's wildest convictions were borne out, most of his men hadn't known how to deal with it. With Xombies swarming the country, the Charm School fell into serious disarray, two thousand hard-ass holy warriors holed up like scared rabbits at their training camp. Believing the Second Coming was really upon them, they went to pieces, some disappearing into the chaos, others throwing their weapons down and devoting their final hours to prayer. They would have died that way, on their knees, if not for Kasim Bendis rallying them to action. It was Bendis who founded the Holy Avengers of Adam—the Adamites. He even came up with their slogan: "Give Me Back My Rib." Then he was immediately dispatched south to mobilize an army of prison convicts— the Reapers.

Bendis presented Sandoval with the key to the city, a marching band struck up "My Country 'Tis of Thee," and together they ventured outside to a tremendous ovation.

Emerging on the green of the Ellipse, near the Zero Milestone, Sandoval was spellbound. The city of Washington was apparently intact, and then some; in fact, it seemed to have reverted to an earlier, more genteel time. There was no automobile traffic, only the quaint sight of electric trolleys, horse-drawn carriages, and bicycle rickshaws ferrying loads of well-dressed burghers about the National Mall.

Strolling onto the grass with Bendis and an entourage of city officials, Sandoval was led to the base of the Washington Monument, which had been turned into an immense hood ornament, a winged colossus representing the First Man. The statue was a framework of iron bars with gas flames burning in its eyes. In its shadow was a tent big enough for a three-ring circus, full of lights, chairs, and buffet-laden tables, where Sandoval was subjected to dozens of toasts and many pious expressions of grace. He joined the toasts but didn't touch the food or drink, blaming a bout of stomach flu. Afterward, he was taken on an all-day tour of the city, culminating in a parade in his honor.

The parade floats were unusual, with sponsors like EX-IT and RED-IT, both appearing to be aerosol deodorants, and there were dancers, jugglers, acrobats, soldiers, and more marching bands, each group flying the flag of Xanadu: a big blue X on a red background with white stars in the blue.

Sandoval asked, "What's Red-It? Looks like some kind of energy drink."

"You might say that. It's what makes all this possible. It's what our whole economy is based on. I believe you in Providence call it the Sacrament. It's simply immune serum in a convenient aerosol form. We have commercialized it a bit more, but it's still the same basic thing. Soon we will begin large-scale exports, and the Xombie problem will be eliminated worldwide."

"Do you plan to give it away free?"

This caused a great eruption of hilarity from all in earshot. People crying with laughter.

Annoyed, Sandoval asked, "Then what's Ex-It?"

"Ah. Now, Ex-It is something we're all very excited about, a time-release cocktail combining the immune factor with an oxygen inhibitor and a specialized strain of the Maenad agent. With that one treatment, we can essentially reboot your body's entire DNA structure in minutes, wiping out a lifetime of accreted cell damage, as well as any disease or injury. Everything is restored to mint condition, meaning that whatever age you are, you are now functionally back to zero, so you get a whole new lifetime. And you can use it again and again! But you already know all this, don't you, Jim? I happen to know you're a major investor in our wonderful products, as well as a customer."

"Yes. Yes, of course. Just making sure you all love the product as much as I do."

"Oh, we do, believe me! Disease and death are things of the past in Xanadu, as are the personality clashes that have led to strife in all other human societies. Ex-It screens out more than ninety percent of subconscious stress factors, all that personal baggage we carry around from childhood, leading to a more homogeneous, receptive personality type. Man will finally be able to rise to his full potential."

"And woman," said Sandoval.

"And woman, of course."

Last stop was the White House.

The White House glowed like a lamp in the settling dark, a civilized beacon of chilled air and electric light. Sandoval's party was led inside and down a carpeted hallway, past elegant sitting rooms full of busts and portraits of former presidents, then through suites of offices. At last they were shown into a room filled with TV cameras and lights, where a man in a suit and tie sat at a table signing papers. No one failed to recognized both the man and the room in which he sat. It was the Oval Office.

"Oh my God," Sandoval muttered.

Alarmed, Bendis said, "What?"

"It's the president!"

"Oh, yes. Quite dignified, isn't he?"

"I saw him shoot himself in the head. During an emergency bulletin."

"Now, Mr. Sandoval. None of the best presidents ever needed a brain, just a signing pen."

Jim Sandoval approached the president's desk. There were several imposing-looking Secret Service agents standing by, but none attempted to stop him or indeed took any notice at all. A bucket brigade of elderly men was busily grabbing papers from an enormous stack, stamping them with the date, passing them to the president to sign, then crimping them with an official seal before piling them onto an even more enormous stack. Carts full of such documents rolled in and out. TV cameras monitored the proceedings.

Sandoval walked behind the president's desk and peered over the man's shoulder as he was handed a document. It was titled, *Amendment to Federal Antitrust Act—Mogul Clause 3381C*. Without reading it, the president automatically scrawled a large X and handed it off. Immediately, another document hit the desk, something about a Mogul bill to reinstate the Articles of Confederation, essentially abolishing all taxes. The president mimed signing those, too, then the next and the next and the next, just like an assembly line.

So this was it, Sandoval realized. All these resurrected Moguls were rewriting bills for the president to sign. The man was a drone—like all the other drones here. They were converted Xombies, brainless ghouls resurrected and trained like monkeys to sign MoCo's wish list into law. The White House had become a factory for rewriting history, manipulating the future by deleting the past. A giant propaganda organ. The dead president was just a puppet, making America safe for permanent Mogul domination.

As they left, Sandoval asked, "Mr. Bendis, who's in charge of all this? You?"

Bendis grinned, suddenly resembling the death's-head he had so recently been. "Oh no, Mr. Chairman."

"Then who is?"

"No one. That's the *point*."

The big ceremony took place that evening, in front of the Lincoln Memorial.

There were tens of thousands of spectators, all of them new converts. The packed field of West Potomac Park was solemn as a cathedral, lit by bonfires that resembled votive candles on a crowded altar. Atop the memorial's promontory, two flatbed trailers were planked over to make a platform for the prisoner.

As Sandoval and his party watched from their places of honor by the stage, a man was led up there, bound, blindfolded, gagged, and chained at the wrists and ankles. It was Chace Dixon. He was remarkably calm, as if expecting nothing other than what he was getting.

The guard pulling Dixon wore a black hood that made him look like a medieval executioner. Once the prisoner was secured to a steel post, the guard removed his blindfolds and gags so Dixon could see the mob staring back at him.

Kasim Bendis climbed the stage to swelling applause. "Good evening, citizens of Xanadu," he said. "We are here tonight to honor James Bernard Sandoval, whose warning of the imminent threat posed by agents of intolerance and discord allowed us to prevent what surely would have been a catastrophic attack on our fair city. Let us put our hands together for this hero of our people. Thank you, Jim!"

Bowing to the cheers, Sandoval stood up and went to the podium. "All of you know now of the dangers you face. The immediate threat is gone, but the hidden danger remains, and lurks right here among you. It is up to every one of you to stop the Moguls from enslaving the human race just to gratify their lust for power. They have destroyed human civilization in their quest for ultimate control of life and death, and now they want to replace it with a society of mindless, groveling serfs. I know the Moguls because I was a Mogul, and all they are interested in is total dominion. They don't want to worship God, they want to be worshipped *as* gods! You must not abet them in this!"

The crowd was silent.

Dixon stood up out of his chains, and asked Kasim Bendis, "May I?"

"Please," said Bendis.

It was an elaborate trap. Sandoval was suddenly very conscious of gun muzzles pressed into his back. Chace Dixon addressed the assembly:

"Jim Sandoval, everyone," he quipped, applauding tepidly. "Jim, this little speech has been interesting, but all of us here have worked too hard and sacrificed too much to stop what we've begun. Just because it doesn't meet your high moral standards? This from a man who betrayed his sacred oath and sold out his brethren? I don't think so. These fine people won't allow it. God won't allow it. *I* won't allow it.

"No, we are going back to the old ways, the good old days, when men were men and women knew their proper place as child-bearers, guardians of home and hearth. Think of Genesis. Was it an accident that Agent X struck women first, and that they spread it to men? Was it an accident that most of the men who survived were in protected hideaways that traditionally shunned women? Official police and military forces were gone; no coed organization on Earth survived Sadie Hawkins Day, a clear signal that God is done with Political Correctness. What you so disparagingly call the Moguls are merely the protectors of ancient tradition, a tradition which is the very foundation of Western Civilization. Xanadu represents a New Genesis. Though we love and honor women, we must never again allow Satan to convince us that the sexes are equal. Equal Rights are off the table; to quote the immortal James Brown, it's a man's world.

"Until recently, we had limited success contacting the South, likely due to the warmer weather conditions—the extreme winter of the Northeast was a big help in suppressing Hellion activity. This 'chill factor' was yet another sign of God's favor. Now, of course, I only wish we had known sooner what you folks had going down here.

"It is a historic day. We stand today on green grass, but it has been no picnic. It was war—the bitterest test of our faith. Let history never forget the battles we fought and lost before we achieved Grace. Clearly, normal rules of combat don't apply to demons, so we tried other means, faith-based means, such as prayer and exorcism . . . and burning. The scientists, of course, had other ideas. Early in the outbreak, they discovered that pure oxygen had a limited effect on Agent X, so a great deal of time and energy was wasted on that. But without a constant supply it was worse than useless, inspiring nothing but false hope since there wasn't enough available to treat the billions of Hellions roaming the Earth. So much for science!

"In the end, the answer came from the unlikeliest of places: Women. The root of all evil turned out to be the source of our salvation. Yes, we must never forget that women not only cursed us but also saved us . . . and in so doing saved themselves. Pious women admitted their guilt, accepted their *responsibility*, and for this act of holy contrition, they earned God's blessing upon us all. He bestowed upon us the Immunes, and thus we were able to again walk fearlessly upon the land. All is finally going as the good Lord intended."

"Jesus Christ," Sandoval said.

"Guilty! Blasphemer, I pronounce you guilty as charged." Pointing his finger at Sandoval, he bellowed, "Guilty, guilty, guilty, guilty!"

*"I'll be the judge of that,"* said a muffled voice.

It was the masked guard who had led Dixon up there. He pulled off his hood, revealing an intense, bearded face . . . and a crown of thorns. The spectators gasped, then fell absolutely silent. The wind ruffled his hair.

After an initial start, Dixon seethed. "Who are you? Who is this man?"

"Don't you know me, Chace?" asked the stranger. He was something out of a black velvet painting, with wavy brown curls and gold highlights in his beard. His eyes shone strangely bright, their whites luminous. Droplets of blood were visible on his brow.

"I know who you're pretending to be, but you're going to find we don't appreciate imposters, much less spies and vandals. Arrest this blasphemer!"

As guards warily approached from both sides, the

stranger held out his hands in mild supplication, revealing open wounds in both palms. The wounds were deep vertical slits, grisly but totally bloodless. Pinkish light shone through them.

The soldiers stopped as if hitting a wall, some dropping to their knees and others piling up behind in confusion.

"Somebody please just shoot him," Dixon beseeched, crossing to the opposite side of the stage. Kasim Bendis drew a pistol that had been used by Teddy Roosevelt to deliver the coup de grace to enemy soldiers on San Juan Hill. Bendis was a dead shot, and the bullets traversed the bearded stranger to strike the great statue of Lincoln just beyond. Lincoln didn't flinch . . . and neither did the stranger.

"Oh, ye of little faith," the man said, pulling open his robe to reveal his exposed, beating heart.

"It's a miracle!" someone cried.

"It's Him!" yelled someone else.

"Hallelujah! Praise Jesus!" The field echoed with men begging forgiveness, throwing down their weapons and falling on their faces, to weep and drool into the mud.

Impatiently, Dixon stalked across the stage and shoved his forked scepter into the stranger's side. The rod was adapted from an electric cattle prod. It was an effective crowd-control device, delivering a hundred thousand volts on contact.

There was a bright blue spark, and suddenly the stranger underwent a bizarre transformation. The flesh of his face rippled smooth, wiped of its features like a sandcastle in the surf. Eyes, nose, mouth, beard, thorns—all abruptly fluttered, dissolved, then changed into another face altogether, an old man's face, clean-shaven and angular, with deep-set eyes and a shock of silver hair. Dixon thought he looked like Jimmy Carter. His pierced hands also aged, their wounds miraculously healing shut.

Uncertain about what it meant, but feeling vindicated by

his own evident power, Dixon fired consecutive shocks from his staff, yelling, "Look! Look! He's a phony! A fake! He's possessed by demons—a wolf in sheep's clothing! Stop groveling like dogs and get him!"

With a loud *snap*, the power went out. Someone had pulled the plug. Before anyone could react, an ugly mutt ran out from under the stage and disappeared around the Memorial.

The crowd murmured in confusion. Even with his rod disconnected, Chace kept on jabbing until the stranger seized the weapon, and said, "Quit it." The holy visage re-asserted itself, wounds and all, smiling sadly upon the congregation. "Father forgive them, for they know not what they do."

"Shut up! I don't know who you are, but you're not going to get away with it!"

Dixon charged to tackle the stranger, confident in his im-munity. He wanted to humiliate him and prove him false. The thought of kowtowing to this soft-voiced hippie was unbearable; it was impossible, absolutely ridiculous, to think that this queer could be his Lord and Savior. Jesus—if He really existed—was a *man*. A man's man, who could bench-press three hundred pounds and pin Chace Dixon to the floor with His massively muscled thighs. *That* was a Jesus worth surrendering to.

The stranger did not flinch from the attack but met his attacker head-on, ducking beneath Chace's outstretched arms and flipping the bigger man over his back. Dixon was shocked—no Xombie should be able to touch him! But after the initial alarm, he realized he was pissed off. Dixon had been a championship wrestler in college and a dabbler in mixed martial arts, so he was not about to let himself go down without a fight. Lunging upward, he managed to lock arms around his prancing opponent's legs so that both men became halves of a human cartwheel, a rolling yin and yang that tumbled off the platform.

Landing hard, they came up fighting, each one gripping the other's shirt with one hand and furiously punching with the other. Locked together in a brutal tango, they grappled for advantage as the assembly watched in awe.

Shouts rang out: "Bust his face! Kick him in the balls! Hit him with a left, a left! Whup his ass!"

To break the stalemate, the fighters commenced kicking, trying to trip one another, but in spite of their size difference, they seemed evenly matched. Bendis hesitated to intervene without a direct command.

The stranger grunted, "Karma's a bitch, ain't it?"

"Who the hell are you?" Chace demanded.

"A man . . . a plan . . . a canal—Panama."

"Phony!" Dixon snarled.

"Hypocrite!"

"You're not the Savior!"

"Neither are you!"

"But I've been anointed by God!"

"Oh really? Then how come I can do *this*?" The stranger kneed Dixon in the groin. "Or *this*?" He head-butted him in the mouth, splitting Dixon's lower lip. The crowd went wild. "You know what I think?" the bearded stranger said. "I think you got a bad batch. I think you got some blood from a boy—a boy in drag."

"You shut up, shut up! Shut your filthy mouth!"

Crazed with anger, Dixon delivered a knockout punch, a hard uppercut that coldcocked his opponent. The newcomer went down like a ton of bricks.

Gasping for breath, bloodied but unbowed, Chace climbed back onstage and turned to his audience, awaiting their cheers. He became aware that no one was looking at him. All eyes were focused on the top of the Washington Monument. Dixon followed their gaze, and he, too, saw the source of the disturbance.

It was the obelisk's winged colossus—it was moving. Someone was crouching atop the tower, using a blowtorch to cut through the suspension cables. Showers of sparks rained down, and wires twanged, causing the wings of corrugated steel to wobble. Suddenly, the cable let go, and the whole thing toppled down the side of the building and crashed to the ground.

The crowd gasped. Appalled, Dixon shrieked, "Find whoever did that and catch them! *Scourge* them! Don't let them escape!" Bendis ran to comply.

Chace was still looking up, afraid to blink lest he lose sight of this phantom. "Get some lights on him!" In a feverish voice, he muttered, "There you are, there you are . . ."

At the very apex of the obelisk, an Olympian figure with a golden spear gleamed heroically in the floodlights. It was the statue of the Independent Man—the very statue Dixon had removed from the Rhode Island State House!

Except that it was no statue. It was *alive*. And the stranger was gone, vanished from the stage.

"Hallelujah!" someone cried. "Praise the Lord!" A furious murmuring swept through the crowd, many people babbling, "It's Him! It's our Lord and Savior!" Others crossed themselves, and yelled, "It's Satan, it's Satan!"

"It's not God or Satan," yelled Dixon. "It's just a freak in gold paint! Someone shoot him, and you'll see!"

Gunfire crackled, peppering the Monument. The range was too far, having no effect on the golden man, who stared down like a disappointed Oscar as spent ammo pelted the crowd, causing mass casualties. Then he hefted his spear, raised it high, and cast it like a thunderbolt.

Kasim Bendis was halfway to the tower with a squad of sharpshooters. He saw the spear coming but did not try to run or dodge because it was simply too absurd to think a thrown spear could single him out amid so many others, not from such a height and distance, even if it was aimed at him, which it surely was not.

Girded by the confidence of his disbelief, Bendis stood fast as his soldiers scattered. "Stand fast, dogs!" he barked, shooting a fleeing man in the back half a second before he was stuck fast, diagonally pinned to the ground by a twelve-foot-long, gold-plated pole through his chest.

At first he didn't understand, trying to walk and getting nowhere, but then his hands found the icy-cold shaft like a tree trunk through his ribs, and he thought, *Damn.* Oddly enough, there was no blood and little pain, just a bit of difficulty breathing, like a stitch in his side, so that his discomfiture was mainly related to the practical challenge of getting loose. The men around him gaped in horror, afraid to touch him. Wriggling like a hooked worm, he wanted to say, *I've been dead before; it's nothing.*

From up on the stage, Chace Dixon heard distant sounds of shooting and hoarse screams of grown men. The screams became a chorus, and in an instant he could see most of his security cordon in flight, scattering like poultry. In another second, he saw exactly what they were fleeing:

*There!* From the direction of Constitution Avenue, a host of women appeared, moving strangely fast, strangely *strange.* They were not women but Hellions—horrific blue Maenads. It quickly became apparent that even the more-human-looking ones were not human, running so erratically that the snipers couldn't get a bead on them. The blizzard of ammo cut zigzagging holes in the crowd, people toppling like dominoes as they ran for cover or leaped into the Reflecting Pool. Tracer gunfire poured down like fireworks, chewing a few Xombies to bits as others swept in right over them, stabbing right and left with the bayonets of their rifles.

*Rifles?* Chace thought. Since when had Xombies ever carried guns?

They were so damn fast, it was already too late; most of the sentries never saw what hit them. As Chace started to give the order to fall back, he spotted more inhuman creatures rushing in from behind the Memorial, cutting off his escape route—it looked like hundreds of them. They whipped across the stage like a high wind, snatching his men off their feet and spiriting them into the dark. Seemingly no one was immune.

Chace ordered someone to hand him the microphone. As he started to speak, the marching band struck up a slow number, "Greensleeves," and he realized the musicians had all been replaced by a band of naked Maenads.

"Fool me once, shame on you; fool me twice, shame on me. We've been wimps, and God is justly punishing us for our weakness. Women pretend to be weak in order to gain sympathy, but there is a difference between being weak and being *willing*. They *desire* to be seduced; it's their nature. Come on now, this is no surprise. Their unclean loins are instruments of Satan's will—always have been. Women are too easily possessed . . . and they too easily possess *us*, leading us into sympathy and temptation, using our charity against us, making us their minions. And Satan laughs to collect our souls. Look around you! How many millions of men have joined the Enemy because they hesitated in the face of a mother, a daughter, a sister, a wife? That is why Satan loves the ladies! They are his public-relations dream team, his spokesmodels. As men of purity, we must be immune to their witchcraft. Because that's what it is, people; let's be real. Faith is no longer required for belief. We are in the time of Revelation, it's no fairy tale, and we can no longer hide from the inconvenient truth: The only Global Warming we need worry about is the fire down below. Witches and demons roam the Earth. The Antichrist himself is afoot, raising his army for the last battle. As soldiers of God, we have inherited a mission, to purify this land and make of it a kingdom worthy of the Savior's return, so that He may lead us in the final battle between Heaven and Hell. The greatest mission ever known. The second-greatest story ever told, but the greatest mission ever known . . . and the soul you save may be your own. As much as we would all like to practice compassion on these miserable creatures, we simply don't have that right. Such days are past. There have been holy women, yes, but they most of all would tell you it is Woman's affinity for sin that brought Man's fall from grace, and Woman's appetite that has again destroyed us. From now on, their appetite for our dutiful souls must be matched by our appetite for their blood!"

While he was talking, his bodyguards started to slip away. Attempting to stop them, Dixon felt a cold hand on his shoulder.

"Don't leave now, man," said the spitting image of Elvis Presley. "The show's just gettin' started."

Unhinged with rage, Chace said, "Go back to Graceland," and stuck a commando knife into Elvis's heart. He stabbed him again and again, venting all of his frustration and terror on this charlatan, following the King to the floor until absolutely sure he was dead.

It felt good to lie there for a moment and catch his breath. There was pain now, a deep sorrow for all that was gone, but also relief. Chace sobbed a little for his long-lost mother. She had been such a decent, hardworking soul, salt of the Earth, and as a child he had always hoped to make her proud. But she learned of the sickness in his soul when she caught him with another man, and it was not something she could either forgive or forget. She never spoke to him again.

"Come on, sir! This way!"

It was one of Kasim Bendis's tin soldiers, a handsome young man, half out of his mind with fear. Dixon allowed himself to be hustled into the cover of the Lincoln Memorial, where a number of green troops were making a last stand against the encroaching blue enemy.

As the snipers fired and reloaded, fired and reloaded, they were astonished to find themselves under fire. Some of these men were accustomed to fighting Xombies, even crafty Maenads . . . but not *armed* ones. For the first time ever, the Hellions were shooting back! It was a very discouraging development since everyone knew Exes could not be killed, only damaged enough to temporarily slow them down. Then, hopefully, one could dismember them at leisure; crush them, freeze them, burn them to a puddle of black tar. But if they had *guns* . . . well, a guy simply stood no chance.

"This can't be happening!" men cried, and, "We're immune, we're immune!"

On every side, surprised men were shot, clubbed, or stabbed by Xombies. Some shot themselves, witnessing that hopeless scene of Xombies firing guns, Xombies riding motorcycles, Xombies driving trucks. One was even wearing a flamethrower.

As Chace watched the last of his forces go down and the Maenads overrun their positions, he was approached by the last person on Earth he needed to see just then. It was Jim Sandoval. Sandoval's guards had disappeared, and the man looked calm and utterly cheerful amid the wholesale panic. "Isn't this something?" he said brightly. "Look at 'em go!"

Chace grabbed a gun off the ground. "Jim, you don't believe in anything, do you? Never did."

"Dix, you've got me all wrong." Sandoval's flesh suddenly rippled, a wave that started at his scalp and passed down the length of his body, seeming to strip off his outer layer of skin and clothing to reveal an entirely different person—a *woman*. Not a grotesque blue Maenad, but seemingly a living woman. And in an ordinary woman's voice, she said, "I'm not Jim." She leaned down and shouldered a flamethrower abandoned by his men. "My name's Brenda."

Dixon tried to shoot, but the gun was out of bullets. Throwing the gun at her, he pulled a cheap two-way radio from his pocket and hit the emergency signal. He had one last thing to do before they got him.

"This is Chace Dixon," he croaked. "Just do it!"

"Just do it?" the radio squawked. "Is that a go?"

"Yes, go! Now!"

The woman paused over Dixon. The light of her weapon's pilot flame guttered in her eyes, barely illuminating her expression of inscrutable fascination. Chace realized it wasn't her looking at him, but someone else looking through her eyes. She was just a window . . . but who was on the other side? Then she pulled the trigger and everything flared bright as day, the heat blowing her hair back.

At that same exact moment, Washington, DC, froze in the glare of a newborn sun.

# CHAPTER **TWENTY-SIX**

## MONS POPULI

It was slow going. All routes to DC were choked with dead vehicles, and pileups cluttered every intersection, blackened wrecks reeking of burnt rubber. Big Ed Albemarle used the truck like a bulldozer, pushing cars aside and clearing a path for the buses. I rode shotgun, wielding a road map and scanning for openings. We drove freely on the sidewalk, across parks or backyards, or plowed through fences—the fastest route was usually off-road—but then urban congestion increased to the point where driving was simply impossible.

At a place called Indian Head, we cut through a fenced Navy installation and traded the battered vehicles for a fleet of shallow-draft police skiffs, gunning them up the wide Potomac. The sinking sun turned deeper and deeper red, staining the whole sky and landscape the same color. Layers of mist hung over the river, swirling as the boat cut through.

There was a lot of trash in the water, but the first real sign of damage was the collapsed span of the I-95 highway bridge—the southernmost link of the Beltway—which lay toppled on its side as if pushed over by a giant hand. Cars and trucks were scattered like bathtub toys in the shallows or lurked just below the surface to gut our boats. Then there were massive chunks of the bridge itself, bristling with exposed rebar—it was one of these that gashed a couple of

our aluminum hulls and struck off one propeller—but some
of the men jumped in the water, heedless of crabs (of which
there appeared to be none), and after several hours of makeshift repairs and careful maneuvering in the dark, we
cleared the wreckage and continued upriver.

The channel narrowed, the air grew stagnant and humid,
and the ground fog thickened. A dusky orange dawn started
to come up. Through the haze, we had occasional glimpses
of swampy shoreline and piles of overgrown debris—the
view was not of a city but of a jungle, vast piles of rubble swallowed up in Amazonian greenery. The profusion of
life made it hard to tell if there were any human auras.
There certainly didn't appear to be a building left standing.

"Where is it?" I asked Coombs.

"Where is what?"

"The city. Washington."

"You're looking at it. We just passed the Anacostia and
are approaching the Tidal Basin and the Thomas Jefferson
Memorial."

"Washington, DC, doesn't look anything like this."

"It does now."

"But there's nothing here."

"That's because it's been bombed flat. Nuked."

"That's impossible. It would be wasteland, not a rain
forest. This looks more like some ancient Mayan ruin or
something."

"I've read it was similar after Hiroshima: The radiation
stimulated plant growth, so you had beautiful flowers
blooming amid the destruction. This kudzu and knotweed
has had all spring and summer to grow unchecked over the
lawns. Doesn't take long."

"But why bomb it, for heaven's sake?"

"Who knows? People are capable of anything, which is
why they need to be saved from themselves."

Easing the boat into a dense wall of foliage, we got out
and pushed through the marsh until we came to sparser

thickets. The pulverized remains of the Bureau of Engraving and Printing blocked our way east, but after a few hundred yards the fishbone rebar and hills of fractured marble gave way to open ground. Just beyond, the thickest stone walls of the Department of Agriculture were still standing, but for the most part buildings were razed to their foundations, just mangled trunks of pipe sticking up.

Using the directional antenna as if it were a dowsing rod, I increased my pace, watching the indicator gauge. It was close. The fog thickened as we made our way among muddy pools that once were basements. Grand stone steps led to tumbled ruins, a vision out of Ephesus or Pergamum. For a little way, there was almost a path, but a bit farther on, the way was blocked with an epic tangle of wreckage, a rusty steel thicket of buildings, cars, human bones—all scorched, shattered, and rolled up together like a colossal tumbleweed.

"Wait here," I said.

Taking the radio receiver, I made my way to the mountainous deadfall. The air was warm and thick with decay. Refraining from breathing, I entered the junk pile and started climbing. It was not easy to avoid injury; I got a number of cuts and splinters, and was partially impaled when a loose foothold gave way.

Little Bobby Rubio caught me, having discreetly followed. I couldn't very well tell him to get lost. My dress was ruined. Freeing myself, I finally came to the top, where Bobby and I were able to stand upright on a canted slab of steel-reinforced concrete, straining to see through the fog.

This was it.

Beyond that muffling caul of vapor, I could see activity—a lot of activity. None of it human.

It was Xanadu.

Xombies were at work here; Xombies were *busy*. They seethed dimly in the haze, parades of blue ants spiraling in and around a bizarre anthill—a huge mound of rubble rising from the center of a flooded crater, partially divided into two lobes and split open at the fat end like an overripe fruit. The dome was at least a hundred feet high, with a column of blurred heat issuing from a recessed pit at its summit. The sides were bushy with twisted rebar, giving the artificial hill even more resemblance to an exotic fruit or seedpod, something spiny and subtropical.

A causeway of packed gravel exuded from its woundlike opening, crossing the water and branching into several feeder roads that splayed in all directions like rhizomes. The whole thing gave the impression of organic function—the fractal architecture of nature.

Above it all hung a strange, living balloon, a thousand-foot-long Xeppelin that rippled and pulsated like a gigantic grub. Attached by a fat umbilicus to the dome, it slowly rose to the end of its tether as it filled with heat, then settled back down as it cooled—over and over again.

The inflated flesh bag was translucent as a fetus, shot through with purplish blue veins and connective tissue. A beardlike mass of filaments hung from its bottom rim like stinging tentacles. In its cycles of rising and falling, expanding and contracting, the Xeppelin was weirdly lifelike, appearing to feed on the dome's exhaust.

Everything else was still under construction, expanding outward and upward. Xombies were building their temple brick by brick, stone by stone, bone by bone, from the surrounding rubble. Only workers who didn't sleep or need rest could have built so much, so fast. They used no concrete, simply fitting the pieces together by hand and pounding hot tar into the cracks. Somehow, it held together.

The overhanging walls of the V-shaped entrance portal all but defied gravity, its builders not being overly concerned with the laws of physics or even basic geometry. For a busy construction site, it was surprisingly quiet—there were no engines of any kind, and the naked Xombies labored silently, ceaselessly.

I was paralyzed by a strange feeling I didn't understand, but Bobby didn't wait—without a word, he was off and running. I watched him go down, curiously following his progress as he leaped to the muddy field. The outside edge of the work zone was only a few hundred yards away, a plain of mudflats surrounding a moat of stagnant water. Raised highways of packed debris crossed the moat, and long lines of Xombie-drawn wagons were traveling to and from the site. Morphing his skin blue, Bobby joined an inbound convoy, his alien presence unnoticed by the laboring multitude.

I followed him down, not knowing what to do, certain only that I had to do something. Cautiously approaching a raised road, I immediately realized the workers passing above had no interest in me at all—or in anything other than their plodding task. Their job was Egyptian, biblical, endless slave trains pulling wobbly carts full of raw materials, mostly charred bones and resin-encased mummies, hard as rock.

Certainly this would have been a hellish chore for human beings—they would drop like flies from the heat alone—but Xombies showed no signs of strain, nor so much as a drop of sweat. They had no boots, no helmets, no gloves, nothing, yet were impervious to pain.

Upon closer inspection, the carts were weird agglomerations of steel and flesh, self-loading meat wagons made of interlocked limbs and interwoven bone, marching in lockstep on ranks of severed legs. They looked like giant bugs. Even to my jaded sensibilities, the versatility of Xombie bodies was marvelous and hideous.

My caravan merged with others as the various roads joined together at the main entrance ramp. This broad avenue crossed the moat and humped over a retaining dam, then sloped downward through the yawning gap beyond, a wedge-shaped defile buttressed by arches of human bone. It was like entering a narrow river gorge, with only a crack of sky to light the way. Above, I could see the tentacles of the Xeppelin raising buckets of black slop. The air became even more densely humid, reeking of something I recognized well: the smell of ichor—Xombie blood. My blood. The whole structure was saturated with it, plastered with it, oozing purple-black extract from the very walls. Not tar, but gore. It was literally the glue that held the joint together.

At long, irregular intervals, the whole structure seemed to settle, wheezing with a deep bass throb as it compressed like a huge bellows . . . or a gigantic heart . . . before expanding once more. I had to stop in awe. Not only the builders but the building itself was undead, a million-ton golem lying helpless as a beached whale.

Now the grisly mule trains began breaking off, bearing their loads up wavy ledges that climbed the inner walls. After that, they disappeared from view. All the traffic was inward; there was no exit route that I could see, no train of empty carts.

I continued downward along the main path, heading for the low archway at the end, a wavering glimmer of light. The air was being sucked that way, rushing like a river into the depths. All angles were askew, all edges rounded, all lines twisted, forming crudely sinuous curves and shapes. Random patterns became grotesque reliefs—gaping mouths, eyes, whole faces that writhed and dissolved as I looked at them. Snatches of words and gibberish emanated from the walls, so many that they combined into a roar, as though I were emerging from a tunnel into a packed stadium. There was even light at the end of the tunnel.

I walked through.

Suddenly, I was no longer in that booming cavern but walking down a peaceful, sunlit street. There were palm trees and parked cars and hibiscus bushes and rows of houses, many of them Spanish-style bungalows with roofs of clay tiles. The white concrete sidewalk sparkled at my feet, sown with mica glitter. In the middle distance was a range of brown hills. I was wearing sneakers, and the hand

holding mine did not burn because we were both alive. I
looked back, and the tunnel was gone.

"Lulu, look! That's our new home!"

I looked up at the smiling, beautiful woman holding my
hand, and she was familiar to me. Not from life, but from
some photographs Fred Cowper once gave me. I had hated
her in those photos because her life looked so perfect and
orderly and above all *normal*, everything mine was not.

"You're Brenda," I said. "You're my sister."

She nodded in surprise, but pleasantly. "How did you
find out?"

"Fred and my mother—I mean, our mother. They told me
some things, and I've just been putting the pieces together."

"Why don't you come inside? There is someone here
who's very eager to see you." She opened a low wrought-
iron gate and led me through a tiled patio full of greenery to
a door like the arched portal of a miniature castle, made of
wood planks with heavy iron bolts and fittings. There was a
welcome mat that said, MI CASA ES SU CASA.

We went inside. "Wait here a sec," she said, disappearing through another arched doorway.

The living room was cool and breezy, with bare white
walls and rustic furnishings of dark wood and bloodred
leather. It echoed. The only decorations were a few pieces
of glazed pottery and a small crucified Jesus. I heard footsteps and looked up. There was a big, dark-eyed boy looking
at me, and for a second I didn't know why my heat-tempered
heart suddenly turned molten.

"Hi, Lulu," he said shyly.

"H-Hector," I said.

"Hey."

It was Hector Albemarle, the boy who saved my life.
The boy who loved me. But Hector died right before my
eyes, blown to bits in the cold hell of Thule.

"Hector," I asked, "what are you doing here?"

"Same thing you are. We came here together, Lulu."

"What do you mean?"

"I mean I'm part of you." He stepped forward and gently touched my stomach. "Right in there."

I stepped back. "What are you talking about?"

"Don't you remember? You took me inside you, Lulu. And I've been there ever since, growing bigger and bigger."

Shaking my head, I started to argue, *But we never did that*, and then something dawned on me. Something so beyond even my Xombie comprehension that it made me shriek. "Hector! Do you mean—? No!"

He nodded sadly, sweetly, exactly the way he always did in life. "Yes."

It came back to me, the madness I felt witnessing his death on that muddy field. The grief and horror that caused me to lose my mind and dive for his shattered remains, trying to gather them together, save him as he had me, and when that wasn't possible . . . when that wasn't possible . . .

I ate him.

Not much of him. Just one little piece before Jake and Julian dragged me away. But was it perhaps enough to have taken root inside my living body, lying dormant until I became a Xombie? I could definitely feel something unusual in there, a tough mass like a tumor. Except Xombies didn't get tumors, Xombies didn't get anything. Or did they? Was I going to give birth to a clone of Hector Albemarle?

"I'm sorry, Lulu," he said. "I know it's weird."

"No," I said, feeling strangely dreamy. I looked at him, at his poor sad face, and couldn't help smiling. "No, Hector. I think it's wonderful."

He beamed hopefully, his brown eyes welling with tears. "Seriously?"

"Yeah." Now I was weeping, too. "Come here, you big dummy."

Bobby ripped me out of my stupor.

*"Lulu, wake up! Lulu, Lulu, Lulu, Lulu! Wake up, wake up, wake up!"*

Bobby was shaking me, pinching me, pulling my hair. I was not in sunny California. I was in a cavernous domed chamber, perhaps a hundred feet deep and twice as wide. Suspended within it like a steel kraken was some kind of blast furnace, an infernal-looking contraption fed by numerous twisting ramps, down which trains of Xombies marched to their white-hot reward. They were its fuel, its lifeblood, and it was their cannibal god.

Beneath the furnace was a black pool, like a tar pit, fed by the slow melting of the walls and ceiling. At Bobby's urging, I turned to see a creature of tar leaning over me—a black-dipped Medusa with black lips, black teeth, shining spider eyes, and skin as sickly iridescent as crude oil. With her overgrown nails and crazed hair, she was an intimidating presence . . . even to me. Compared to her, I looked like a blue kewpie doll. But I still recognized her.

"Brenda," I said.

# CHAPTER **TWENTY-SEVEN**

## OOBLECK

Trying to contain my disquiet, I asked, *"Why?"*

"Why?" The Ex-Brenda looked blank. I could see her mind stumble, like someone groping in sudden dark.

"Yes, why? What is all this? What is it for?"

Everything stopped.

The chamber went awesomely quiet, absent that roar of voices. Even the blast furnace and the churning of the pool were muted. There was a noise beyond hearing, however, a silent alarm that required no ears to hear, but which rang in Maenad cells like a billion dinner bells. I heard it loud and clear, and at once sensed millions of eyes staring at me, probing not just with those eyes but with the rude fingers of their minds, as if I were in a tank full of invisible eels fondling my body, trying to worm inside my deepest self.

*Back off,* I thought, slapping them away with the force of my will.

Distracted, I was caught off guard by the vise grip of the her sharp-nailed hand on my upper arm. *Hey!* I flailed with inhuman agility, kicking, twisting, but the Ex-woman was twice my size, double my strength, and equally impervious to hurt. Our flesh crackled at the point of contact, the familiar Xombie repulsion effect known as the Solomon Principle.

"Because we have to," she said. "The future depends on it."

"Depends on what? Whose idea was this?"

"Uri Miska's."

That knocked me cold. We, too, were following a vision of Uri Miska; he was the father of us Xombies, the man who had created Agent X as a means of insulating mankind from the coming cataclysm of the Big Enchilada, which would wipe out all mortal life. It was the whole point of our submarine mission.

Shocked, I said, "Miska! Why?"

"Why? Why? What do you mean, *why*?" The woman shook her head as if wracked by some powerful inner turmoil.

"I mean I don't understand! Let go!"

"Where did you come from? How did you get in here?"

"*Tonic!*" hissed a voice from behind us. "She is a spy! She has the agent of free will!"

Oh no. It was another familiar face, and not a pretty one: Major Kasim Bendis—Uncle Spam. He pulled clear of the wall, and I realized these creatures were subsets of the whole vast structure, extruded at will.

I knew Kasim well from my brief time with the Reapers, when he looked like a pile of leftover barbecue with a hat, so this was a step up. I hadn't been in such great shape back then either, with huge holes bored through my head and torso, but at least I didn't have to come back as a drip sculpture. Clearly there were worse things than being a Xombie.

"Hey, man," I said, "pull yourself together."

"Get her! *Get* her!"

Well, this was quite a coincidence . . . or was it? Come to think of it, I had been led here, *lured* here in remembrance of things past. But was it deliberate? If so, who was dropping the crumbs? Bendis? He certainly didn't look capable of anything so interesting, being just another Xombie drone. In the presence of human beings, he would no doubt step lively, but amid all these Mogul Xombies, he was basically cheap labor . . . until I came along and upset the applecart.

Apparently, all this talk had shocked him to action, or perhaps someone else was pulling his strings. Either way, he was suddenly a maniacal dervish, grabbing me by my neck and yanking me against his chest. Brenda stepped forward as if to intervene, then suddenly went stiff, twitching in place.

Other goop-monsters joined in, pinning my limbs, pulling my hair. One of them was the former president of the United States.

Repeating, "She's the Tonic, the Tonic!" the Ex-president took a handsome fountain pen from his scorched coat pocket and jabbed its sharp nib into my jugular, instantly filling the ink reservoir with my purplish black blood. As all the others watched in fascination, he tipped back his head and raised the pen over his open mouth, thumb poised to flip the release.

Before he could do so, he was hit by a thing like a hairy medieval mace, which rammed the pen into his mouth and out the back of his throat, where my captive blood burst free, spraying Kasim Bendis in the face.

As Bendis flailed backward, the mace whirled in the air and struck the other Moguls in turn, splatting them like fudge-filled treats. Now I could see it was not a mace but Bobby Rubio's head, studded with hornlike spikes and attached to a freakishly elongated neck. The rest of Bobby's body had changed as well, three of his limbs anchored to the ground while the fourth—his right forearm—had lengthened and split apart into a double-bladed scythe, a giant pair of shears, literally cutting Xombies off at the knees. The boy resembled a giant fiddler crab. But as I joined the fight, I could see all the other Ex-Moguls being birthed from side alcoves, a hundred or more. It was hopeless.

While Bobby's body returned to normal human proportions, I grabbed his hand, and we ran. As we approached the main entrance portal, it shrank like a stony sphincter, the archway and surrounding wall bunching up and contracting in grinding spasms, sprouting long black thorns. We were cornered.

Looking for a way out, I felt someone touch my arm. It was Brenda. She had followed us up the entrance ramp and was mutely pointing at a series of openings high in the ceiling, from which Xombie catwalks descended into the plasma oven, chutes for the endless lemming parade.

"I think she wants us to go that way," Bobby said. Brenda nodded wildly.

"How?" I asked.

Battling some inner demon, black veins popping in her forehead, Brenda croaked, *"Climb."*

"We can't climb up there!"

"Sure we can," Bobby said. "Come on!"

"Is there even a way out up there?"

"Is there a way out down here?"

"Good point."

Bobby led the way, with me following on his heels and Brenda picking up the rear. In seconds, Bobby was way ahead of us, finding handholds among the gore and charnel rebar. The kid was a spider.

Having never been overly coordinated, I moved forward in fits and starts. It was easier than I thought. The surface was more irregular than any cliff face, a conglomeration of organic and inorganic debris held together by a blood pudding made from a million nuked Xombies. Ichor oozed from every crevice, dangling in long black drips that hung halfway to the floor. When I brushed against them, I got a static shock, and they retracted like sensitive tendrils. Slug eyes.

Avoiding contact with flesh and bone, I seized upon all manner of other junk: heavy machinery, trucks, highway signs, dinosaur skeletons, planes, trains, automobiles. It could have been the nest of some gigantic packrat. Except that it *moved*. The whole thing heaved up and down in a slow, rolling motion, vines swaying eerily.

Beneath the furnace, filling the deep bottom of the hollow, was that black pool of ichor that began to churn and erupt like a vast cauldron of boiling oil. In the center of this pit was an island, a peculiar mound banked with marble columns and statuary, steaming and glowing green from within. I could make out the head of Abraham Lincoln. The radiation in the chamber was intense; no human being could have survived it for more than a few minutes.

It occurred to me that the pile of rubble was a crude nuclear reactor, using uranium from the dry-docked sub at Norfolk and the power plant at Calvert Cliffs to generate the plasma arc in the furnace. There was a brain behind all this, and it smelled human.

The ichor was not boiling from heat so much as from restless, restless life—it moved like a living thing, a vast, seething mollusk. The room was actually relatively cool, most of the heat wicked away by the porous walls or ventilated out a huge stone chimney that rose to the ceiling and supported both domes. Like the uranium fuel rods, that chimney was preapocalyptic, a cracked relic of human craftsmanship. I recognized it at once as the base of the Washington Monument. All that remained of the famous obelisk was its stump.

The sickly light radiating from underneath the plasma kiln silhouetted Xombies laboring at its base. Rows of railroad tracks led to the pool, with sludge carts going in and out, in and out, dragged by lines of workers, who then shoveled the heavy gunk into metal buckets as if it were toxic waste. But it wasn't toxic waste; it was industrial product. This was the source of the ichor—the black pitch of which the whole place was built. Even the Xeppelin was made of this stuff, blown up like so much oobleck. A million Xombies boiled down for glue.

But oobleck was not the only product there. As I watched, I could see buckets of it being lowered into supercooled wells in the floor, shooting fountains of dry-ice vapor, and this frozen material then returned to the furnace to be blasted again by the plasma arc. In this way it was disinte-grated, crystallized, reduced to a fraction of its former mass. Rendered to its pure nanoparticles—dust to dust. The ultra-fine white powder was then transferred to a deep concrete tunnel, perhaps part of an old government fallout shelter built during the Cold War.

I suddenly realized I knew how this all worked because I had seen it before—I had seen it while I was linked to all the other Maenads, jacked into the Hex.

Through all this, Moguls were being hatched. The black cocoons that I had seen outside were cracked open in the nuclear pool, and their withered residents granted freedom—the freedom to slave away in service of the all-consuming fire. Once titans of industry, they were now merely drones, existing to service that infernal queen.

I remembered seeing those plastic-encased mummies at Thule, then later in Miska's secret lab, all being kept in cold storage until Agent X could be perfected; my queasy feeling as Dr. Chandra Stevens explained to me that they were all sick and elderly men who paid to be inoculated with the disease. Their brains had been chilled to protect them from the effects of oxygen starvation, but they still had the manic need to share their "gift," so MoCo scientists laminated them in carbon-fiber shells for safekeeping. Bottled Moguls betting on a better life—the ultimate golden parachute. But they never got the Tonic they ordered, an eternal youth of permanent bliss. Instead, this was their final reward: hauling sludge in Hades.

Clearly, somebody up there had a sense of humor.

What began as a wall quickly became the ceiling, our butts dangling in space. The thought of falling obviously didn't bother Bobby at all. *That's right, we dead.* Following his lead, I worked my way along the overhang, clinging firmly to the least little protrusion, my body molded to the slimy, jagged surface as though making love to it. In a matter of seconds, I was fifty feet above the reactor pool. Looking up, I could see Bobby scuttling into the first opening above the incinerator chute, pushing past leaping Xombies to get inside.

Someone grabbed my leg. Not someone—some*thing*: Kasim Bendis. He was back, with the president's pen wedged between his neck vertebrae. Now he had one more problem: The bone and tissue had fused around it; he would have to break his own neck to get it out.

Trying to talk, he could only make a horrible gargling sound: *"Gluurgggaaaaaachhh! Gglarghaaachhhh!"*

I tried to pull free, but Bendis had gravity on his side. With one hard tug, he yanked both of us off the wall. Falling, I grabbed hold of the first thing I found: a handful of black tendrils. They stretched long, then instantly recoiled, pulling me upward and dragging Bendis after me.

He swung from my ankle like a trapeze artist, both of us swaying wide over the seething pit. Above us, Brenda was following Bobby toward a shaft of sunlight.

I realized I couldn't escape. However much I kicked and fought, Bendis was too strong. The only real choice was whether to hang on or let go. The thought of falling no longer scared me, or even made me sad. It was just . . . irritating. Whatever happened, I couldn't be hurt, much less killed.

I had a sudden revelation: Even if they reduced me to my bare molecules, I would still exist, and at some point in eternity I would even exist again as myself. Not just once, but infinite times. This was true of everything in the Universe, alive or dead—you didn't have to be a Xombie. Everything lived forever. The curse of the Xombie was that we *remembered*.

And suddenly I did remember. I remembered that I was not alone.

Letting go with one hand, I reached over my shoulder and unzipped my Hello Kitty backpack. It was squeezed tightly between us, Bendis's body now enfolding mine like a hungry starfish around a clam.

"Come on, honey baby," he said, his charred-bacon lips mashed against my ear. "Won't you share a little of your sweet nectar with Kasim? So we can both be freeeeeee."

"Sounds like somebody's got a sweet tooth," said a rusty voice from my backpack.

Bendis looked down in surprise, and a jagged set of jaws sprang shut on his face like a bear trap.

It was Fred Cowper. Fred's hideous head thrashed like a shark tearing at a piece of meat, engulfing Bendis's entire face. Kasim let go of my body, fighting to pull his head away, but Cowper was relentless. With an explosive snap, his neck tendrils sprang erect, ripping the backpack open and kicking me and Bendis apart. The major clawed furiously, hand over hand, but suddenly he had nothing to hang on to but the slippery cords of Fred Cowper's severed neck.

Cowper bit his face off. Released to gravity, Bendis plummeted to the reactor pit, bouncing off the marble cladding and into the oobleck. Shed of the weight, I recoiled upward, using the momentum to propel myself over the ledge. Brenda caught me and pulled me in.

"Thanks," I said.

"What's a sister for?"

It looked like we were home free, only a short tunnel away from daylight. Bobby was already there, waving us through. But as Brenda and I moved forward, the opening closed around us, folding shut like a giant, spiny sea anemone.

Just before the spines pierced our bodies, Brenda shoved me through the disappearing gap. In doing so, she sacrificed herself, stuck fast by the contracting spikes.

"Run!" she cried. "Run fast!" She held up a small spray bottle, some kind of atomizer, and shot it off. Hissing vapor engulfed her, and immediately her riven body turned human, all punctured flesh dying red.

The spray had an instant effect on the walls, turning the spines to red goop and burning through the connective ichor like a coal fire. A bloody fissure appeared as the blue-black tissues retracted, melting and undermining the mass of rubble. Blood poured down like red paint into the black pool—a lot of blood.

This liquid was literally the building's lifeblood: thousands of gallons of coolant and hydraulic muscle, pumped at high pressure through branching arteries in the dome wall, a hidden web of living plasma ducts that supported the weight of the ceiling.

As the flesh retreated, the bone framework sloughed away, and the blood broke through. A steaming torrent of gore burst upon the chamber. It resembled a volcanic eruption, a scarlet flow of meat pulp and grinding debris that crushed Xombies and tumbled the steel blast furnace like a tin toy. Crimson sludge battered the hot reactor, causing the banked marble to crack and explode, releasing all its stored energy in one massive explosion. With the entrance portal blocked, there was only one outlet for the enormous pressure: up the shaft of the Washington Monument.

This makeshift chimney prolapsed with a geyser of gore and flame that billowed higher than the original Monument, a false obelisk that obliterated the Xeppelin above. But it was not nearly enough to release the explosive pressure within the mound. For this, the roof itself burst, expelling a jet of superheated gas from its weakest point: the chute above the kiln, our exit, which was the terminal end of the fissure between the mound's two lobes. This passage now ruptured outward, releasing a fountain of glowing ejecta high into the sky.

Bobby and I rode this bubble of force, cartwheeling upward like scraps of pounded gristle. Soaring far and wide, we were flung clear of the dome to land in the deep mud of the moat.

"Ow," Bobby said.

Sitting up in the knee-deep scum, we gathered our wits, assessed our multifarious dings, and pulled out the more egregious bits of shrapnel. Actually, the damage wasn't nearly as bad as I would have expected, but we weren't going anywhere. The alarm had gone out on us. Xombies and robots were closing in on all sides, even from above— aerial drones swooping in to destroy the saboteurs.

Bobby got up first, trying to drag me by my broken arm. "Come on, we gotta go!"

I got up, willing my bones to mend faster, wobbling forward on the rubbery new shoots. Both of us were hobbled by the mud—the stuff had a life of its own, sucking at us like putrid quicksand. Bobby was fast and light enough to walk above the stuff. It was heavy and slippery, a toxic mixture of clay, soil, radioactive ash, and contaminated rainwater, all churned to a thick gray batter by countless Xombie imagineers. A human being would have quickly floundered, become exhausted, and suffocated like a fly in amber, but we could not tire, could not drown.

Unable to run, we swam, slithering through the muck like salamanders, disappearing from targeting systems so that the incoming missiles missed us, exploding harmlessly in the mud. Reaching dry land, we pulled ourselves from the mire and ran, shedding clods of gunk. It was no use; we were surrounded. As if on command, every Ex had turned away from the Xombie mountain's majesty, ditching their burdens and charging across the fruitless plain. All descended upon us.

Then they stopped.

The ground shook. A titanic force rocked the mound from within, making it wobble like an immense aspic. Within the Mons, something new was happening. Buried beneath the catastrophic destruction, the steel hatch to the underground silo had warped and cracked. It was a small crack, but still a crack—just enough for a trickle of bloody water to enter, water red as barn paint, which soaked into the pure white powder at the bottom.

The microscopic particles, each one an independent crystalline spore, began locking together, growing, multiplying, building webs of water and protein that mimicked cell membranes, then furnishing those membranes with hardy clockwork. This reconstituted mass, representing the flesh of over four thousand rendered Clears, themselves each a colony organism, expanded like yeasty dough, quickly filling the concrete silo and blowing the lid off. What came out amid the fire and steam was twenty tons of pure id. A literal living will: thought translated to shape, and shape to action.

With a deafening scream, it rose from the breached citadel.

"Now, that's something you don't see every day," I said, as all the puppet Xombies and robots went berserk, blinded by the massive electromagnetic discharge, attacking one another or just crashing to earth. Amid all this, something very large and very hard to look at was being birthed from its shell.

"Let's go," Bobby said, taking my hand.

I wiped mud off his face. "Go where?" I asked.

"Back to the boats. They're waiting for us."

"Okay."

**PART V**

Sesame Street

# CHAPTER **TWENTY-EIGHT**

### LIVE

Throttling away from shore, we hurtled out of the inlet and veered south down the Potomac. It was much faster going downriver than it had been coming up, not only because the stream was with us but because we knew all the major obstacles, and the best routes through them. Soon we were out of view of the madness happening behind us and started focusing on what was ahead. Stopping along the Virginia shore to refuel, we briefly surveyed the town of Mount Vernon. From a distance it looked like every other town, its rooftops rising from groves of shade trees, the fall leaves rustling in the breeze. I could see a main street lined with pubs and restaurants. It could have been a quiet Sunday morning.

Looking closer, the evidence of long neglect became more apparent: streets littered with abandoned cars and blown debris—roof tiles, broken glass, fallen tree limbs. As in Washington, plants had run rampant: Huge thickets of knotweed and thistle filled every patch of earth—lawns were extinct. Seams in the pavement were shaggy with greenery, and larger cracks sprouted actual trees. In places, the city had given way to swamp, storm drains backed up and the stagnant water clotted with algae. Here and there amid the refuse could be seen shoes, clothes, New Year's Eve decorations. Just shit. The town was dead, we were

dead, and we felt no urge to pretend otherwise. Not anymore. We returned to the boats.

Following a sharp eastward bend in the river, we paused
at Blossom Point to ditch two of our faltering skiffs for a
big power cruiser. The boat was sitting on a trailer in the
dockyard, all fueled up and still hitched to the car that had
backed it halfway down the launch ramp. Whatever had
happened to the unfortunate boat owner, his loss was our
gain.

As we rounded Smith Point and turned south into the
vastness of Chesapeake Bay, there it was.

From a distance, it could have been our submarine, that
winged tower on its black peninsula, but as we drew closer,
there was no mistaking the differences. It was five thousand
tons lighter and a hundred feet shorter than our boat. This
was not the USS *No-Name*, resurrected from its murky
grave. It was not an American sub at all, but a French boomer
of the *Triomphante* class.

And it appeared to be abandoned.

The ship was wide open to the elements, adrift in the
middle of the channel like a floating log. Humans had recently been here, we could sense them, but it was only a
vague aftertaste. There were no spotters on the bridge or
escort vessels. The periscope and radar masts were not deployed. Bay and sky were clear as far as the eye could
see . . . and our Xombie eyes could see very far indeed.

"Think they're coming back?" Coombs asked.

"Only one way to find out," I said.

We pulled alongside and boarded the ship. I was surprised by how normal it felt to be on a submarine again.

One by one, we entered the hatch, climbing down the
ladder to the deck below. We moved quickly, headfirst, agile
as cockroaches as we searched out every corner. There was
no obstruction, no resistance, no reaction to our trespassing.
No alarms whatsoever.

The interior of the French sub was different from what

we were used to, me especially, but even I recognized the basic function of almost everything in sight. Most submarine technology is fundamentally the same: up, down; forward, aft; port, starboard; fast, slow. Beyond those basics, every control was in the service of the power plant, the weapons, or the life-support systems—the last having recently fallen into disuse on our vessel.

Compared to the barren shell of our boat, this submarine was a warm and cozy womb. I could smell coffee and fresh-baked rolls with butter, men's aftershave, minty soaps, clean bedding, ironed clothes, and patent leather shoes. The smell evoked a whole dead culture, one I had never really experienced and therefore didn't realize it was possible to yearn for: the solace of a first-class ticket.

"I feel like I'm in Paris," I said.

The hatches slammed shut.

There was a whoosh of powerful compressors, creating a vacuum that sucked the stale air into holding tanks. As the cabin pressure dropped, we could feel it in our bodies—not as pain, but a sensation of tightness, as if our heads were going to pop. We could also hear it affecting the boat, its pressure hull flexing like an empty beer can. Just before our fluids boiled and eyeballs started flying, a human voice ordered, "Close all outboard valves and open $O_2$ reserve!"

Pure oxygen flooded in. It was an extraordinary feeling. All of us suddenly opened our mouths as if remembering a question of desperate importance . . . then froze in place, our blue faces flushing bright red, our bloodshot eyes gaping as their pupils dilated to pinpricks. Then, one by one, we all took a long, ragged breath of air—a veritable backward scream—and collapsed to the deck.

A moment later, we began to rise. Shakily, painfully, we sat up, staring around like survivors of some terrible catastrophe. Dr. Langhorne was the first to speak, and she articulated what all of us were feeling in every quailing, agonized nerve fiber.

"Oh my God," she sobbed. "I'm *alive!*"

I, too, was wracked with the smothering horror of it. As depressing as eternity could be, I was not ready to give it up so soon. To be human again? So scared and fragile and cramped by time? The very thought was terrifying—perhaps the only thought that could terrify a Xombie.

Several men appeared, strolling from the aft hatch and looking down at us with curiosity and pity. Their faces were blurred by air masks, and they wore foreign military uniforms—the uniforms of French naval officers.

*"Bonjour,"* said the leader. *"Bienvenue à* Le Terrible— although I prefer to call it the *Apocalypso.* Welcome aboard; we hope you enjoy your stay with us. My name is Alaric Despineau, and I will be your captain today."

My jump-started heart almost stalled. Alaric? It was a name I knew all too well. Not least because it was my middle name: Louise Alaric Pangloss.

"Hi, Pops," I groaned.

# CHAPTER **TWENTY-NINE**

## SESAME STREET

"Lulu. Yes, of course." Stunned, Captain Despineau said, "*Mon Dieu*, it is so wonderful to finally meet you, you have no idea. I have wished for this a long time."

"You and me both, bub," I croaked, sitting up and propping myself against the forward bulkhead. "I'd love to catch up on old times—oh, right, there weren't any."

My body felt carbonated, every cell fizzing painfully. I hadn't felt pain in a long time. It kind of sucked. But there was also something amazing about it—I was physically present in a way I had forgotten possible. I truly *existed*.

Fred Cowper's head was discovered in my backpack, and I freaked out a bit because it was just a lifeless head—Fred was dead!—but I didn't have the strength to really get upset . . . or perhaps there was still too much Agent X in me. Before I could start screaming, Despineau gently took the pack from my hands and ordered someone to stick it in a freezer.

He sat with us as we faded in and out of consciousness, the pressurized oxygen suffusing our tissues, neutralizing the artificial Maenad organism. It would only stay dormant as long as the oxygen was applied, but in the meantime, we were mortal again . . . meaning weak as kittens.

Over the next few hours, the submarine traveled back to the mouth of Chesapeake Bay, the southern shipping channel. It was easy to find because of the huge abandoned oil platform jutting from the sea. That was our destination, Despineau explained.

"We're going on an oil rig?" I asked.

"Not on. *Under.*"

"Under?"

"Petropolis was designed with certain unusual features, such as an undersea docking port and a large decompression chamber. So was the Bridge Tunnel. All we had to do was connect them."

"That seems awfully . . . convenient," Alice Langhorne said.

"Not at all. They're both emergency depots for the storage of sensitive personnel and materials."

"SPAM," I said.

"Yes, SPAM."

"In other words, you planned for all this?"

"Lulu, I know your mother taught you about the Five P's. Come on, what are the Five P's?"

"Prior Planning Prevents Poor Performance."

*"Voilà!"*

There was bumping and grinding as the sub docked, then the forward hatch popped open. Despineau led us up into a horizontal steel tunnel about ten feet in diameter. It echoed. I knew the boat had not surfaced; this tunnel was still deep underwater. At the end of the tunnel was a door like a bank vault, opening into a vertical chamber perhaps twenty feet in diameter and forty feet high, with a spiral stair and six decks of seats, enough for over a hundred people.

On the wall were three lit buttons. The top button was labeled PETROPOLIS, the middle button read APOCALYPSO, and the down button read SESAME STREET. Despineau pushed the bottom button, and, with a pneumatic hiss, we descended.

Sitting between Langhorne and me, he said, "Now you know."

"What?" I asked.

"How to get to Sesame Street."

The elevator stopped with a hiss, and the heavy door opened. We filed through into another short tunnel, then a watertight hatch protected by a giant ball valve. There was noise coming from the other side—the sound of many people.

"The Bridge Tunnel," Despineau said delightedly. "I call it the Metro: ten miles of tunnel sheltering twenty thousand people, separated from land by ten miles of fortified bridges that double as airstrips. It is an ideal arrangement. Or it was, until somebody I know torpedoed the south causeway."

"Sorry."

It looked like a campground on the Fourth of July. The cavernous highway tunnel seemed to stretch to infinity, one of its two lanes occupied by a line of RVs and the other open to walkers, skaters, and bicycle traffic. Patches of plastic grass had been laid down as little parks for games of Frisbee and touch football. Hundreds of people were out in the road or just sitting in lawn chairs enjoying the view. I could understand why—it was a beautiful sight: men and women of all ages and all colors living together in harmony, staring at us not in fear but in simple curiosity. We who had so recently been Xombies wept to see them . . . and to be them.

"Whoa," said Sal DeLuca, eyeing the bikes and skateboards with envy. "Blast from the past."

A squadron of golf carts zipped toward us and squealed to a stop. The lead driver, a wiry-haired older woman in a brightly colored ski suit, jumped out to greet Captain Despineau, then started at the sight of Alice Langhorne.

"Dr. Stevens, I presume?"

"Alice?" the woman said. "Is that really you?"

"I'm not quite sure yet. Give me a few more minutes."

They shook hands and fake-kissed. I remembered Dr. Chandra Stevens well . . . too well. She was the cheerful scientist who had supervised my torture at Thule. And she remembered me.

"*Lulu!* Hello! Alice, you should have warned me! Just kidding. Welcome! So *nice* to see you all, come on in. Would you like something to drink? Some nice iced tea, maybe? Oh, a tall glass of iced tea sounds good, doesn't it? With a little sprig of mint—I always like that. And maybe some finger sandwiches and deviled eggs, what do you think? The eggs are *super* fresh; you should try them."

My father, Captain Despineau, said, "Everyone, this is a good friend of mine, Dr. Chandra Stevens. Chandra, I believe you know many of these folks. You'll have to excuse their long faces; they've just been through quite an ordeal."

"Of course, I understand! I know there are some people here who have been very worried about you."

From one of the carts at the rear, a tall, bald man approached. "Alice!" he called.

"Jim . . . ?" Langhorne said doubtfully.

"Alice!" cried the man.

It was Mogul Chairman James Sandoval.

*Sandoval,* I thought. Jim Sandoval was a handsome older man whom I had originally found charming in a Daddy Warbucks kind of way. That was before he tried to sell me to the other Moguls as a human Fountain of Youth.

But Jim Sandoval was *dead.*

The last I had seen of the man, he was freezing to death in the Arctic with two crushed legs and a headless Xombie going for his throat. Now he seemed fully recovered, not a wrinkle on his brow or his elegant gray suit. His steely eyes beamed with amusement.

Alice Langhorne tottered toward him. She knew Sandoval even better than I did, having married and divorced him. They had a troubled daughter who had died prior to the Maenad Pandemic, a daughter about my age, but in a real sense their only child was Agent X, for it was Jim and Alice's partnership that financed Uri Miska's longevity experiments.

Her voice ragged, Langhorne said, "Jim. I thought you were dead." She swayed forward as if to hug him, then swung a weak punch at his face.

He caught and held her, stroking her silver-blond hair. "Don't you mean you left me for dead?" He grinned ruefully. "That's all right, I probably deserved it."

"What do you think you're *doing* down here?" Langhorne asked.

"What's it look like I'm doing?" Sandoval replied. "Same thing I've always done: Trying to make my daddy proud."

"You mean being a Mogul."

This made Sandoval laugh until he was blue in the face. "Honey, you have got me so wrong."

"How in God's name did you manage to survive?"

"After my submarine was hijacked and I was left on an ice floe to die, a fellow Mogul very kindly arranged for new transportation, courtesy of our French connections. You may know her, Lulu. I know Alice does."

"Who?" Langhorne asked.

"Chandra Stevens, of course."

"Of course" Alice groaned. "Another MoCo alum."

Twinkling, Sandoval said, "Oh yeah. It's a regular Old Home Day. But look at the bright side, honey."

"And what would that be?"

"I did it all for you."

Langhorne trembled and averted her face, fighting some inner turmoil. Without warning, she grabbed his head in both hands and pressed her face to his, snarling viciously. Alarmed, Sandoval tried to pull away, but she gripped him tight as a Xombie, her nails digging into his flesh, and in that frenzy she kissed him. He flinched in terror . . . then surrendered. And as he surrendered, so did she, so did we all. They melted together, tearfully, blissfully kissing like they were in a Hollywood movie.

When the kiss finally ended, Sandoval came over to me, and said, "Well, if it isn't the unsinkable Lulu Pangloss."

"Mr. Sandoval," I said, "why did you never tell me you knew my father?"

He did an exaggerated double take. To Captain Despineau, he said, "No. You're not the father of Lulu *Pangloss*?"

"Yes, I am . . . her father. Or at least I hope she will allow me to earn that fortunate appellation."

Before I could respond, two other familiar faces arrived, one sunny with blond dreadlocks and the other darker and straight-haired. They both looked like they had been through a lot . . . as I suppose I did myself. We stared at each other for a second, trying to place the familiar faces. Then it clicked for me: Todd Holmes and Ray Despineau.

"Todd! Ray! Oh my God!"

"Lulu, you're alive!"

"Where have you guys *been*?" I asked.

"Don't ask."

"I thought you were dead!"

"We thought *you* were dead."

We laughed and cried, and then Captain Despineau came up behind us, and said, "Lulu, I want you to meet someone you should have met a long time ago. This is my son, Raymond."

"Of course I know Ray." My eyes went wide. "Oh shit. Your *son*? I *knew* that name sounded familiar! Ray, you are *not* my brother?"

He nodded sheepishly.

"That means Brenda is your sister? Our sister?"

His face crashed. "Yeah . . . well, there's something you should know about that. Brenda died, Lulu."

"I know. I'm sorry."

"How do you know?"

"I saw her. While I was . . . one of them. You know no one ever really dies, right? Xombie or not."

Ray and I hugged awkwardly. Then something broke loose, and suddenly we were both crying, gripping each other as if for dear life. Captain Despineau was weeping, too.

"I can't believe I really have a brother," I sobbed.

"And I have a sister," Ray said.

"And I now have a son as well as a daughter," the captain added, warmly clutching us both. *"Tout comprendre c'est tout pardonner."*

Someone behind us said, "Bullshit!"

It was my ex-Ex-mother, Grace Pangloss. *Here we go,* I thought. As a Xombie, my mom had never spoken much, but even though she had only been human a few hours, Mummy was already back to being her former self.

"Grace," said Captain Despineau stiffly. "I hope you are well."

"Hello, Al," my mother said. "Oh, I'm great. It's nice to see you having this little family reunion with the children you abandoned."

"I didn't abandon them! You waited until I was at sea, and then you kidnapped them and moved to the States!"

"I had postpartum depression! I was suicidal! I was alone in a foreign country with no one to turn to, and we weren't even married. You were my only support, and I couldn't so much as call you on the phone for months at a time! I couldn't take it anymore!"

"Yes, but then you also drive Brenda away, so the whole family is *tant pis.*"

"Don't start about Brenda! Don't you *dare*. Brenda was another one who needed you while you were out joyriding around the seven seas, so don't even start with me about Brenda, mister."

"I had my duties; I had no choice! Maybe if you had tried telling me this—"

"I did try! I tried till I was blue in the face, but you refused to listen. You're like every man I've ever known: selfish, irresponsible, egotistical, obnoxious—"

"Somebody talkin' about me?"

We all turned at the impossible gruff voice.

*No. No. Come on.*

But it was. Standing behind me was Fred Cowper. Head and body reunited.

At first I couldn't believe what I was seeing . . . then I almost jumped out of my new pink skin. Fred was *whole*. More than whole—he looked twenty years younger, as if losing and regaining his head was the best thing that ever happened to him. I was too stunned to speak; all I could do was gape.

As if realizing it was her cue, Dr. Stevens leaped in. "Wonderful! Wonderful! So nice to meet you all. Come on, let's go!"

Reeling from the shock, we allowed ourselves to be nudged aboard the carts.

As we took our seats, Dr. Stevens said, "I can't *wait* to show you around."

There were more reunions along the way. Moving on, we came to a neighborhood of Immunes, including the two girls who had traveled with Todd, Ray, Sandoval, and Chandra Stevens all the way from Providence: Fran and Deena.

As a Xombie, I had taken great interest in Immunes. In fact, they were the major reason I was here at all. Would I have continued so long with this absurd voyage if not for the dream of somehow liberating these doomed, forbidden beings? Unfortunately, they were not nearly as fascinating to my human consciousness—just regular people, after all.

Sandoval gestured at the door with a flourish. "Step right up," he said.

We went inside. The room was empty except for a couch facing a bank of television screens. Each screen showed a strange mound like the one I had seen in Washington, with thousands of Xombies filing in, and the same black blimps suspended overhead.

A man in a space suit was sitting on the couch between Fran and Deena, his body wired to a fuse box. The two women were very happy to have company. There were hugs and introductions all around.

"Uri," Sandoval said, "you have visitors."

Miska shifted his helmet slightly to see us, which allowed us to see his blue face through the visor. "Hello, Bobby," he said. "Hey, man, turn that frown upside down. Deena, could you be a sweetheart and get my friend Bobby a Yoo-hoo?"

Sandoval said, "Uri's working for us now. He's been very useful in maneuvering the Xombies wherever we need them to be, and as *whoever* we need them to be. For instance, I've been able to operate in several places at once. So has Miska. We've also been able to find all the X-infected Moguls in their hidden vaults and move them to one secure facility. Not so secure anymore, unfortunately, thanks to your visit, Lulu."

"Sorry," I said. "What the hell were you doing to them there?"

"Since Agent X cannot be 'killed,' and we have yet to find a means of treating five billion Xombies worldwide, it is necessary to isolate the threat. In this colony we have a certain number of Immunes who donate the blood factor we require to remain human. It goes into the drinking water here, so we all live together under the illusion of normalcy. Eventually, we expect to have fully immune children—a number of women are pregnant right now. But in order for human civilization to continue in the meantime, we *have* to deal with the existing Xombies. And we've decided that the best way to do that is by reducing them to a concentrated, crystalline form and converting that to organic biomass."

"How do you manage that?" Langhorne asked.

"We pour it into the bay. The shellfish population is thriving."

"Mr. Sandoval?" There was a woman in camouflage fatigues at the door. "Major Hammersmith requests you come to the Command Center right away. It's urgent."

"Hold that thought," Sandoval said, hurrying out the door.

We followed him down the tunnel to a row of humming

tractor-trailers. The people there were too busy to pay any attention to us. They were frantically manning banks of computer workstations and cockpit simulators, from which scores of aerial and surface drones were being remote-controlled. These were the same lethal gadgets that had so recently attacked *us* . . . but, of course, we were Xombies then.

There was some kind of major operation going on, all the drones swarming a strange shimmering mass—on the monitors it looked like an iridescent bluish black sea slug, an immense nudibranch covered with glassy tendrils. It was mountainous.

"What is that?" Langhorne asked.

"That's what I was hoping Lulu could tell us," said Dr. Stevens. "It came out of the Mons right after she did."

All I could do was shake my head. As I watched, the thing reared up and projectile-vomited a rope of pale, wormy innards hundreds of feet into the air. The seething mass flew in a high arc, unraveling as it avalanched to the ground, its lashing tendrils seizing any living thing in its path. But it didn't pull the prey back to its body. Instead, the rear end poured into the front, pulsing forward like a giant maggot. In its wake it left nothing but a trail of scorched earth.

With a grimace, Captain Despineau muttered, *"Écrasez l'infâme."*

Stevens said, "It's been moving in fits and starts, averaging about fifteen miles an hour, and that speed has remained relatively stable even as the thing has grown in bulk. We hoped it would eventually stop moving, but it just keeps crawling along, growing bigger and bigger."

"How big is it?" I asked.

"We estimate it has grown over ten thousand times its original mass, so it's gotta be in the millions of tons by now. It's vacuuming up every bit of organic matter in its path. It keeps collapsing under its own weight, then pulling itself together again—sort of like a volcanic lava dome. We're expecting it to melt down completely at any time, but if it reaches the open ocean, all bets are off."

Sandoval asked, "Where is it now?"

"It came south down the Maryland peninsula and crossed the Potomac River at Blossom Point. It then entered Virginia and began veering eastward south of the Rappahannock. It is now approaching the York River at Gloucester Point. That's right on the lower Chesapeake, and less than forty miles away from us here. Which is why we're throwing everything we've got at it. So far, no good."

"And you have no idea what it is?" I asked.

Sandoval said, "Oh, we have *some* idea." He gestured back in the direction of Miska's trailer. "This is Miska's Big Enchilada—the end of the world he was predicting. Except that because it didn't exist outside of his head, he needed an opportunity to create it . . . which Lulu generously provided."

"It's not like I *meant* to," I said.

"No, it was our fault for putting all our eggs in one basket. Miska's crazy as a damn doodlebug, and this is his ultimate madness unleashed—the finale to Agent X. I don't know if he's even consciously controlling it, but I guarantee he is linked to that thing."

"Then you should be able to kill it by killing him," I said.

"No, then we'll lose control of the Xombies. Like it or not, we *need* him."

# CHAPTER **THIRTY**

## LEVIATHAN

With nothing to do but wait, I found cots for Bobby and myself and slept the sleep of the living. The dead never sleep.

We were awakened some twenty hours later by an alarm in the tunnel. Sitting up on our cots, we rubbed sand from our eyes and tried to figure out what was happening. It was like the scene of a fire: All the tunnel residents were out of their trailers, chattering in anxious groups.

Bobby took my hand. "What's going on, Lulu?"

"I don't know."

In the distance, we could hear beeping as vehicles forced their way through the crowds. As they got nearer, the lane was cleared to make room for them, and in a minute we could see a convoy of electric buses. They were full of people, but as they came abreast of us, they stopped. The doors wheezed open and a man leaned out—Sandoval. I could see Miska sitting in the front seat like a derelict spaceman.

Over a loudspeaker, Sandoval shouted, "All those who depend on Agent X inhibitors are asked to board the buses at once. Thank you."

"Why?" someone asked.

"It's a precautionary evacuation, just in the event that we lose power. You're temporarily being moved to Petropolis. A little vacation in the fresh air."

Without the least quibble, I jumped up and got on a bus. So did everyone else from the boat, as well as a number of tunnel residents. It just seemed like a good idea; we didn't question it. If someone had said to me, *You are being controlled like a hand puppet*, I would have said, *No I'm not*.

Sandoval escorted us back to the bathyscaphe elevator and loaded us in like cattle. Next thing we knew, we were stepping out into the bright sky of Petropolis. There was something dreamlike about it, going from that tunnel to high above the blue of Chesapeake Bay.

Shading my eyes, I asked Sandoval, "Why exactly are we up here? What's going on?"

"Ask him," he said, nodding at Uri Miska. "It was his idea."

He went to Miska and unclamped the man's helmet. No one thought to stop him—perhaps we were all dreaming. Or sharing Miska's dream. In a minute, the blue man was out of his pressure suit and standing completely free, wearing only space boots and long johns.

"*That's* better," Miska said. "Thank you, Jim."

Pointing at me, Sandoval said, "She wants to know why we're up here."

Miska grinned amiably. "Tell her she's got a ticket to ride."

I nodded as if that made all the sense in the world.

Miska led us to the west side of the platform, facing the far Virginia shore. There was something going on out there, a disturbance on the horizon like a dark waterspout. Tiny flashes crackled around it, darts of lightning in a bruised sky, and the whole bay was unsettled with heavy surf. Petropolis shook from the blows.

I knew what this was. Wormwood. The World-Devourer; the Big Enchilada. It was coming. It was growing. Soon it would arrive at the mouth of the bay and break through to the open Atlantic. Just an embryo in an amniotic sea, the

Earth one big womb. Unchecked, it would take over the surface of the planet—here, there, and everywhere.

A shadow passed over, and I suddenly noticed all the strange black clouds. They were not clouds, I realized, but Xombie airships—Xeppelins.

"Where are they going?" Bobby asked me.

"They're leaving," I said.

Bobby started to weep.

Maybe they heard him. One of the weirdly shaped bubbles was closer than the others—clearer, as if I could reach up and touch it. Closer and closer by the minute, swelling to enormous size, it scudded toward us over the bay, trailing black ribbons and casting its shadow on the water.

It hove to Petropolis as though the massive oil rig was its hitching post, then hung its billowing muzzle over us. Sighing hugely, it unfurled veinous blue curtains and carpets of tender flesh. Through that entrance we could see a cathedral of dark glass, and the honeycombed bedchamber that would be our eternal resting place, safe from Earth's impending ruin.

We just had to be Xombies again.

Miska entered. "All aboard," he said, waving us in.

Bobby went first—Bobby went gladly. Slightly less eagerly, the rest started to follow . . . though I held back, and my Dreadnauts with me. The florid walls trembled with the desire to receive us.

And then we heard something. Music. A familiar tune from somewhere far away and below the sea:

*All you need is love . . .*

Across the bay, the World-Devourer listened, too, Wormwood spreading its long pale tubers in search of those human vibrations. It swept the Virginia shore, plumbing the entrance to Hampton Roads and sending tsunami waves through the deserted streets of Norfolk until it found the source.

And it screamed.

The leviathan had stumbled upon a hornets' nest. All at once the water was alive with a monstrous scourge that swarmed over the behemoth and burrowed inside it like a plague of chiggers: a trillion feeding crabs. The X-altered crabs filled that corner of the bay, their age-old spawning grounds, attracted by the lure of Xombie flesh, dangled before them inside a thick-hulled submarine. There were more crabs there than water, all fighting to get at the Fab Four, driven to frenzy by the sound of long-dead music.

The Big Enchilada had no such steel shell to protect it.

It sought to retreat, withdrawing its amorphous limbs into itself, but they tore from the strain as thousands of tons of crabs infested them. The Devourer became the devoured. Rotten with parasites, Wormwood tried to flee its attackers by crawling ashore, but the weight of its riddled body in the shallows caused it to crack and shiver apart like a glacier of gelatin, and the carcass fell to the crabs. The crabs ate it; the crabs contained it; the crabs neutralized it. It was a good year for crabs—they would be delicious.

I stepped back from the lip of the Xeppelin, and my friends stayed with me. We raised our arms and waved as its bow rose from the platform and swelled shut around Miska's shocked face. Like a slow eclipse, the gargantuan shadow passed, leaving us standing in daylight.

My baby would be human.

# EPILOGUE

## HEROES

It's a rum business, being a zombie and all. Excuse me, I meant a "Xombie." All very ridiculous, when you think about it. When we were alive we called them Blue Meanies, but now we know there's nothing mean about it. If anything, we're generous to a fault. My mates and I—Dick, Wally, Phil, and I'm Reggie—came by this fate in a most peculiar way: We'd been playing small clubs for years, specializing in old-school hardcore for West Britain's drunk and disorderly, but our youthful dreams of record deals and international fame had given way to the reality of living on a diet of take-away curry and greasy chips. We were knackered. Aside from the traveling minstrel bullshit, it wasn't easy being "bloody Paki" in post 9/11 England, much less four bloody Pakis traveling about the countryside in an unmarked delivery van. We had tried painting the band's name on the side of the lorry, but punters kept letting air out of the tyres, and it likely didn't help that our group was at that time called the Golliwogs. Anyway, one day we decided to do a show dressed all in Sgt. Pepper kit, just having a laugh, but the audience went bloody mad, especially when we did an actual Beatles number—"Yellow Submarine," I remember it well. Just a lark. Word got round, and suddenly we were jamming to packed halls everywhere we went—in a trice we found ourselves playing more Beatles and less

Golliwogs. Whole different audience, that, one a bit less prone to head-butting, property damage, and public urination. Fewer skinheads. More family-like, I suppose, and we were ready for a bit of gentility, having had our fill of race riots—it was nice to play a whole set without a bloomin' row breaking out in the bloomin' front row. To be honest, we'd all been about to quit the band, find some steady work, settle down, and start families. All we needed was a regular gig, and this Beatles shtick was it, man. Dick found an advert for cruise lines seeking music acts, but they told us our band name was too "inflammatory." Thus, the Blackpudlians were born, and the rest is history.

Who would have thought four lads from Blackpool would save the human race?

## ABOUT THE AUTHOR

Walter Greatshell has lived in five countries and worked many odd jobs across America, including painting houses, writing for a local newspaper, managing a quaint old movie house, and building nuclear submarines. For now, he has settled in Providence, Rhode Island, with his wife, Cindy; son, Max; and cat, Reuben. Visit Walter's website at www.waltergreatshell.com.

*It's the end of the world—unless you're a zombie.*

# XOMBIES:
## APOCALYPSE BLUES

### by Walter Greatshell

When the Agent X plague struck, it infected women first, turning them into mindless killers intent on creating an army of "Xombies" by spreading their disease.

Running for her life, seventeen-year-old Lulu is rescued by the only father she has never known and taken aboard a refitted nuclear submarine that's crew has one mission: to save a little bit of humanity.

*Now available from Ace Books!*

penguin.com